NOT TO BE REMOVED
FROM THE LIBRARY

POPULAR RHYMES AND
NURSERY TALES OF ENGLAND

UNIFORM WITH THIS EDITION

The Nursery Rhymes of England
James Orchard Halliwell

Popular Tales from the Norse
Peter C. Asbjörnsen and Jörgen I. Moe

Celtic Fairy Tales
Joseph Jacobs

English Fairy Tales
Joseph Jacobs

POPULAR RHYMES & NURSERY TALES OF ENGLAND

Collected by

JAMES ORCHARD HALLIWELL

Decorations by
MAUREEN ROFFEY

THE BODLEY HEAD
LONDON SYDNEY
TORONTO

Popular Rhymes and Nursery Tales was first published
in 1849 by John Russell Smith, 4 Old Compton Street,
Soho Square.
(See Publisher's Note on p. *vi*)

ISBN 0 370 01255 0
Illustrations © The Bodley Head Ltd 1970
Printed and bound in Great Britain for
The Bodley Head Ltd
9 Bow Street, London WC2
by W. & J. Mackay & Co Ltd, Chatham
Set in 'Monotype' Ehrhardt
This edition first published 1970

Tales of my Nursery! shall that still loved spot,
That window corner, ever be forgot,
Where through the woodbine when with upward ray
Gleam'd the last shadow of departing day,
Still did I sit, and with unwearied eye,
Read while I wept, and scarcely paused to sigh!
In that gay drawer, with fairy fictions stored,
When some new tale was added to my hoard,
While o'er each page my eager glance was flung,
'Twas but to learn what female fate was sung;
If no sad maid the castle shut from light,
I heeded not the giant and the knight.
 Sweet Cinderella, even before the ball,
How did I love thee—ashes, rags, and all!
What bliss I deem'd it to have stood beside,
On every virgin when thy shoe was tried!
How long'd to see thy shape the slipper suit!
But, dearer than the slipper, lov'd the foot.

ANON.

PUBLISHER'S NOTE

Popular Rhymes and Nursery Tales was first published in 1849 and according to the Halliwell Bibliography (*Halliwelliana*, 1879) was not reprinted until it was put with *The Nursery Rhymes* in one large collection by Warne *c*. 1870. *Halliwelliana* however does record that "a copy with MS. notes and corrections for new edition was advertised in Halliwell's 1857 sale and withdrawn." This second collection made by James Orchard Halliwell was published seven years after the Percy Society edition of *The Nursery Rhymes of England*, and these two volumes of rhymes, tales and "vernacular scraps" have served for over a century as source books for countless readers and students of nursery and folk lore. Joseph Jacobs for example chose eight of Halliwell's stories for inclusion in his *English Fairy Tales* and *More English Fairy Tales* some forty years later.

Halliwell himself made no claim to be a specialist and in a charming note at the end of this book he says: "Our collection of vernacular scraps, which, like the 'brave beggars of Coudingham fair', have been gathered from the lanes and by-ways, is now brought to a conclusion. They are, it must be confessed, but literary vagrants at the best; but they breathe of country freshness, and may impart some of their spirit to our languishing home-life . . ."

As a young man Halliwell was something of a prodigy, publishing his first book, a life of Sir Samuel Morland, in 1839 when he was only eighteen. In that same year he attempted to sell to the book collector Sir Thomas Phillipps some manuscripts that were later believed to have been stolen from the library of Trinity College, Cambridge, where Halliwell had matriculated in 1837, and which were subsequently sold to the British Museum. In 1845 the matter was made public and although Halliwell was by now a noted Shakespearean scholar he was barred from the British Museum and his reader's ticket withdrawn. However the lawyers of the Museum and of Trinity College "fell out" over the prosecution and the case was abandoned in 1846, Halliwell once again being given access to the Museum. In 1842 he had eloped with Phillipps' daughter, Henrietta, and on the death of her father in 1872 was forced to change his name to Halliwell-Phillipps in order to be eligible to inherit the old man's considerable fortune.

Contents

Preface

It were greatly to be desired that the instructors of our children could be persuaded how much is lost by rejecting the venerable relics of nursery traditional literature, and substituting in their place the present cold, unimaginative,—I had almost said, unnatural,—prosaic good-boy stories. "In the latter case," observes Sir Walter Scott, "their minds are, as it were, put into the stocks, like their feet at the dancing-school, and the moral always consists in good conduct being crowned with success. Truth is, I would not give one tear shed over Little Red Riding Hood for all the benefit to be derived from a hundred histories of Jemmy Goodchild. I think the selfish tendencies will be soon enough acquired in this arithmetical age; and that, to make the higher class of character, our own wild fictions—like our own simple music—will have more effect in awakening the fancy and elevating the disposition, than the colder and more elaborate compositions of modern authors and composers."

Deeply impressed with this truth, and firmly convinced of the "imagination-nourishing" power of the wild and fanciful lore of the old nursery, I have spared no labour in collecting the fragments which have been traditionally preserved in our provinces. The object is not so much to present to the reader a few literary trifles, though even their curiosity and value in several important discussions must not be despised, as to rescue in order to restore; a solemn recompense due from literature for having driven them away; and to recall the memory to early associations, in the hope that they who love such recollections will not suffer the objects of them to disappear with the present generation.

In arranging the materials gathered for this little volume, I have followed, in some respects, the plan adopted by Mr Robert Chambers, in his elegant work, the "Popular Rhymes of Scotland"; but our vernacular anthology will be found to contain so much which does not occur in any shape in that of the sister country, that the two collections have not as much similarity as might have been expected. Together, they will eventually contain nearly all that is worth preserving of what may be called the natural literature of Great Britain. Mr Chambers, indeed, may be said to have already exhausted the subject for his own land in the last edition of his interesting publication, but no systematic attempt has yet been made in the same direction for this country; and although the curiosity and extent of the relics I have been enabled to collect have far exceeded my expectations, I am fully aware how much more can yet be accomplished.

An additional number of foreign synonymes could also, no doubt, be collected; though perhaps more easily by foreigners, for continental works which contain notices of traditional literature are procured with difficulty in England. The following pages, however, contain sufficient of these to exhibit the striking similarities between rhymes prevalent over England, and others which exist in the North of Europe.

The collection of Nursery Tales is not as extensive as could have been wished, but the difficulty of procuring the brief traditional stories which were current some century since, now for the most part only recollected in obscure districts, is so great, that no apology is necessary for the apparent deficiency of that section. The few which have been obtained are of considerable curiosity and interest; and I would venture to suggest to all readers of these pages the great obligation they would confer by the communication of any additions. Stories of this kind are undoubtedly to be obtained from oral tradition, and perhaps some of literary importance may yet be recovered.

The compiler's best thanks are due to Captain Henry Smith for the very interesting communication of rhymes current in the Isle of Wight; to Mr George Stephens for several curious fragments, and valuable references to Swedish songs; and to many kind correspondents who have furnished me with rhymes current in the various districts in which they reside. It is only by a large provincial correspondence that a collection of this kind can be rendered complete, and the minutest information on any of our popular tales or rhymes, forwarded to the address given below, would be most thankfully and carefully acknowledged.

Brixton Hill, Surrey   JAMES ORCHARD HALLIWELL
April, 1849

ONE

Nursery Antiquities

Although the names of Scott and Grimm may be enumerated amongst the writers who have acknowledged the ethnological and philosophic value of traditional nursery literature, it is difficult to impress on the public mind the importance of a subject apparently in the last degree trifling and insignificant, or to induce an opinion that the jingles and simple narratives of a garrulous nurse can possess a worth beyond the circle of their own immediate influence.

But they who despise the humbler sources of literary illustration must be content to be told, and hereafter to learn, that traces of the simplest stories and most absurd superstitions are often more effectual in proving the affinity of different races, and determining other literary questions, than a host of grander and more imposing monuments. The history of fiction is continually efficacious in discussions of this kind, and the identities of puerile sayings frequently answer a similar purpose. Both, indeed, are of high value. The humble chap-book is found to be descended not only from mediaeval romance, but also not unfrequently from the more ancient mythology, whilst some of our simplest nursery-rhymes are chanted to this day by the children of Germany, Denmark, and Sweden, a fact strikingly exhibiting their great antiquity and remote origin.

The subject, however curious and interesting, is far too diffuse to be investigated at any length in a work like the present; and, indeed, the materials are for the most part so scattered and difficult of access, that it would require the research of many years to accomplish the task satisfactorily. I shall, then, content myself with indicating a few of the most striking analogies between the rhymes of foreign countries and those of our own, for this portion of the inquiry has been scarcely alluded to by my predecessors. With regard to the tales, a few notices of their antiquity will be found in the prefaces or notes to the stories themselves, and few readers will require to be informed that Whittington's cat realized his price in India, and that Arlotto related the story long before the Lord Mayor was born; that Jack the Giant-killer is founded on an Edda; or that the slipper of Cinderella finds a parallel in the history of the celebrated Rhodope. To enter into these discussions would be merely to repeat an oft-told tale, and I prefer offering a few Notes which will be found to possess a little more novelty.

Of the many who must recollect the nursery jingles of their youth, how few in number are those who have suspected their immense age, or that they were ever more than unmeaning nonsense; far less that their creation belongs to a period before that at which the authentic records of our history commence. Yet there is no exaggeration in such a statement. We find that the same trifles which erewhile lulled or amused the English infant are current in slightly varied forms throughout the North of Europe; we know that they have been sung in the northern countries for centuries, and that there has been no modern outlet for their dissemination across the German Ocean. The most natural inference is to adopt the theory of a Teutonic origin, and thus give to every genuine child-rhyme, found current in England and Sweden, an immense antiquity. There is nothing improbable in the supposition, for the preservation of the relics of primitive literature often bears an inverse ratio to their importance. Thus, for example, a well-known English nursery rhyme tells us,

> There was an old man,
> And he had a calf,
> And that's half;
> He took him out of the stall,
> And put him on the wall,
> And that's all.

A composition apparently of little interest or curiosity; but Arwidsson, unacquainted with the English rhyme, produces the following as current in Sweden, Svenska Fornsånger, iii. 488, which bears far too striking a similarity to the above to have had a different origin,

> Gubben och gumman hade en kalf,
> Och nu är visan half!
> Och begge så körde de halfven i vall,
> Och nu är visan all!

We could not, perhaps, select a better instance of this kind of similarity in nepial songs as current throughout the great northern states of Europe than the pretty stanza on the lady-bird. Variations of this familiar song belong to the vernacular literature of England, Germany, Denmark, and Sweden. The version at present current in the North of England is as follows:

> Lady-cow, lady-cow, fly thy way home,
> Thy house is on fire, thy children all gone;
> All but one that ligs under a stone,
> Fly thee home, lady-cow, ere it be gone!*

These lines are said by children, when they throw the beautiful little insect into the air, to make it take flight. Two Scottish variations are given by Mr Chambers, p. 170. In Germany it is called the Virgin Mary's chafer, *Marienwürmchen*, or the May-chafer, *Maikäferchen*, or the gold-bird, *Guldvogel*. In Sweden, gold-hen, gold-cow, or the Virgin Mary's maid. In Denmark, our Lord's hen, or our Lady's hen. We may first mention the German song translated by Taylor, as frequently alluded to by writers on this subject. The second verse is the only one preserved in England.

> Lady-bird! lady-bird! pretty one! stay!
> Come sit on my finger, so happy and gay;
> With me shall no mischief betide thee:

---

* In Norfolk the lady-bird is called *burney-bee*, and the following lines are current:
> Burnie bee, burnie bee,
> Tell me when your wedding be.
> If it be to-morrow day,
> Take your wings and fly away.

3

No harm would I do thee, no foeman is near,
I only would gaze on thy beauties so dear,
   Those beautiful winglets beside thee.

Lady-bird! lady-bird! fly away home;
Thy house is a-fire, thy children will roam!
   List! list! to their cry and bewailing!
The pitiless spider is weaving their doom,
Then lady-bird! lady-bird! fly away home!
   Hark! hark! to thy children's bewailing.

Fly back again, back again, lady-bird dear!
Thy neighbours will merrily welcome thee here;
   With them shall no perils attend thee!
They'll guard thee so safely from danger or care,
They'll gaze on thy beautiful winglets so fair,
   And comfort, and love, and befriend thee!

In Das Knaben Wunderhorn, Arnim und Brentano, 1808, iii. 82, 83, 90, we have three German songs relating to the lady-bird. The first two of these are here given:

Der Guldvogel

Guldvogel, flieg aus,
Flieg auf die Stangen,
Käsebrode langen;
Mir eins, dir eins,
Alle gute G'sellen eins.

"Gold-bird, get thee gone, fly to thy perch, bring cheese-cakes, one for me, one for thee, and one for all good people."

Maikäferchen, Maikäferchen, fliege weg!
Dein Häusgen brennt,
Dein Mütterchen flennt,
Dein Vater sitzt auf der Schwelle,
Flieg in Himmel aus der Hölle.

"May-bird, May-bird, fly away. Thy house burns, thy mother weeps, thy father stays at his threshold, fly from hell into heaven!"

4

The third is not so similar to our version. Another German one is given in Kuhn und Schwark, Norddeutsche Sagen, 1848, p. 375:

> Maikäferchen, fliege,
> Dein Vater ist im Kriege,
> Dein Mutter ist in Pommerland,
> Pommerland ist abgebrannt!
> Maikäferchen, fliege.

"May-bird, fly. Thy father is in the war, thy mother is in Pomerania, Pomerania is burnt! May-bird, fly."—See, also, Erk und Irmer, Die Deutschen Volkslieder, Berlin, 1839, iv. 7, Das Maikäferlied. For the two pretty Swedish songs which follow I am indebted to the MS. of Mr Stephens. The first is common in the southern part of that country, the other in the northern.

> Guld-höna, guld-ko!
> Flyg öster, flyg vester,
> Dit du flyger der bor din älskade!

"Gold-hen, gold-cow! fly east, fly west, you will fly where your sweetheart is."

> Jungfru Marias Nyckelpiga!
> Flyg öster, flyg vester,
> Flyg dit der min käresta bor!*

"Fly, our holy Virgin's bower-maid! fly east, fly west, fly where my loved-one dwelleth." In Denmark they sing (Thiele, iii. 134):

> Fly, fly, our Lord's own hen!
> To-morrow the weather fair will be,
> And eke the next day too.†

Accumulative tales are of very high antiquity. The original of "the House that Jack built" is well known to be an old Hebrew hymn in Sepher Haggadah. It is also found in Danish, but in a

---

* This is a very remarkable coincidence with an English rhyme:
> Fly, lady-bird, fly!
>   North, south, east, or west;
> Fly to the pretty girl
>   That I love best.

† "The lady-bird," observes Mr Chambers, "is always connected with fine weather in Germany and the north."

somewhat shorter form; (See Thiele, Danske Folkesagn, II. iii. 146, *Der har du det Huus som Jacob bygde*); and the English version is probably very old, as may be inferred from the mention of "the priest all shaven and shorn". A version of the old woman and her sixpence occurs in the same collection, II. iv. 161, *Konen och Grisen Fick*, the old wife and her piggy Fick,—"There was once upon a time an old woman who had a little pig hight Fick, who would never go home late in the evening. So the old woman said to her stick:

> 'Stick, beat Fick, I say!
> Piggie will not go home to-day!' "

This chant-tale is also common in Sweden. One copy has been printed by N. Lilja in his Violen en Samling Jullekar, Barnsånger och Sagor, i. 20, *Gossen och Geten Näppa*, the boy and the goat Neppa,—"There was once a yeoman who had a goat called Neppa, but Neppa would never go home from the field. The yeoman was therefore forced to promise his daughter in marriage to whoever could get Neppa home. Many tried their fortune in vain, but at last a sharp boy offered to ward the goat. All the next day he followed Neppa, and when evening came, he said, 'Now will we homeward go?' but Neppa answered, 'Pluck me a tuft or so,'" &c. The story is conducted in an exactly similar manner in which the *dénoûement* is brought about in the English tale.*

The well-known song of "There was a lady loved a swine" is found in an unpublished play of the time of Charles I in the Bodleian Library, MS. Bodl. 30:

> There was a lady loved a hogge;
> Hony, quoth shee,
> Woo't thou lie with me to-night?
> Ugh, quoth hee.

A similar song is current in Sweden, as we learn from Arwidsson, "Svenska Fornsånger", iii. 482, who gives a version in which an

---

* Two other variations occur in Arwidsson, "Svenska Fornsånger", 1842, iii. 387–8, and Mr Stephens tells me he has a MS. Swedish copy entitled the Schoolboy and the Birch. It is also well known in Alsace, and is printed in that dialect in Stöber's "Elsassisches Volksbüchlein", 1842, pp. 93–5. Compare, also, Kuhn und Schwark, "Norddeutsche Sagen, Märchen und Gebräuche", 1848, p. 358, "Die frâ, dos hippel un dos hindel."

old woman, who had no children, took a little foal, which she called Longshanks, and rocked and nursed it as if it had been her own child:*

> Gumman ville vagga
>   Och inga barn hade hon;
>   Då tog hon in
>   Fölungen sin,
>   Och lade den i vaggan sin.
>   Vyssa, vyssa, långskånken min,
>   Långa ben har du;
>   Lefver du till sommaren,
>   Blir du lik far din.

Another paradoxical song-tale, respecting the old woman who went to market, and had her petticoats cut off at her knees "by a pedlar whose name was Stout", is found in some shape or other in most countries in Europe. A Norwegian version is given by Asbjörnsen og Moe, "Norske Folkeevantyr", 1843, and, if I recollect rightly, it is also found in Grimm.

The riddle-rhyme of "Humpty Dumpty sat on a wall" is, in one form or other, a favourite throughout Europe. A curious Danish version is given by Thiele, iii. 148:

> Lille Trille
> Laae paa Hylde;
> Lille Trille
> Faldt ned af Hylde.
> Ingen Mand
> I hele Land
> Lille Trille curere kan.

Which may be thus translated:

> Little Trille
> Lay on a shelf:
> Little Trille
> Thence pitch'd himself:
> Not all the men
> In our land, I ken,
> Can put Little Trille right again.

---

* It is still more similar to a pretty little song in Chambers, p. 188, commencing, "There was a miller's dochter".

And Mr. Stephens has preserved two copies in his MS. Swedish collections. The first is from the province of Upland:

> Thille Lille
>   Satt på take';
> Thille Lille
>   Trilla' ner;
> Ingen läkare i hela verlden
> Thille Lille laga kan.

> (Thille Lille
>   On the roof-tree sat;
> Thille Lille
>   Down fell flat;
> Never a leech the world can show
> That Thille Lille can heal, I trow.)

Another from the province of Småland:

> Lille Bulle
> Trilla' der å skulle;
> Ingen man i detta lan'
> Lille Bulle laga kan.

> (Down on the shed
> Lille Bulle rolled;
> Never a man in all this land
> Lille Bulle helpen can.)

It will now only be necessary to refer to the similarities pointed out in other parts of this work, to convince the reader that, at all events, a very fair case is made out of the truth of the positions we have contended for, if, indeed, sufficient evidence of their absolute truth is not adduced. They who are accustomed to researches of this kind are too well aware of the facility with which the most plausible theories are frequently nullified by subsequent discovery; but there appears in the present case to be numerous conditions insoluble by any other supposition than that of a common origin, and we are therefore fully justified in adopting it as proved.

Turning to the nursery rhymes of our own country, it will tend materially to strengthen the results to which we have arrived, if we succeed in proving their antiquity in this island. We shall be enabled to do so satisfactorily, and to show that they are not the modern nonsense some folks may pronounce them to be. They illustrate the history and manners of the people for centuries. Here, for instance, is a relic in the form of a nursery rhyme, but in reality part of a political song, referring to the rebellious times of Richard II:*

> My father he died, I cannot tell how,
> But he left me six horses to drive out my plough!
> With a wimmy lo! wommy lo! *Jack Straw, blazey-boys*!
> Wimmy lo! wommy lo! wob, wob, wob!

An infant of the nineteenth century recalling our recollection to Jack Straw and his "blazey-boys!" Far better this than teaching history with notes "suited to the capacity of the youngest". Another refers to Joanna of Castile, who visited the court of Henry VII in 1506:

> I had a little nut-tree, nothing would it bear
> But a golden nutmeg and a silver pear;
> The King of Spain's daughter came to visit me,
> And all for the sake of my little nut-tree.

We have distinct evidence that the well-known rhyme,†

> The King of France went up the hill,
>   With twenty thousand men:
> The King of France came down the hill,
>   And ne'er went up again—

was composed before 1588. It occurs in an old tract called "Pigges Corantoe", 1642, where it is entitled "Old Tarlton's Song",

---

* I am here, and in a few other cases, quoting from myself. It may be necessary to say so, for my former collections on this subject have been appropriated—"convey, the wise it call"—in a work by a learned Doctor, the preface to which is an amusing instance of plagiarism.

† An early variation occurs in MS. Sloane, 1489:
>   The King of France, and four thousand men,
>   They drew their swords, and put them up again.

referring to Tarlton the jester, who died in 1588. The following one belongs to the seventeenth century:

> As I was going by Charing Cross,
> I saw a black man upon a black horse;
> They told me it was King Charles the First;
> Oh dear, my heart was ready to burst!

Political nursery rhymes or rather political rhymes of a jingling character, which, losing their original application, are preserved only in the nursery, were probably common in the seventeenth century. The two just quoted have evidently an historical application. The manuscript miscellanies of the time of James I and Charles I contain several copies of literal rhymes not very unlike "A, B, C, tumble down D". In the reign of Charles II political pasquinades constantly partook of the genuine nursery character. We must select the following example, of course put into the mouth of that sovereign, preserved in MS. Douce 357, f. 124, in the Bodleian Library:

> See-saw, sack-a-day;
> Monmouth is a pretie boy,
>   Richmond is another,
> Grafton is my onely joy,
> And why should I these three destroy
>   To please a pious brother?

"What is the rhyme for porringer?" was written on occasion of the marriage of Mary, the daughter of James, Duke of York, afterwards James II, with the young Prince of Orange; and the following alludes to William III and George, Prince of Denmark:

> William and Mary, George and Anne,
> Four such children had never a man:
> They put their father to flight and shame,
> And call'd their brother a shocking bad name.

Another nursery song on King William is not yet obsolete, but its application is not generally known. My authority is the title of it in MS. Harl. 7316:

10

As I walk'd by myself,
And talked to myself,
  Myself said unto me,
Look to thyself,
Take care of thyself,
  For nobody cares for thee.

I answer'd myself,
And said to myself,
  In the self-same repartee,
Look to thyself,
Or not look to thyself,
  The self-same thing will be.

To this class of rhymes I may add the following on Dr. Sacheverel, which was obtained from oral tradition:

Doctor Sacheverel
Did very well,
But Jacky Dawbin
Gave him a warning.

When there are no allusions to guide us, it is only by accident that we can hope to test the history and antiquity of these kind of scraps, but we have no doubt whatever that many of them are centuries old. The following has been traced to the time of Henry VI, a singular doggerel, the joke of which consists in saying it so quickly that it cannot be told whether it is English or gibberish:

In fir tar is,
In oak none is,
In mud eel is,
In clay none is,
Goat eat ivy,
Mare eat oats.

"Multiplication is vexation", a painful reality to schoolboys, was found a few years ago in a manuscript dated 1570; and the memorial lines, "Thirty days hath September", occur in the "Return from Parnassus", an old play printed in 1606. Our own reminiscences of such matters, and those of Shakespeare, may thus have been identical! "To market, to market, to buy a plum-bun", is partially quoted in Florio's "New World of Words", 1611, in v. "Abómba". The old song of the "Carion Crow sat on an Oak", was discovered by me in MS. Sloane 1489, of the time of Charles I, but under a different form:

> Hic, hoc, the carrion crow,
> For I have shot something too low:
> I have quite missed my mark,
> And shot the poor sow to the heart;
> Wife, bring treacle in a spoon,
> Or else the poor sow's heart will down.

Joseph Mede, Chr. Coll. July 1, 1626, (MS. Harl. 390, f. 85):

> There was a crow sate on a stone,
>   He flew away and there was none.
> There was a man that ran a race,
>   When he ran fast, he ran apace.
> There was a mayd, that eate an apple,
>   When she eate two she eate a couple.
> There was an ape sate on a tree,
>   When he fell downe, then downe fell hee.
> There was a fleet that went to Spaine,
>   When it return'd it came againe.

"Sing a song of sixpence" is quoted by Beaumont and Fletcher. "Buz, quoth the blue fly", which is printed in the nursery half-penny books, belongs to Ben Jonson's Masque of "Oberon"; the old ditty of "Three Blind Mice" is found in the curious music book entitled "Deuteromelia, or the Second Part of Musicke's Melodie", 1609; and the song, "When I was a little girl, I wash'd my mammy's dishes", is given by Aubrey in MS. Lansd. 231. "A swarm of bees in May", is quoted by Miege, 1687. And so on of others, fragments of old catches and popular songs being constantly traced in the apparently unmeaning rhymes of the nursery.

Most of us have heard in time past the school address to a story-teller; the proverb occurs in "Gammer Gurton's Needle" *ad fin.*:

> Liar, liar, lick dish,
> Turn about the candlestick.

Not very important lines, one would imagine, but they explain a passage in Chettle's play of the "Tragedy of Hoffman, or a Revenge for a Father", 4to. Lond. 1631, which would be partially inexplicable without such assistance:

> Lor.　By heaven! it seemes hee did, but all was vaine;
> 　　　The flinty rockes had cut his tender scull,
> 　　　And the rough water wash't away his braine.
> Luc.　Lyer, lyer, licke dish!

The intention of the last speaker is sufficiently intelligible, but a future editor, anxious to investigate his author minutely, might search in vain for an explanation of *licke dish*. Another instance* of the antiquity of children's rhymes I met with lately at Stratford-on-Avon, in a MS. of the seventeenth century, in the collection of the late Captain James Saunders, where, amongst common-place memoranda on more serious subjects, written about the year 1630, occurred a version of one of our most favourite nursery songs:

> I had a little bonny nagg,
> 　His name was Dapple Gray;
> And he would bring me to an ale-house
> 　A mile out of my way.

"Three children sliding on the ice" is founded on a metrical tale published at the end of a translation of Ovid "de Arte Amandi", 1662.† The lines,

> There was an old woman
> Lived under a hill,
> And if she ben't gone,
> She lives there still,

form part of an old catch, printed in the "Academy of Complements", ed. 1714, p. 108. The same volume (p. 140) contains the original words to another catch, which has been corrupted in its passage to the nursery:

---

* A dance called "Hey, diddle, diddle", is mentioned in the play of "King Cambises", written about 1561, and the several rhymes commencing with those words may have been original adaptations to that dance-tune.
† See the whole poem in my "Nursery Rhymes of England".

There was an old man had three sons,
Had three sons, had three sons;
There was an old man had three sons,
    Jeffery, James, and Jack.
Jeffery was hang'd and James was drown'd,
And Jack was lost, that he could not be found,
And the old man fell into a swoon,
    For want of a cup of sack!

It is not improbable that Shakespeare, who has alluded so much and so intricately to the vernacular rural literature of his day, has more notices of nursery rhymes and tales than research has hitherto elicited. I am only acquainted with one reference to the former: "Pillicock sat on Pillicock hill", which is quoted by Edgar in "King Lear", iii. 4, and is found in "Gammer Gurton's Garland", and in most modern collections of English nursery rhymes. The secret meaning is not very delicate, nor is it necessary to enter into any explanation on the subject. It may, however, be worthy of remark, that the term *pillicock* is found in a manuscript (Harl. 913) in the British Museum of the thirteenth century.

English children accompanied their amusements with trivial verses from a very early period, but as it is only by accident that any allusions to them have been made, it is difficult to sustain the fact by many examples. The "Nomenclator or Remembrancer of Adrianus Junius", translated by Higins, and edited by Fleming, 8vo. 1585, contains a few notices of this kind; p. 298, "βασιλινδα, the playe called one penie, one penie, come after me; χυτρινδα, the play called the selling of peares, or how many plums for a penie; p. 299, χοινοφιλινδα, a kinde of playe called

    Clowt, clowt,
    To beare about,

or my hen hath layd: ιποστρακισμος, a kind of sport or play with an oister shell or a stone throwne into the water, and making circles yer it sinke, &c.; it is called,

    A ducke and a drake,
    And a halfe penie cake."

This last notice is particularly curious, for similar verses are used by boys at the present day at the game of water-skimming. The amusement itself is very ancient, and a description of it may be seen in Minucius Felix, Lugd. Bat 1652, p. 3. There cannot be a doubt but that many of the inexplicable nonsense-rhymes of our nursery belonged to antique recreations, but it is very seldom their original application can be recovered. The well-known doggerel respecting the tailor of Bicester may be mentioned as a remarkable instance of this, for it is one of the most common nursery rhymes of the present day, and Aubrey, MS. Lansd. 231, writing in the latter part of the seventeenth century, preserved it as part of the formula of a game called *Leap-candle*. "The young girls in and about Oxford have a sport called Leap-Candle, for which they set a candle in the middle of the room in a candlestick, and then draw up their coats into the form of breeches, and dance over the candle back and forth, with these words:

> The tailor of Biciter,
> He has but one eye,
> He cannot cut a pair of green galagaskins,
> If he were to die.

This sport in other parts is called *Dancing the Candle Rush*." It may be necessary to observe that *galagaskins* were wide loose trousers.

In the "London Cuckolds", a comedy of the date 1682, we find this rhyme:

> There was a lady loved a swine, hunny, quoth she,
> Pig-hog wilt thou be mine—Hunh—quoth he—

The rhyme of Jack Horner has been stated to be a satire on the Puritanical aversions to Christmas pies and such-like abominations. It forms part of a metrical chap-book history, founded on the same story as the Friar and the Boy, entitled "The Pleasant History of Jack Horner, containing his witty tricks, and pleasant pranks, which he played from his youth to his riper years: right pleasant and delightful for winter and summer's recreation", embellished with frightful wood-cuts, which have not much connection with the tale. The pleasant history commences as follows:

> Jack Horner was a pretty lad,
> Near London he did dwell,

His father's heart he made full glad,
    His mother loved him well.
While little Jack was sweet and young,
    If he by chance should cry,
His mother pretty sonnets sung,
    With a lul-la-ba-by,
With such a dainty curious tone,
    As Jack sat on her knee,
So that, ere he could go alone,
    He sang as well as she.
A pretty boy of curious wit,
    All people spoke his praise,
And in the corner would he sit
    In Christmas holydays.
When friends they did together meet,
    To pass away the time—
Why, little Jack, he sure would eat
    His Christmas pie in rhyme.
And said, Jack Horner, in the corner,
    Eats good Christmas pie,
And with his thumbs pulls out the plumbs,
    And said, Good boy am I!

Here we have an important discovery! Who before suspected that the nursery rhyme was written by Jack Horner himself?

Few children's rhymes are more common than those relating to Jack Sprat and his wife, "Jack Sprat could eat no fat", &c.; but it is little thought they have been current for two centuries. Such, however, is the fact, and when Howell published his collection of Proverbs in 1659, p. 20, the story related to no less exalted a personage than an archdeacon:

    Archdeacon Pratt would eat no fatt,
        His wife would eat no lean;
    'Twixt Archdeacon Pratt and Joan his wife,
        The meat was eat up clean.

On the same page of this collection we find the commencement of the rigmarole, "A man of words and not of deeds", which in the next century was converted into a burlesque song on the battle of Culloden!*

> Double Dee Double Day,
> Set a garden full of seeds;
> When the seeds began to grow,
> It's like a garden full of snow.
> When the snow began to melt,
> Like a ship without a belt.
> When the ship began to sail,
> Like a bird without a tail.
> When the bird began to fly,
> Like an eagle in the sky.
> When the sky began to roar,
> Like a lion at the door.
> When the door began to crack,
> Like a stick laid o'er my back.
> When my back began to smart,
> Like a penknife in my heart.
> When my heart began to bleed,
> Like a needleful of thread.
> When the thread began to rot,
> Like a turnip in the pot.
> When the pot began to boil,
> Like a bottle full of oil.
> When the oil began to settle,
> Like our Geordies bloody battle.

* The following nursery game, played by two girls, one personating the mistress and the other a servant was obtained from Yorkshire, and may be interpreted as a dialogue between a lady and her Jacobite maid:

Lady. Jenny, come here! So I hear you have been to see that man.
Maid. What man, madam?
Lady. Why, the handsome man.
Maid. Why, madam, as I was a-passing by,
Thinking no harm, no not in the least, not I,
I did go in,
But had no ill intention in the thing,
For, as folks say, a cat may look at a king.
Lady. A king do you call him? You rebellious slut!
Maid. I did not call him so, dear lady, but—
Lady. But me none of your buttings, for not another day
Shall any rebel in my service stay;
I owe you twenty shillings—there's a guinea!
Go, pack your clothes, and get about your business, Jenny.

The earliest copy of the saying, "A man of words and not of deeds", I have hitherto met with, occurs in MS. Harl. 1927, of the time of James I. Another version, written towards the close of the seventeenth century, but unfitted for publication, is preserved on the last leaf of MS. Harl. 6580.

In "Love Without Interest", a play dating 1699, is found this nursery rhyme:

> (Jon. *pulls out several Papers, flings 'em by slightly, while he sings.*)
> And when I was a little boy I wash'd my mother's dishes,
> I put my fingers in the pail, and pull'd out little fishes.

Many of the metrical nonsense-riddles of the nursery are of considerable antiquity. A collection of conundrums formed early in the seventeenth century by Randle Holmes, the Chester antiquary, and now preserved in MS. Harl. 1962, contains several which have been traditionally remembered up to the present day. Thus we find versions of "Little Nancy Etticoat in a white petticoat", "Two legs sat upon three legs", "As round as an apple", and others.*

During the latter portion of the seventeenth century numerous songs and games were introduced which were long remembered in the English nursery. "Questions and Commands" was a common game, played under various systems of representation. One boy would enact king, and the subjects would give burlesque answers, *e.g.*:

> *K.* King I am!
> *S.* I am your man.
> *K.* What service will you do?
> *S.* The best and worst, and all I can!

A clever writer in the "Gentleman's Magazine" for 1738, says this was played during the Commonwealth in ridicule of sovereignty! He humourously adds, continually quoting games then current: "During all Oliver's time, the chief diversion was, 'The parson hath lost his fuddling cap', which needs no explanation. At the Restoration succeeded love-games, as 'I love my love with an

---

* A vast number of these kind of rhymes have become obsolete, and old manuscripts contain many not very intelligible. Take the following as a specimen:
> Ruste duste tarbotell,
> Bagpipelorum hybattell.—*MS. Harl.* 7332, xvij. cent.

A', a 'Flower and a lady', and 'I am a lusty wooer', changed in the latter end of this reign, as well as all King James II's, to 'I am come to torment you'. At the Revolution, when all people recovered their liberty the children played promiscuously at what game they liked best. The most favourite one, however, was 'Puss in the corner'." The same writer also mentions the game of "I am a Spanish merchant".

The following nursery rhyme is quoted in Parkin's Reply to Dr. Stukeley's second number of the "Origines Roystonianæ", 4to. 1748, p. 6, but I am not aware that it is still current:

> Peter White will ne'er go right,
>   And would you know the reason why?
> He follows his nose where'er he goes,
>   And that stands all awry.

The song of the Lion and the Unicorn is mentioned in "Useful Transactions in Philosophy", 8vo. 1709, p. 56.

"Four and twenty fiddlers all in a row" is quoted in the play of "Vice Reclaimed", 4to. 1703, p. 18.

The tale of Old Mother Hubbard is undoubtedly of some antiquity, were we merely to judge of the rhyme of *laughing* to *coffin* in the third verse.* "There was an old woman toss'd up in a blanket" is supposed to be the original song of "Lilliburlero, or Old Woman, whither so high?" the tune to which was published in 1678.† "Come, drink old ale with me", a nursery catch, with an improper meaning now lost, is found in MS. Harl. 7332, of the seventeenth century. "Round about, round about, maggotty pie" is probably as old, magot-pie being an obsolete term for magpie. For a similar reason, the antiquity of "Here am I, little Jumping Joan", may be inferred. Jumping Joan was the cant term for a lady of little reputation.‡ The well-known riddle, "As I was going to St. Ives", occurs in MS. Harl. 7316, of the early part of the last century; and the following extract from Poor Robin's Almanack for 1693 may furnish us with the original of the celebrated ballad on Tom of

---

* The first three verses are all the original. The rest is modern, and was added when Mother Hubbard was the first of a series of eighteen-penny books published by Harris.
† Chappell's National Airs, p. 89.
‡ Beaumont and Fletcher. ed. Dyce, viii. 176. The tune of Jumping Joan is mentioned in MS. Harl. 7316, p. 67.

Islington, though the latter buried his troublesome wife on Sunday: "How one saw a lady on the Saturday, married her on the Sunday, she was brought to bed on the Monday, the child christened on the Tuesday, it died on the Wednesday, was buried on the Thursday, the bride's portion was paid on the Friday, and the bridegroom ran clear away on the Saturday!"

"Little Tommy Tucker" was the name of the Christmas prince at St. John's College, Oxford, in the year 1607.

The antiquity of a rhyme is not unfrequently determined by the use of an obsolete expression. Thus it may be safely concluded that the common nursery address to the white moth is no modern composition, from the use of the term *dustipoll*, a very old nickname for a miller, which has long fallen into disuse:

> Millery, millery, dustipoll,
> How many sacks have you stole?
> Four and twenty and a peck:
> Hang the miller up by his neck!

The expression is used by Robin Goodfellow in the old play of "Grim, the Collier of Croydon", first printed in 1662, but written considerably before that period:

> Now, miller, miller, dustipole,
> I'll clapper-claw your jobbernole!*

"Ride a cock horse to Banbury Cross" is probably ancient, the cross having been pulled down in the seventeenth century.

"I went to the toad that lies under the wall", Ben Jonson, vol. 7, p. 132.

A very curious ballad, written about the year 1720, in the possession of Mr. Crofton Croker, establishes the antiquity of the rhymes of "Jack-a-Dandy", "Boys and girls come out to play", "Tom Tidler's on the Friar's ground", "London bridge is broken

---

* "Oh, madam, I will give you the keys of Canterbury", must be a very ancient song, as it mentions chopines, or high cork shoes, and appears, from another passage, to have been written before the invention of bell-pulls. The obsolete term *delve*, to dig, exhibits the antiquity of the rhyme "One, two, buckle my shoe". *Minikin* occurs in a rhyme printed in the "Nursery Rhymes of England", p. 145; *coif, ibid.* p. 150; *snaps*, small fragments, *ibid.* p. 190; *moppet*, a little pet, *ibid.* p. 193, &c.

down", "Who comes here? A grenadier", and "See, saw, sacra-down", besides mentioning others we have before alluded to. The ballad is entitled, "Namby Pamby, or a Panegyric on the New Versification, addressed to A. F., Esq."

> Nanty Panty, Jack-a-Dandy,
> Stole a piece of sugar-candy,
> From the grocer's shoppy shop,
> And away did hoppy hop.

In the course of the ballad, the writer thus introduces the titles of the nursery rhymes,

> Namby Pamby's double mild,
> Once a man, and twice a child;
> To his hanging sleeves restor'd,
> Now he fools it like a lord;
> Now he pumps his little wits
> All by little tiny bits.
> Now, methinks, I hear him say,
> Boys and girls, come out to play,*
> Moon do's shine as bright as day:
> Now my Namby Pamby's† found
> Sitting on the Friar's ground,
> Picking silver, picking gold,—
> Namby Pamby's never old:
> Bally-cally they begin,
> Namby Pamby still keeps in.
> Namby Pamby is no clown—
> London bridge is broken down:
> Now he courts the gay ladee,
> Dancing o'er the Lady Lee:‡
> Now he sings of Lickspit Liar,
> Burning in the brimstone fire;

* Mentioned, with a variation, in "Useful Transactions in Philosophy", 8vo. 1709, p. 44.
† Namby Pamby is said to have been a nickname for Ambrose Phillips. Another ballad, written about the same time as the above, alludes to the rhyme of "Goosy Goosy, Gander".
‡ "Dance over the Lady Lea", alluded to in "Have at you All, or the Drury Lane Journal", 1752, p. 103.

Lyar, lyar, Lickspit, lick,
Turn about the candlestick.
Now he sings of Jacky Horner,
Sitting in the chimney corner,
Eating of a Christmas pie,
Putting in his thumb, oh! fie!
Putting in, oh! fie, his thumb,
Pulling out, oh! strange, a plumb!
Now he acts the grenadier,
Calling for a pot of beer:
Where's his money? He's forgot—
Get him gone, a drunken sot!
Now on cock-horse does he ride,
And anon on timber stride,
Se and saw, and sack'ry down,
London is a gallant town!

This ballad is a very important illustration of the history of these puerile rhymes, for it establishes the fact that some we might aptly consider modern are at least more than a century old; and who would have thought such nonsense as,

Who comes here?
A grenadier!
What do you want?
A pot of beer!
Where's your money?
I've forgot!
Get you gone,
You drunken sot!

could have descended in all its purity for several generations, even although it really may have a deep meaning and an unexceptionable moral?

Having thus, I trust, shown that the nursery has an archaeology, the study of which may eventually lead to important results, the jingles and songs of our childhood are defended from the imputation of exclusive frivolity. We may hope that, henceforth, those who have the opportunity will not consider it a derogatory task to add to these memorials. But they must hasten to the rescue. The antiquities of the people are rapidly disappearing before the spread of education; and before many years have elapsed, they will be lost, or recorded only in the collections of the antiquary, perhaps requiring evidence that they ever existed. This is the latest period at which there is a chance of our arresting their disappearance. If, unfortunately, the most valuable relics of this kind are wholly lost, many, doubtlessly, remain in the remote districts sufficiently curious to reward the collector; and it is to be hoped they will not be allowed to share the fate of Wade and his boat Guingelot.

TWO

Fireside Nursery Stories

The efforts of modern romance are so greatly superior to the best fictions of a former age, that old wives' tales are not so readily tolerated as they were in times past. We question whether any one in these days, save a very grave antiquary, could read two chapters of the Morte Arthure without a yawn. Let us, then, turn to that simpler class of narratives which bears the same relation to novels that rural ballads do to the poem; and ascertain whether the wild interest which, in the primitive tales erewhile taught by nurse, first awakened our imagination, can be so reflected as to render their resuscitation agreeable. We rely a good deal for the success of the experiment on the power of association; for though these inventions may, in their character, be suited to the dawn of intellect, they not infrequently bear the impress of creative fancy, and their imperceptible influence over the mind does not always evaporate at a later age.

Few persons, indeed, there are, even amongst those who affect to be insignificantly touched by the imagination, who can be recalled to the stories and carols that charmed them in their childhood wholly without emotion. An affectation of indifference in such matters is, of course, not unusual, for most thoughts springing from early associations, and those on which so many minds love to dwell, may not be indiscriminately divulged. It is impossible they should be generally appreciated or understood. Most of us, however, are liable to be occasionally touched by allusions breathing of happy days, bearing our memories downward to behold the shadows of joys that have long passed away like a dream. They now serve only "to mellow our occasions", like that "old and antique song" which relieved the passion of the Duke Orsino.

NURSERY TALE

I saddled my sow with a sieve full of buttermilk, put my foot into the stirrup, and leaped nine miles beyond the moon into the land of Temperance, where there was nothing but hammers and hatchets and candlesticks, and there lay bleeding Old Noles. I let him lie, and sent for Old Hippernoles, and asked him if he could grind green steel nine times finer than wheat flour. He said he could not. Gregory's wife was up in the pear-tree gathering nine corns of buttered peas to pay St. James's rent. St. James was in the meadow mowing oat cakes; he heard a noise, hung up his scythe at his heels, stumbled at the battledore, tumbled over the barn-door ridge, and broke his shins against a bag of moonshine that stood behind the stairsfoot door, and if that isn't true you know as well as I.

SIR GAMMER VANS

Last Sunday morning at six o'clock in the evening as I was sailing over the tops of the mountains in my little boat, I met two men on horseback riding on one mare: so I asked them "Could they tell me whether the little old woman was dead yet who was hanged last Saturday week for drowning herself in a shower of feathers?" They said they could not positively inform me, but if I went to Sir Gammer Vans he could tell me all about it. "But how am I to know the house?" said I. "Ho, 'tis easy enough," said they, "for 'tis a brick house, built entirely of flints, standing alone by itself in the middle of sixty or seventy others just like it." "Oh, nothing in the world is easier," said I. "Nothing *can* be easier," said they; so I went on my way. Now this Sir G. Vans was a giant, and bottle-maker. And as all giants who *are* bottle-makers usually pop out of a little thumb-bottle from behind the door, so did Sir G. Vans. "How d'ye do?" says he. "Very well, I thank you," says I. "Have some breakfast with me?" "With all my heart," says I. So he gave me a slice of beer, and a cup of cold veal; and there was a little dog under the table that picked up all the crumbs. "Hang him," says I. "No, don't hang him," says he; "for he killed a hare yesterday. And if you don't believe me, I'll show you the hare alive in a basket." So he took me into his garden to show me the curiosities. In one corner there was a fox hatching eagle's eggs; in another there was an iron apple-tree, entirely covered with pears and lead; in the third there was the hare which the dog killed yesterday alive in the basket; and in the fourth there were twenty-four *hipper switches* threshing tobacco, and at the sight of me they threshed so hard that they drove the plug through the wall, and through a little dog that was passing by on the other side. I, hearing the dog howl, jumped over the wall; and turned it as neatly inside out as possible, when it ran away as if it had not an hour to live. Then he took me into the park to show me his deer: and I remembered that I had a warrant in my pocket to shoot venison for his majesty's dinner. So I set fire to my bow, poised my arrow, and shot amongst them. I broke seventeen ribs on one side, and twenty-one and a-half on the other; but my arrow passed clean through without ever touching it, and the worst was I lost my arrow: however, I found it again in the hollow of a tree. I felt it; it felt clammy. I smelt it: it smelt honey. "Oh, ho!" said I, "here's a bee's nest," when out sprang a covey of partridges. I shot at them; some say I killed eighteen; but I am sure I killed thirty-six, besides a dead salmon which was flying over the bridge, of which I made the best apple-pie I ever tasted.

TEENY-TINY*

Once upon a time there was a teeny-tiny woman lived in a teeny-tiny house in a teeny-tiny village. Now, one day this teeny-tiny woman put on her teeny-tiny bonnet, and went out of her teeny-tiny house to take a teeny-tiny walk. And when this teeny-tiny woman had gone a teeny-tiny way, she came to a teeny-tiny gate; so the teeny-tiny woman opened the teeny-tiny gate, and went into the teeny-tiny churchyard. And when this teeny-tiny woman had got into the teeny-tiny churchyard, she saw a teeny-tiny bone on a

* This simple tale seldom fails to rivet the attention of children, especially if well told. The last two words should be said loudly with a start. It was obtained from oral tradition, and has not, I believe, been printed.

teeny-tiny grave, and the teeny-tiny woman said to her teeny-tiny self, "This teeny-tiny bone will make me some teeny-tiny soup for my teeny-tiny supper." So the teeny-tiny woman put the teeny-tiny bone into her teeny-tiny pocket, and went home to her teeny-tiny house.

Now when the teeny-tiny woman got home to her teeny-tiny house she was a teeny-tiny tired; so she went up her teeny-tiny stairs to her teeny-tiny bed, and put the teeny-tiny bone into a teeny-tiny cupboard. And when this teeny-tiny woman had been to sleep a teeny-tiny time, she was awakened by a teeny-tiny voice from the teeny-tiny cupboard, which said, "Give me my bone!" And this teeny-tiny woman was a teeny-tiny frightened, so she hid her teeny-tiny head under the teeny-tiny clothes, and went to sleep again. And when she had been to sleep again a teeny-tiny time, the teeny-tiny voice again cried out from the teeny-tiny cupboard a teeny-tiny louder, "Give me my bone!" This made the teeny-tiny woman a teeny-tiny more frightened, so she hid her teeny-tiny head a teeny-tiny further under the teeny-tiny clothes. And when the teeny-tiny woman had been to sleep again a teeny-tiny time, the teeny-tiny voice from the teeny-tiny cupboard said again a teeny-tiny louder, "Give me my bone!" And this teeny-tiny woman was a teeny-tiny bit more frightened, but she put her teeny-tiny head out of the teeny-tiny clothes, and said, in her loudest teeny-tiny voice, "Take it!"

THE STORY OF MR. VINEGAR*

Mr. and Mrs. Vinegar lived in a vinegar bottle. Now one day, when Mr. Vinegar was from home, Mrs. Vinegar, who was a very good housewife, was busily sweeping her house, when an unlucky thump of the broom brought the whole house clitter-clatter, clitter-clatter, about her ears. In a paroxysm of grief she rushed forth to meet her husband. On seeing him she exclaimed, "Oh, Mr. Vinegar, Mr. Vinegar, we are ruined, we are ruined: I have knocked the house down, and it is all to pieces!" Mr. Vinegar then said, "My dear, let us see what can be done. Here is the door; I will take it on my back, and we will go forth to seek our fortune." They walked all that day, and at nightfall entered a thick forest. They were both excessively tired, and Mr. Vinegar said, "My love, I will climb up into a tree,

* This story was obtained from oral tradition in the West of England. It is undoubtedly a variation of the "Hans im Glück" of Grimm, which is current in Germany.

drag up the door, and you shall follow." He accordingly did so, and they both stretched their weary limbs on the door, and fell fast asleep. In the middle of the night Mr. Vinegar was disturbed by the sound of voices beneath, and to his inexpressible dismay perceived that a party of thieves were met to divide their booty. "Here, Jack," said one, "here's five pounds for you; here, Bill, here's ten pounds for you; here, Bob, here's three pounds for you." Mr. Vinegar could listen no longer; his terror was so intense that he trembled most violently, and shook down the door on their heads. Away scampered the thieves, but Mr. Vinegar dared not quit his retreat till broad daylight. He then scrambled out of the tree, and went to lift up the door. What did he behold but a number of golden guineas! "Come down, Mrs. Vinegar," he cried, "come down, I say; our fortune's made, our fortune's made! come down, I say." Mrs. Vinegar got down as fast as she could, and saw the money with equal delight. "Now, my dear," said she, "I'll tell you what you shall do. There is a fair at the neighbouring town; you shall take these forty guineas and buy a cow. I can make butter and cheese, which you shall sell at market, and we shall then be able to live very comfortably." Mr. Vinegar joyfully assents, takes the money, and goes off to the fair. When he arrived, he walked up and down, and at length saw a beautiful red cow. It was an excellent milker, and perfect in every respect. Oh! thought Mr. Vinegar, if I had but that cow I should be the happiest man alive; so he offers the forty guineas for the cow, and the owner declaring that, as he was a friend, he'd oblige him, the bargain was made. Proud of his purchase, he drove the cow backwards and forwards to show it. By and by he saw a man playing the bagpipes, Tweedle dum, tweedle de; the children followed him about, and he appeared to be pocketing money on all sides. Well, thought Mr. Vinegar, if I had but that beautiful instrument I should be the happiest man alive—my fortune would be made. So he went up to the man: "Friend," says he, "what a beautiful instrument that is, and what a deal of money you must make." "Why, yes," said the man, "I make a great deal of money, to be sure, and it is a wonderful instrument." "Oh!" cried Mr. Vinegar, "how I should like to possess it!" "Well," said the man, "as you are a friend, I don't much mind parting with it; you shall have it for that red cow." "Done," said the delighted Mr. Vinegar; so the beautiful red cow was given for the bagpipes. He

29

walked up and down with his purchase, but in vain he attempted to play a tune, and instead of pocketing pence, the boys followed him hooting, laughing, and pelting. Poor Mr. Vinegar, his fingers grew very cold, and, heartily ashamed and mortified, he was leaving the town, when he met a man with a fine thick pair of gloves. "Oh, my my fingers are so very cold," said Mr. Vinegar to himself; "if I had but those beautiful gloves I should be the happiest man alive." He went up to the man, and said to him, "Friend, you seem to have a capital pair of gloves there." "Yes, truly," cried the man; "and my hands are as warm as possible this cold November day." "Well," said Mr. Vinegar, "I should like to have them." "What will you give?" said the man; "as you are a friend of mine, I don't much mind letting you have them for those bagpipes." "Done," cried Mr. Vinegar. He put on the gloves, and felt perfectly happy as he trudged homewards. At last he grew very tired, when he saw a man coming towards him with a good stout stick in his hand. "Oh," said Mr. Vinegar, "that I had but that stick! I should then be the happiest man alive." He accosted the man—"Friend! what a rare good stick you have got." "Yes," said the man, "I have used it for many a long mile, and a good friend it has been, but if you have a fancy for it, as you are a friend, I don't mind giving it to you for that pair of gloves." Mr. Vinegar's hands were so warm, and his legs so tired, that he gladly exchanged. As he drew near to the wood where he had left his wife, he heard a parrot on a tree calling out his name —"Mr. Vinegar, you foolish man, you blockhead, you simpleton; you went to the fair, and laid out all your money in buying a cow; not content with that, you changed it for bagpipes, on which you could not play, and which were not worth one-tenth of the money. You fool, you—you had no sooner got the bagpipes than you changed them for the gloves, which were not worth one quarter of the money; and when you had got the gloves, you changed them for a poor miserable stick; and now for your forty guineas, cow, bagpipes, and gloves, you have nothing to show but that poor miserable stick, which you might have cut in any hedge." On this the bird laughed immoderately, and Mr. Vinegar falling into a violent rage, threw the stick at its head. The stick lodged in the tree, and he returned to his wife without money, cow, bagpipes, gloves, or stick, and she instantly gave him such a sound cudgelling that she almost broke every bone in his skin.

THE STORY OF CHICKEN-LICKEN*

As Chicken-licken went one day to the wood, an acorn fell upon her poor bald pate, and she thought the sky had fallen. So she said she would go and tell the king that the sky had fallen. So chicken-licken turned back, and met Hen-len. "Well, hen-len, where are you going?" And hen-len said, "I'm going to the wood for some meat." And chicken-licken said, "Oh; hen-len, don't go, for I was going, and the sky fell upon my poor bald pate, and I am going to tell the king." So hen-len turned back with chicken-licken, and met Cock-lock. "Oh! cock-lock, where are you going?" And cock-lock said, "I'm going to the wood for some meat." Then hen-len said, "Oh! cock-lock, don't go, for I was going, and I met chicken-licken, and chicken-licken had been at the wood, and the sky had fallen on her poor bald pate, and we are going to tell the king."

So cock-lock turned back, and met Duck-luck. "Well, duck-luck, where are you going?" And duck-luck said, "I'm going to the wood for some meat." Then cock-lock said, "Oh! duck-luck, don't go, for I was going, and I met hen-len, and hen-len met chicken-licken, and chicken-licken had been at the wood, and the sky had fallen on her bald pate, and we are going to tell the king."

So duck-luck turned back, and met Drake-lake. "Well, drake-lake, where are you going?" And drake-lake said, "I'm going to the wood for some meat." Then duck-luck said, "Oh! drake-lake, don't go, for I was going, and I met cock-lock, and cock-lock met hen-len, and hen-len met chicken-licken, and chicken-licken had been at the wood, and the sky had fallen on her poor bald pate, and we are going to tell the king."

So drake-lake turned back, and met Goose-loose. "Well, goose-loose, where are you going?" And goose-loose said, "I'm going to the wood for some meat." Then drake-lake said, "Oh! goose-loose, don't go, for I was going, and I met duck-luck, and duck-luck met cock-lock, and cock-lock met hen-len, and hen-len met chicken-licken, and chicken-licken had been at the wood, and the sky had fallen on her poor bald pate, and we are going to tell the king."

So goose-loose turned back, and met Gander-lander. "Well, gander-lander, where you going?" And gander-lander said, "I'm going to the wood for some meat." Then goose-loose said, "Oh!

* A shorter and very different version of this is given by Mr Chambers, p. 211.

gander-lander, don't go, for I was going, and I met drake-lake, and drake-lake met duck-luck, and duck-luck met cock-lock, and cock-lock met hen-len, and hen-len met chicken-licken, and chicken-licken had been at the wood, and the sky had fallen on her poor bald pate, and we are going to tell the king."

So gander-lander turned back, and met Turkey-lurkey. "Well, turkey-lurkey, where are you going?" And turkey-lurkey said, "I'm going to the wood for some meat." Then gander-lander said, "Oh! turkey-lurkey, don't go, for I was going, and I met goose-loose, and goose-loose met drake-lake, and drake-lake met duck-luck, and duck-luck met cock-lock, and cock-lock met hen-len, and hen-len met chicken-licken, and chicken-licken had been at the wood, and the sky had fallen on her poor bald pate, and we are going to tell the king."

So turkey-lurkey turned back, and walked with gander-lander, goose-loose, drake-lake, duck-luck, cock-lock, hen-len, and chicken-licken. And as they were going along, they met Fox-lox. And fox-lox said, "Where are you going, my pretty maids?" And they said, "Chicken-licken went to the wood, and the sky fell upon her poor bald pate, and we are going to tell the king." And fox-lox said, "Come along with me, and I will show you the way." But fox-lox took them into the fox's hole, and he and his young ones soon ate up poor chicken-licken, hen-len, cock-lock, duck-luck, drake-lake, goose-loose, gander-lander, and turkey-lurkey, and they never saw the king to tell him that the sky had fallen!

THE MISER AND HIS WIFE*

Once upon a time there was an old miser, who lived with his wife near a great town, and used to put by every bit of money he could lay his hands on. His wife was a simple woman, and they lived together without quarrelling, but she was obliged to put up with very

---

* "Let us cast away nothing," says Mr. Gifford, "for we know not what use we may have for it." So will every one admit whose reading has been sufficiently extensive to enable him to judge of the value of the simplest traditional tales. The present illustrates a passage in Ben Jonson in a very remarkable manner,

——Say we are robb'd,
If any come to borrow a spoon or so;
I will not have Good Fortune or God's Blessing
Let in, while I am busy.

hard fare. Now, sometimes, when there was a sixpence she thought might be spared for a comfortable dinner or supper, she used to ask the miser for it, but he would say, "No, wife, it must be put by for Good Fortune." It was the same with every penny he could get hold of, and notwithstanding all she could say, almost every coin that came into the house was put by "for Good Fortune".

The miser said this so often, that some of his neighbours heard him, and one of them thought of a trick by which he might get the money. So the first day that the old chuff was away from home, he dressed himself like a wayfaring man, and knocked at the door. "Who are you?" said the wife. He answered, "I am Good Fortune, and I am come for the money which your husband has laid by for me." So this simple woman, not suspecting any trickery, readily gave it to him, and, when her good man came home, told him very pleasantly that Good Fortune had called for the money which had been kept so long for him.

THE THREE QUESTIONS

There lived formerly in the county of Cumberland a nobleman who had three sons, two of whom were comely and clever youths, but the other a natural fool, named Jack, who was generally dressed in a party-coloured coat, and a steeple-crowned hat with a tassel, as became his condition. Now the King of the East Angles had a beautiful daughter, who was distinguished by her great ingenuity and wit, and he issued a decree that whoever should answer three questions put to him by the princess should have her in marriage, and be heir to the crown at his decease. Shortly after this decree was published, news of it reached the ears of the nobleman's sons, and the two clever ones determined to have a trial, but they were sadly at a loss to prevent their idiot brother from going with them. They could not, by any means, get rid of him, and were compelled at length to let Jack accompany them. They had not gone far, before Jack shrieked with laughter, saying, "I've found an egg." "Put it in your pocket," said the brothers. A little while afterwards, he burst out into another fit of laughter on finding a crooked hazel stick, which he also put in his pocket: and a third time he again laughed extravagantly because he found a nut. That also was put with his other treasures.

When they arrived at the palace, they were immediately admitted on mentioning the nature of their business, and were ushered into a room where the princess and her suite were sitting. Jack, who never stood on ceremony, bawled out, "What a troop of fair ladies we've got here!" "Yes," said the princess, "we are fair ladies, for we carry fire in our bosoms." "Do you," said Jack, "then roast me an egg," pulling out the egg from his pocket. "How will you get it out again?" said the princess. "With a crooked stick," replied Jack, producing the hazel. "Where did that come from?" said the princess. "From a nut," answered Jack, pulling out the nut from his pocket. And thus the "fool of the family", having been the first to answer the questions of the princess, was married to her the next day, and ultimately succeeded to the throne.

THE CAT AND THE MOUSE*

> The cat and the mouse
> Play'd in the malt-house:

The cat bit the mouse's tail off. Pray, Puss, give me my tail. No, says the cat, I'll not give you your tail, till you go to the cow, and fetch me some milk:

> First she leapt, and then she ran,
> Till she came to the cow, and thus began,—

Pray, Cow, give me milk, that I may give cat milk, that cat may give me my own tail again. No, said the cow, I will give you no milk, till you go to the farmer and get me some hay.

> First she leapt, and then she ran,
> Till she came to the farmer, and thus began,—

Pray, Farmer, give me hay, that I may give cow hay, that cow may give me milk, that I may give cat milk, that cat may give me my own tail again. No, says the farmer, I'll give you no hay, till you go to the butcher and fetch me some meat.

> First she leapt, and then she ran,
> Till she came to the butcher, and thus began,—

* This tale has been traced back fifty years, but it is probably considerably older.

Pray, Butcher, give me meat, that I may give farmer meat, that farmer may give me hay, that I may give cow hay, that cow may give me milk, that I may give cat milk, that cat may give me my own tail again. No, says the butcher, I'll give you no meat, till you go to the baker and fetch me some bread.

> First she leapt, and then she ran,
> Till she came to the baker, and thus began,—

Pray, Baker, give me bread, that I may give butcher bread, that butcher may give me meat, that I may give farmer meat, that farmer may give me hay, that I may give cow hay, that cow may give me milk, that I may give cat milk, that cat may give me my own tail again.

> Yes, says the baker, I'll give you some bread,
> But if you eat my meal, I'll cut off your head.

Then the baker gave mouse bread, and mouse gave butcher bread, and butcher gave mouse meat, and mouse gave farmer meat, and farmer gave mouse hay, and mouse gave cow hay, and cow gave mouse milk, and mouse gave cat milk, and cat gave mouse her own tail again!

THE PRINCESS OF CANTERBURY

In days of yore, when this country was governed by several sovereigns, amongst them was the King of Canterbury, who had an only daughter, wise, fair, and beautiful. She was unmarried, and according to a custom not unusual in those days, of assigning an arbitrary action for the present of a lady's hand, the king issued a proclamation, that whoever would watch one night with his daughter, and neither sleep nor doze, should have her the next day in marriage; but if he did either, he should lose his head. Many knights attempted to fulfil the condition, and, having failed in the attempt, forfeited their lives.

Now it happened that a young shepherd, grazing his flock near the road, said to his master, "Zur,* I see many gentlemen ride to the court at Canterbury, but I ne'er zee'em return again." "Oh,

---

* The present Kentish dialect does not adopt this form, but anciently some of the peculiarities of what is now the western dialect of England extended all over the southern counties.

shepherd," said his master, "I know not how you should, for they attempt to watch with the king's daughter, according to the decree, and not peforming it, they are all beheaded." "Well," said the shepherd, "I'll try my vorton; zo now vor a king's daughter, or a headless shepherd!" And taking his bottle and bag, he trudged to the court. In his way thither, he was obliged to cross a river, and pulling off his shoes and stockings, while he was passing over he observed several pretty fish bobbing against his feet; so he caught some, and put them into his pocket. When he reached the palace, he knocked at the gate loudly with his crook, and having mentioned the object of his visit, he was immediately conducted to a hall where the king's daughter sat ready prepared to receive her lovers. He was placed in a luxurious chair, and rich wines and spices were set before him, and all sorts of delicate meats. The shepherd, unused to such fare, ate and drank plentifully, so that he was nearly dozing before midnight. "Oh, shepherd," said the lady, "I have caught you napping!" "Noa, sweet ally, I was busy a-feeshing." "A fishing!" said the princess in the utmost astonishment: "Nay, shepherd, there is no fish-pond in the hall." "No matter vor that, I have been feeshing in my pocket, and have just caught one." "Oh me!" said she, "let me see it." The shepherd slyly drew the fish out of his pocket and pretending to have caught it, showed it her, and she declared it was the finest she ever saw. About half an hour after-wards, she said, "Shepherd, do you think you could get me one more?" He replied, "Mayhap I may, when I have baited my hook;" and after a little while he brought out another, which was finer than the first, and the princess was so delighted that she gave him leave to go to sleep, and promised to excuse him to her father.

In the morning the princess told the king, to his great astonish-ment, that the shepherd must not be beheaded, for he had been fishing in the hall all night; but when he heard how the shepherd had caught such beautiful fish out of his pocket, he asked him to catch one in his own. The shepherd readily undertook the task, and bidding the king lie down, he pretended to fish in his pocket, having another fish concealed ready in his hand, and giving him a sly prick with a needle, he held up the fish, and showed it to the king. His majesty did not much relish the operation, but he assented to the marvel of it, and the princess and shepherd were united the same day, and lived for many years in happiness and prosperity.

LAZY JACK*

Once upon a time there was a boy whose name was Jack, and he lived with his mother on a dreary common. They were very poor, and the old woman got her living by spinning, but Jack was so lazy that he would do nothing but bask in the sun in the hot weather, and sit by the corner of the hearth in the winter time. His mother could not persuade him to do anything for her, and was obliged at last to tell him that if he did not begin to work for his porridge, she would turn him out to get his living as he could.

This threat at length roused Jack, and he went out and hired himself for the day to a neighbouring farmer for a penny; but as he was coming home, never having had any money in his possession before, he lost it in passing over a brook. "You stupid boy," said his mother, "you should have put it in your pocket." "I'll do so another time," replied Jack.

The next day Jack went out again, and hired himself to a cow-keeper, who gave him a jar of milk for his day's work. Jack took the jar and put it into the large pocket of his jacket, spilling it all, long before he got home. "Dear me!" said the old woman; "you should have carried it on your head." "I'll do so another time," replied Jack.

The following day Jack hired himself again to a farmer, who agreed to give him a cream cheese for his services. In the evening, Jack took the cheese, and went home with it on his head. By the time he got home the cheese was completely spilt, part of it being lost, and part matted with his hair. "You stupid lout," said his mother, "you should have carried it very carefully in your hands." "I'll do so another time," replied Jack.

The day after this Jack again went out, and hired himself to a baker, who would give him nothing for his work but a large tom-cat. Jack took the cat, and began carrying it very carefully in his hands, but in a short time pussy scratched him so much that he was compelled to let it go. When he got home, his mother said to him, "You silly fellow, you should have tied it with a string, and dragged it along after you." "I'll do so another time," said Jack.

The next day Jack hired himself to a butcher, who rewarded his

* From oral tradition in Yorkshire.

labours by the handsome present of a shoulder of mutton. Jack took the mutton, tied it to a string, and trailed it along after him in the dirt, so that by the time he had got home the meat was completely spoilt. His mother was this time quite out of patience with him, for the next day was Sunday, and she was obliged to content herself with cabbage for her dinner. "You ninnyhammer," said she to her son, "you should have carried it on your shoulder." "I'll do so another time," replied Jack.

On the Monday Jack went once more, and hired himself to a cattle-keeper, who gave him a donkey for his trouble. Although Jack was very strong, he found some difficulty in hoisting the donkey on his shoulders, but at last he accomplished it, and began walking slowly home with his prize. Now it happened that in the course of his journey there lived a rich man with his only daughter, a beautiful girl, but unfortunately deaf and dumb; she had never laughed in her life, and the doctors said she would never recover till somebody made her laugh.* Many tried without success, and at last the father, in despair, offered her in marriage to the first man who could make her laugh. This young lady happened to be looking out of the window, when Jack was passing with the donkey on his shoulders, the legs sticking up in the air; and the sight was so comical and strange, that she burst out into a great fit of laughter, and immediately recovered her speech and hearing. Her father was overjoyed, and fulfilled his promise by marrying her to Jack, who was thus made a rich gentleman. They lived in a large house, and Jack's mother lived with them in great happiness until she died.

THE THREE HEADS OF THE WELL†

Long before Arthur and the Knights of the Round Table, there reigned in the eastern part of England a king who kept his court at Colchester. He was witty, strong, and valiant, by which means he subdued his enemies abroad, and secured peace among his subjects at home. Nevertheless, in the midst of his glory, his queen died,

---

* An incident analogous to this occurs in Grimm, "Die Goldene Gans". See Edgar Taylor's "Gammer Grethel", 1839, p. 5.
† This story is abridged from the old chap-book of the Three Kings of Colchester. The incident of the heads rising out of the well is very similar to one introduced in Peele's "Old Wives' Tale", 1595, and the verse is also of a similar character.

leaving behind her an only daughter, about fifteen years of age. This lady, from her courtly carriage, beauty and affability, was the wonder of all that knew her; but, as covetousness is said to be the root of all evil, so it happened in this instance. The king, hearing of a lady who had likewise an only daughter, for the sake of her riches had a mind to marry; though she was old, ugly, hooked-nosed, and humpbacked, yet all this could not deter him from marrying her. Her daughter, also, was a yellow dowdy, full of envy and ill-nature; and, in short, was much of the same mould as her mother. This signified nothing, for in a few weeks the king, attended by the nobility and gentry, brought his intended bride to his palace, where the marriage rites were performed. They had not been long in the court before they set the king against his own beautiful daughter, which was done by false reports and accusations. The young princess, having lost her father's love, grew weary of the court, and one day meeting with her father in the garden, she desired him, with tears in her eyes, to give her a small subsistence, and she would go and seek her fortune; to which the king consented, and ordered her mother-in-law to make up a small sum according to her discretion. She went to the queen, who gave her a canvas bag of brown bread and hard cheese, with a bottle of beer. Though this was but a very pitiful dowry for a king's daughter, she took it, returned thanks, and proceeded on her journey, passing through groves, woods, and valleys, till at length she saw an old man sitting on a stone at the mouth of a cave, who said, "Good morrow, fair maiden, whither away so fast?" "Aged father," says she, "I am going to seek my fortune." "What hast thou in thy bag and bottle?" "In my bag I have got bread and cheese, and in my bottle good small beer; will you please to partake of either?" "Yes," said he, "with all my heart." With that the lady pulled out her provisions, and bid him eat and welcome. He did so, and gave her many thanks, saying thus: "There is a thick thorny hedge before you, which will appear impassable; but take this wand in your hand, strike three times, and say, 'Pray, hedge, let me come through,' and it will open immediately; then, a little further, you will find a well; sit down on the brink of it, and there will come up three golden heads, which will speak: pray do whatever they require." Promising she would follow his directions, she took her leave of him. Arriving at the hedge, and pursuing the old man's directions, it divided, and gave her a passage: then, going

39

to the well, she had no sooner sat down than a golden head came up singing—

> Wash me, and comb me,
> And lay me down softly,
> And lay me on a bank to dry,
> That I may look pretty
> When somebody comes by.

"Yes," said she, and putting forth her hand, with a silver comb performed the office, placing it upon a primrose bank. Then came up a second and a third head, making the same request, which she complied with. She then pulled out her provisions and ate her dinner. Then said the heads one to another, "What shall we do for this lady who hath used us so kindly?" The first said, "I will cause such addition to her beauty as shall charm the most powerful prince in the world." The second said, "I will endow her with such perfume, both in body and breath, as shall far exceed the sweetest flowers." The third said, "My gift shall be none of the least, for, as she is a king's daughter, I'll make her so fortunate that she shall become queen to the greatest prince that reigns." This done, at their request she let them down into the well again, and so proceeded on her journey. She had not travelled long before she saw a king hunting in the park with his nobles; she would have avoided him, but the king having caught a sight of her, approached, and what with her beauty and perfumed breath, was so powerfully smitten, that he was not able to subdue his passion, but commenced his courtship immediately, and was so successful that he gained her love, and, conducting her to his palace, he caused her to be clothed in the most magnificent manner.

This being ended, and the king finding that she was the King of Colchester's daughter, ordered some chariots to be got ready, that he might pay the king a visit. The chariot in which the king and queen rode was adorned with rich ornamental gems of gold. The king, her father, was at first astonished that his daughter had been so fortunate as she was, till the young king made him sensible of all that happened. Great was the joy at court amongst all, with the exception of the queen and her club-footed daughter, who were ready to burst with malice, and envied her happiness; and the greater was their madness because she was now above them all.

Great rejoicings, with feasting and dancing, continued many days. Then at length, with the dowry her father gave her, they returned home.

The deformed daughter perceiving that her sister had been so happy in seeking her fortune, would needs do the same; so disclosing her mind to her mother, all preparations were made, and she was furnished not only with rich apparel, but sweetmeats, sugar, almonds, &c., in great quantities, and a large bottle of Malaga sack. Thus provided, she went the same road as her sister, and coming near the cave, the old man said, "Young woman whither so fast?" "What is that to you?" said she. "Then," said he, "what have you in your bag and bottle?" She answered, "Good things, which you shall not be troubled with." "Won't you give me some?" said he. "No, not a bit, nor a drop, unless it would choke you." The old man frowned, saying, "Evil fortune attend thee." Going on, she came to the hedge, through which she espied a gap, and thought to pass through it, but, going in, the hedge closed, and the thorns ran into her flesh, so that it was with great difficulty that she got out. Being now in a painful condition, she searched for water to wash herself, and, looking round, she saw the well; she sat down on the brink of it, and one of the heads came up, saying, "Wash me, comb me, and lay me down softly, &c." but she banged it with her bottle, saying, "Take this for your washing." So the second and third heads came up, and met with no better treatment than the first; whereupon the heads consulted among themselves what evils to plague her with for such usage. The first said, "Let her be struck with leprosy in her face." The second, "Let an additional smell be added to her breath." The third bestowed on her a husband, though but a poor country cobbler. This done she goes on till she came to a town, and it being market day, the people looked at her, and seeing such an evil face, fled out of her sight, all but a poor country cobbler (who not long before had mended the shoes of an old hermit, who having no money, gave him a box of ointment for the cure of the leprosy, and a bottle of spirits for a bad breath). Now the cobbler having a mind to do an act of charity, was induced to go up to her and ask her who she was. "I am," said she "the King of Colchester's daughter-in-law." "Well," said the cobbler, "if I restore you to your natural complexion, and make a sound cure both in face and breath, will you in reward take me for a husband?" "Yes, friend,"

41

replied she, "with all my heart." With this the cobbler applied the remedies, and they worked the effect in a few weeks, and then they were married, and after a few days they set forward for the court of Colchester. When the queen understood she had married a poor cobbler, she fell into distraction, and hanged herself for vexation. The death of the queen was not a source of sorrow to the king, who had only married her for her fortune, and bore her no affection; and shortly afterwards he gave the cobbler £100 to take the daughter to a remote part of the kingdom, where he lived many years mending shoes, while his wife assisted the housekeeping by spinning, and selling the results of her labour at the country market.

THE MAIDEN AND THE FROG*

Many years ago there lived on the brow of a mountain, in the North of England, an old woman and her daughter. They were very poor, and obliged to work very hard for their living, and the old woman's temper was not very good, so that the maiden, who was very beautiful, led but an ill life with her. The girl, indeed, was compelled to do the hardest work, for her mother got their principal means of subsistence by travelling to places in the neighbourhood with small articles for sale, and when she came home in the afternoon she was not able to do much more work. Nearly the whole domestic labour of the cottage devolved therefore on the daughter, the most wearisome part of which consisted in the necessity of fetching all the water they required from a well on the other side of the hill, there being no river or spring near their own cottage.

It happened one morning that the daughter had the misfortune, in going to the well, to break the only pitcher they possessed, and

* The tale of the frog-lover is known in every part of Germany, and is alluded to by several old writers of that country. It is the tale "Der Froschkönig, oder der Eiserne Heinrich", in Grimm. "These enchanted frogs," says Sir W. Scott, "have migrated from afar, and we suspect that they were originally crocodiles; we trace them in a tale forming part of a series of stories entitled the 'Relations of Ssidi Kur,' extant among the Calmuck Tartars." Mr. Chambers has given a Scotch version of the tale, under the title of "The Well o' the Warld's End", in his "Popular Rhymes", p. 236. The rhymes in the copy given above were obtained from the North of England, without, however, any reference to the story to which they evidently belong. The application, however, is so obvious to any one acquainted with the German and Scotch tale, that the framework I have ventured to give them cannot be considered incongruous; although I need not add how very desirable it would be to procure the traditional tale as related by the English peasantry. Perhaps some of our readers may be enabled to supply it.

having no other utensil she could use for the purpose, she was obliged to go home without bringing any water. When her mother returned, she was unfortunately troubled with excessive thirst, and the girl, though trembling for the consequences of her misfortune, told her exactly the circumstance that had occurred. The old woman was furiously angry, and, so far from making any allowance for her daughter, pointed to a sieve which happened to be on the table, and told her to go at once to the well and bring her some water in that, or never venture to appear again in her sight.

The young maiden, frightened almost out of her wits by her mother's fury, speedily took the sieve, and though she considered the task a hopeless one to accomplish, almost unconsciously hastened to the well. When she arrived there, beginning to reflect on the painful situation in which she was placed, and the utter impossibility of her obtaining a living by herself, she threw herself on the brink of the well in an agony of despair. Whilst she was in this condition, a large frog came up to the top of the water, and asked her for what she was crying so bitterly. She was somewhat surprised at this, but not being the least frightened, told him the whole story, and that she was crying because she could not carry away water in the sieve. "Is that all?" said the frog: "cheer up, my hinny! for if you will only let me sleep with you for two nights, and then chop off my head, I will tell you how to do it." The maiden thought the frog could not be in earnest, but she was too impatient to consider much about it, and at once made the required promise. The frog then instructed her in the following words:

> Stop with fog (*moss*),
> And daub with clay;
> And that will carry
> The water away.

Having said this, he dived immediately under the water, and the girl, having followed his advice, got the sieve full of water, and returned home with it, not thinking much of her promise to the frog. By the time she reached home the old woman's wrath was appeased; but as they were eating their frugal supper very quietly, what should they hear but the splashing and croaking of a frog near the door, and shortly afterwards the daughter recognised the voice of the frog of the well saying—

Open the door, my hinny, my heart,
Open the door, my own darling;
Remember the words you spoke to me,
In the meadow by the well-spring.

She was now dreadfully frightened, and hurriedly explained the matter to her mother, who was also so much alarmed at the circumstance, that she dared not refuse admittance to the frog, who, when the door was opened, leapt into the room, exclaiming:

Go wi' me to bed, my hinny, my heart,
Go wi' me to bed, my own darling;
Remember the words you spoke to me,
In the meadow by the well-spring.

This command was also obeyed, although, as may be readily supposed, she did not much relish such a bedfellow. The next day, the frog was very quiet, and evidently enjoyed the fare they placed before him,—the purest milk and the finest bread they could procure. In fact, neither the old woman nor her daughter spared any pains to render the frog comfortable. That night, immediately supper was finished, the frog again exclaimed:

Go wi' me to bed, my hinny, my heart,
Go wi' me to bed, my own darling;
Remember the words you spoke to me,
In the meadow by the well-spring.

She again allowed the frog to share her couch, and in the morning, as soon as she was dressed, he jumped towards her, saying:

Chop off my head, my hinny, my heart,
Chop off my head, my own darling;
Remember the words you spoke to me,
In the meadow by the well-spring.

The maiden had no sooner accomplished this last request, than in the stead of the frog there stood by her side the handsomest prince in the world, who had long been transformed by a magician, and who could never have recovered his natural shape until a beautiful virgin had consented, of her own accord, to make him her bedfellow for two nights. The joy of all parties was complete; the girl and the prince were shortly afterwards married, and lived for many years in the enjoyment of every happiness.

THE STORY OF MR. FOX*

Once upon a time there was a young lady called Lady Mary, who had two brothers. One summer they all three went out to a country seat of theirs which they had not before visited. Among the other gentry in the neighbourhood who came to see them was a Mr. Fox, a bachelor, with whom they, particularly the young lady, were much pleased. He used often to dine with them, and frequently invited Lady Mary to come and see his house. One day, when her brothers were absent elsewhere, and she had nothing better to do, she determined to go thither, and accordingly set out unattended. When she arrived at the house and knocked at the door, no one answered. At length she opened it and went in, and over the portal of the door was written:

Be bold, be bold, but not too bold.

She advanced, and found the same inscription over the staircase; again at the entrance of the gallery; and lastly, at the door of a chamber, with the addition of a line:

Be bold, be bold, but not too bold,
Lest that your heart's blood should run cold!

She opened it, and what was her terror and astonishment to find the floor covered with bones and blood. She retreated in haste, and coming down stairs, she saw from a window Mr. Fox advancing towards the house with a drawn sword in one hand, while with the other he dragged along a young lady by the hair of her head. Lady Mary had just time to slip down, and hide herself under the stairs, before Mr. Fox and his victim arrived at the foot of them. As he pulled the young lady up stairs, she caught hold of one of the bannisters with her hand, on which was a rich bracelet. Mr. Fox cut it off with his sword: the hand and bracelet fell into Lady

---

* A simple, but very curious tale, of considerable antiquity. It is alluded to by Shakespeare, and was contributed to the variorum edition by Blakeway. Part of this story will recall to the reader's memory the enchanted chamber of Britomart.

Mary's lap, who then contrived to escape unobserved, and got safe home to her brother's house.

A few days afterwards Mr. Fox came to dine with them as usual. After dinner the guests began to amuse each other with extra-ordinary anecdotes, and Lady Mary said she would relate to them a remarkable dream she had lately had. I dreamt, said she, that as you, Mr. Fox, had often invited me to your house, I would go there one morning. When I came to the house, I knocked at the door, but no one answered. When I opened the door, over the hall I saw written, "Be bold, be bold, but not too bold". But, said she, turning to Mr. Fox, and smiling, "It is not so, nor it was not so." Then she pursued the rest of the story, concluding at every turn with, "It is not so, nor it was not so," till she came to the discovery of the room full of bones, when Mr. Fox took up the burden of the tale, and said:

It is not so, nor it was not so,
And God forbid it should be so!

which he continued to repeat at every subsequent turn of the dreadful story, till she came to the circumstance of his cutting off the young lady's hand, when, upon his saying, as usual,

It is not so, nor it was not so,
And God forbid it should be so!

Lady Mary retorts by saying,

But it is so, and it was so,
And here the hand I have to show!

at the same moment producing the hand and bracelet from her lap. Whereupon the guests drew their swords, and instantly cut Mr. Fox into a thousand pieces.

THE OXFORD STUDENT*

Many years ago there lived at the University of Oxford a young student, who, having seduced the daughter of a tradesman, sought to conceal his crime by committing the more heinous one of murder. With this view, he made an appointment to meet her one evening in a secluded field. She was at the rendezvous considerably

* Obtained in Oxfordshire from tradition.

before the time agreed upon for their meeting, and hid herself in a tree. The student arrived on the spot shortly afterwards, but what was the astonishment of the girl to observe that he commenced digging a grave. Her fears and suspicions were aroused, and she did not leave her place of concealment till the student, despairing of her arrival, returned to his college. The next day, when she was at the door of her father's house, he passed and saluted her as usual. She returned his greeting by repeating the following lines:

> One moonshiny night, as I sat high,
> Waiting for one to come by,
> The boughs did bend; my heart did ache
> To see what hole the fox did make.

Astounded by her unexpected knowledge of his base design, in a moment of fury he stabbed her to the heart. This murder occasioned a violent conflict between the tradespeople and the students, the latter taking part with the murderer, and so fierce was the skirmish, that Brewer's Lane, it is said, ran down with blood. The place of appointment was adjoining the Divinity Walk, which was in time past far more secluded than at the present day, and she is said to have been buried in the grave made for her by her paramour.

According to another version of the tale, the name of the student was Fox, and a fellow-student went with him to assist in digging the grave. The verses in this account differ somewhat from the above.

> As I went out in a moonlight night,
> I set my back against the moon,
> I looked for one, and saw two come;
> The boughs did bend, the leaves did shake,
> I saw the hole the Fox did make.

JACK HORNBY*

In the reign of King Arthur there lived near the Land's End, in Cornwall, a wealthy farmer, who had an only son, commonly called Jack Hornby. He was of a brisk and ready wit, and he was never known to be outwitted in any transaction.

* This little tale was most likely copied from the commencement of the original edition of Jack the Giant-killer, where similar incidents are related of that renowned hero.

One day, when he was no more than seven years of age, his father sent him into the field to look after his oxen. While he was attending to them, the lord of the manor came across the field, and as Jack was known to be a clever boy, he began asking him questions. His first was, "How many commandments are there?" Jack told him there were nine. The lord corrected him, saying there were ten. "Nay," quoth Jack, "you are wrong there: it is true there were ten, but you broke one of them when you stole my father's cow for your rent." The lord of the manor was so struck by this answer, that he promised to return the poor man's cow.

"Now," quoth Jack, "it is my turn to ask a question. Can you tell me how many sticks go to build a crow's nest?" "Yes," said he, "there are as many go as are sufficient for the size of the nest." "Oh!" quoth Jack, "you are out again; there are none go, for they are all carried!"

Jack Hornby was never more troubled with questions by the lord of the manor.

MALLY DIXON AND KNURRE-MURRE

Stories of fairies appearing in the shape of cats are common in the North of England. Mr. Longstaffe relates that a farmer of Staindrop, in Durham, was one night crossing a bridge, when a cat jumped out, stood before him, and looking him full in the face, said:

> Johnny Reed! Johnny Reed!
> Tell Madam Momfort
> That Mally Dixon's dead.

The farmer returned home, and in mickle wonder recited this awfu' stanza to his wife, when up started their black cat, saying, "Is she?" and disappeared for ever. It was supposed she was a fairy in disguise, who thus went to attend a sister's funeral, for in the North fairies do die, and green shady spots are pointed out by the country folks as the cemeteries of the tiny people. An analogous story is found in the people-literature of Denmark.

Near a town called Lyng is the hill of Brondhoë, inhabited by the trold-folk, or imps. Amongst these trolds was an old sickly devil, peevish and ill-tempered, because he was married to a young wife.

This unhappy trold often set the rest by the ears, so they nicknamed him Knurre-Murre, or Rumble-Grumble. Now it came to pass, that Knurre-Murre discovered that his young wife was inclined to honour him with a supplemental pair of horns; and the object of his jealousy, to avoid his vengeance, was compelled to fly for his life from the cavern, and take refuge, in the shape of a tortoise-shell cat, in the house of Goodman Platt, who harboured him with much hospitality, let him lie on the great wicker chair, and fed him twice a day with bread and milk out of a red earthenware pipkin. One evening the goodman came home, at a late hour, full of wonderment. "Goody," exclaimed he to his wife, "as I was passing by Brondhoë, there came out a trold, who spake to me saying:

> Hör du Plat,
> Süg til din cat
> At Knurre-Murre er död.

> (Hear thou, Platt,
> Say to thy cat
> That Knurre-Murre is dead.)

The tortoise-shell cat was lying on the great wicker chair, and eating his supper of bread and milk out of the red earthenware pipkin, when the goodman came in; but as soon as the message was delivered he jumped bolt upright upon his two hind legs, for all the world like a Christian, and kicking the red earthenware pipkin and the rest of the bread and milk before him, he whisked through the cottage door, mewing, "What! is Knurre-Murre dead? then I may go home again!"*

THE RED BULL OF NORROWAY†

> To wilder measures next they turn:
> The black black bull of Norroway!
> Sudden the tapers cease to burn,
> The minstrels cease to play!

* This analysis of the Danish tale is taken from an article in the "Quarterly Review", xxi. 98.
† This is a modern version, taken down from recitation, of the very old tale of the "Black Bull of Norroway", mentioned in the "Complaynt of Scotland", 1548. It is here taken, by the author's kind permission, from the "Popular Rhymes of Scotland", by Mr. Robert Chambers, the most delightful book of the kind ever published.

Once upon a time there lived a king who had three daughters; the two eldest were proud and ugly, but the youngest was the gentlest and most beautiful creature ever seen, and the pride not only of her father and mother, but of all in the land. As it fell out, the three princesses were talking one night of whom they would marry. "I will have no one lower than a king," said the eldest princess; the second would take a prince, or a great duke even. "Pho, pho," said the youngest, laughing, "you are both so proud; now, I would be content with the Red Bull o' Norroway." Well, they thought no more of the matter till the next morning, when, as they sat at breakfast, they heard the most dreadful bellowing at the door, and what should it be but the red bull come for his bride. You may be sure they were all terribly frightened at this, for the red bull was one of the most horrible creatures ever seen in the world. And the king and queen did not know how to save their daughter. At last they determined to send him off with the old henwife. So they put her on his back, and away he went with her till he came to a great black forest, when, throwing her down, he returned, roaring louder and more frightfully than ever. They then sent, one by one, all the servants, then the two eldest princesses; but not one of them met with any better treatment than the old henwife, and at last they were forced to send their youngest and favourite child.

On travelled the lady and the bull through many dreadful forests and lonely wastes, till they came at last to a noble castle, where a large company was assembled. The lord of the castle pressed them to stay, though much he wondered at the lovely princess and her strange companion. When they went in among the company, the princess espied a pin sticking in the bull's hide, which she pulled out, and, to the surprise of all, there appeared not a frightful wild beast, but one of the most beautiful princes ever beheld. You may believe how delighted the princess was to see him fall at her feet, and thank her for breaking his cruel enchantment. There were great rejoicings in the castle at this; but, alas! at that moment he suddenly disappeared, and though every place was sought, he was nowhere to be found. The princess, however, determined to seek through all the world for him, and many weary ways she went, but nothing could she hear of her lover. Travelling once through a dark wood, she lost her way, and as night was coming on, she thought she must now certainly die of cold and hunger; but seeing a light through the trees, she went on till she came to a little hut, where an old woman lived, who took her in, and gave her both food and shelter. In the morning, the old wifie gave her three nuts, that she was not to break till her heart was "like to break, and owre again like to break"; so, showing her the way, she bade God speed her, and the princess once more set out on her wearisome journey.

She had not gone far till a company of lords and ladies rode past her, all talking merrily of the fine doings they expected at the Duke o' Norroway's wedding. Then she came up to a number of people carrying all sorts of fine things, and they, too, were going to the duke's wedding. At last she came to a castle, where nothing was to be seen but cooks and bakers, some running one way, and some another, and all so busy that they did not know what to do first. Whilst she was looking at all this, she heard a noise of hunters behind her, and some one cried out, "Make way for the Duke o' Norroway!" and who should ride past but the prince and a beautiful lady! You may be sure her heart was now "like to break, and owre again like to break", at this sad sight; so she broke one of the nuts, and out came a wee wifie carding. The princess then went into the castle, and asked to see the lady, who no sooner saw the wee wifie so hard at work, than she offered the princess anything in her castle for it. "I will give it to you," said she, "only on condition that you put off for one day your marriage with the Duke o' Norroway, and that I may go into his room alone tonight." So anxious was the lady for the nut, that she consented. And when dark night was come, and the duke fast asleep, the princess was put alone into his chamber. Sitting down by his bedside, she began singing:

> Far hae I sought ye, near am I brought to ye;
> Dear Duke o' Norroway, will ye no turn and speak to me?

Though she sang this over and over again, the duke never awakened, and in the morning the princess had to leave him, without his knowing she had ever been there. She then broke the second nut, and out came a wee wifie spinning, which so delighted the lady, that she readily agreed to put off her marriage another day for it; but to the princess came no better speed the second night than the first, and, almost in despair, she broke the last nut, which contained a wee wifie reeling; and on the same condition as before the lady got possession of it. When the duke was dressing in the morning, his man asked him what the strange singing and moaning that had been heard in his room for two nights meant. "I heard nothing," said the duke; "it could only have been your fancy." "Take no sleeping-draught tonight, and be sure to lay aside your pillow of heaviness," said the man, "and you will also hear what for two nights has kept me awake." The duke did so, and the princess coming in, sat down sighing at his bedside, thinking this the last time she might ever see him. The duke started up when he heard the voice of his dearly-loved princess; and with many endearing expressions of surprise and joy, explained to her that he had long been in the power of an enchantress, whose spells over him were now happily ended by their once again meeting. The princess, happy to be the instrument of his second deliverance, consented to marry him, and the enchantress, who fled that country, afraid of the duke's anger, has never since been heard of. All was hurry and preparation in the castle, and the marriage which now took place at once ended the adventures of the Red Bull o' Norroway and the wanderings of the king's daughter.

PUSS IN BOOTS*

There was a miller, who left no more estate to his three sons than his mill, his ass, and his cat. The partition was soon made, neither scrivener nor attorney being sent for. They would soon have eaten up all the patrimony. The eldest had the mill, the second the ass, and the youngest nothing but the cat.

The poor young fellow was quite downcast at so poor a lot. "My brothers," said he, "may get their living handsomely enough by joining their stocks together, but for my part, when I have eaten up my cat, and made me a muff of his skin, I must die with hunger." The cat, who heard all this, yet made as if he did not, said to him, with a grave and serious air, "Do not thus afflict yourself, my good master; you have nothing else to do but give me a bag, and get a pair of boots made for me, that I may scamper through the dirt and

---

* One of the tales of Perrault, 1697. The plot was taken from the first novel of the eleventh night of Straparola. Its moral is that talents are equivalent to fortune. We have inserted this in our collection, although generally remembered, as a specimen of the simple tales founded by Perrault on older stories, and which soon became popular in this country. The others, as Blue Beard, and Little Riding Hood, are vanishing from the nursery, but are so universally known that reprints of them would be superfluous.

the brambles, and you shall see that you have not so bad a portion as you imagine." Though he did not build very much upon what the cat said, he had however often seen him play a great many cunning tricks to catch rats and mice: as when he used to hang by the heels, or hide himself in the meal, and make as if he were dead; so that he did not altogether despair of his affording him some help in his miserable condition. When the cat had what he asked for, he booted himself very gallantly; and putting the bag about his neck, held the string of it in his two fore-paws, and went into a warren where there was a great abundance of rabbits. He put bran and sowthistles into the bag, and stretching himself out at length, as if he had been dead, he waited for some young rabbits not yet acquainted with the deceits of the world to come and rummage his bag for what he had put into it.

Scarce was he laid down, but he had what he wanted; a rash and foolish young rabbit jumped into his bag, and Monsieur Puss immediately drawing the strings close, took and killed him without pity. Proud of his prey, he went with it into the palace, and asked to speak with his majesty. He was shown up stairs into the king's apartment, and, making a low reverence, said to him, "I have brought you, Sire, a rabbit of the warren, which my noble lord, the Marquis of Carabas (for that was the title which Puss was pleased to give his master), has commanded me to present to your majesty from him." "Tell thy master," said the king, "that I thank him, and he does me a great deal of pleasure."

Another time he went and hid himself amongst some standing corn, holding his bag open; and when a brace of partridges ran into it, he drew the strings, and so caught them both. He went and made a present of these to the king, as he had done before of the rabbit. The king received the partridges with great pleasure, and ordered him some money for drink.

The cat continued, for two or three months, to carry game to his majesty. One day in particular, when he knew that the king was to take the air along the river side, with his daughter, the most beautiful princess in the world, he said to his master, "If you will follow my advice, your fortune is made; you have nothing else to do, but go and wash yourself in the river, in that part I shall show you, and leave the rest to me." The Marquis of Carabas did what the cat advised, without knowing why or wherefore.

While he was washing, the king passed by, and the cat began to cry out, as loud as he could, "Help! help! my Lord Marquis of Carabas is going to be drowned!" At this noise the king put his head out of the coach-window, and finding it was the cat who had so often brought him such good game, he commanded the guards to run immediately to the assistance of his lordship the Marquis of Carabas.

While they were drawing the poor marquis out of the water, the cat came up to the coach and told the king, that, while his master was washing, there came by some rogues who went off with his clothes, though he had cried out "Thieves! thieves!" several times, as loud as he could. (This cunning cat had hidden them under a great stone.) The king immediately commanded the officers of his wardrobe to run and fetch one of his best suits for the Lord Marquis of Carabas.

The king caressed him after a very extraordinary manner, and as the fine clothes he had given him extremely set off his good mien (for he was well-made and very handsome in his person), the king's daughter took a secret inclination to him, and the Marquis of Carabas had no sooner cast two or three respectful and tender glances, but she fell in love with him to distraction; and the king would have him come into his coach. The cat, overjoyed to see his project begin to succeed, marched on before, and meeting with some countrymen who were mowing a meadow, he said to them, "Good people, if you do not tell the king that the meadow you mow belongs to the Marquis of Carabas, you shall be chopped as small as herbs for the pot."

The king did not fail to ask the mowers to whom the meadow they were mowing belonged. "To my Lord Marquis of Carabas," answered they all together; for the cat's threats had made them terribly afraid. "You see, sir," said the marquis, "this is a meadow that never fails to yield a plentiful harvest every year." The cat, who still went on before, met with some reapers, and said to them, "Good people, you who are reaping, if you do not tell the king that all this corn belongs to the Marquis of Carabas, you shall be chopped as small as herbs for the pot." The king, who passed by a moment after, would needs know to whom all that corn did belong. "To my Lord Marquis of Carabas," replied the reapers; and the king was very well pleased with it, as well as the marquis, whom he congratulated thereupon. The master cat went always before, saying the same words to all he met; and the king was astonished at the vast estates of my Lord Marquis of Carabas. Monsieur Puss came at last to a stately castle, the master of which was an ogre, the richest that had ever been known; for all the lands the king had then gone over belonged to him. The cat, having taken care to inform himself who this ogre was, and what he could do, asked to speak to him, saying, "he could not pass so near his castle, without having the honour of paying his respects to him."

The ogre received him as civilly as an ogre could do, and made him sit down. "I have been assured," said the cat, "that you have the gift of being able to change yourself into all sorts of creatures you have a mind to; you can, for example transform yourself into a lion or elephant, and the like." "This is true," answered the ogre, very briskly, "and to convince you, you shall see me now become a lion." Puss was so sadly terrified at the sight of a lion so near him, that he immediately got into the gutter, not without great trouble and danger, because of his boots, which were of no use at all to him in walking upon the tiles. A little while after, when Puss saw that the ogre had resumed his natural form, he came down, and owned that he had been very much frightened.

"I have been moreover informed," said the cat, "but I know not how to believe it, that you have also the power to take upon you the smallest animals, for example, to change yourself into a rat or a mouse, but, I must own to you, I take this to be impossible." "Impossible!" cried the ogre, "you shall see that presently"; and at the same time changed himself into a mouse, and began to run about the floor. Puss no sooner perceived this, but he fell upon him, and ate him up.

Meanwhile the king, who saw as he passed this fine castle of the ogre's, had a mind to go into it. Puss, who heard the noise of his majesty's coach running over the drawbridge, ran out, and said to the king, "Your majesty is welcome to this castle of the Lord Marquis of Carabas." "What! my lord marquis," cried the king, "and does this castle also belong to you? there can be nothing finer than this court, and all the stately buildings which surround it: let us go into it, if you please."

The king went up first, the marquis, handing the princess, following; they passed into a spacious hall, where they found a magnificent collation the ogre had prepared for his friends, who dared not enter, knowing the king was there. His majesty was perfectly charmed with the good qualities of the marquis, and his daughter was violently in love with him. The king, after having drank five or six glasses, said to him, "My lord marquis, you will be only to blame, if you are not my son-in-law." The marquis, making several low bows, accepted the honour his majesty conferred upon him, and forthwith the very same day married the princess.

Puss became a great lord, and never ran after mice any more but only for his diversion.

JACK AND THE GIANTS

[The present copy of this tale is taken, with a few necessary alterations, from the original editions, which differ very considerably from the modern versions; and it is worthy of preservation in its antique costume, for the story is undoubtedly of Teutonic origin. "Jack, commonly called the Giant Killer," says Sir W. Scott, "and Thomas Thumb landed in England from the very same keels and war-ships which conveyed Hengist and Horsa, and Ebba the Saxon." One incident in the romance exactly corresponds to a device played by the giant Skrimner, when he and Thor travelled to Utgard Castle, related in the Edda of Snorro. Skrimner placed an immense rock on the leafy couch where Thor supposed he was sleeping, and when the latter, desiring to rid himself of his companion, heard the giant snore, he struck the rock with his tremendous hammer, thinking it was the monster's head. "Hath a leaf fallen upon me from the tree?" exclaimed the awakened giant. He went to sleep again, and snoring louder than ever, Thor gave a blow which he thought must have cracked his skull. "What is the matter?" quoth Skrimner, "hath an acorn fallen on my head?" A third time the snore was heard, and a third time the hammer fell with redoubled force, insomuch that Thor weened the iron had buried itself in Skrimner's temples. "Methinks," quoth the giant, rubbing his cheek, "some moss hath fallen on my face!" Jack's invisible coat, his magic sword, and his shoes of swiftness, are also undoubtedly borrowed from Northern romance.*

* The last is also found in the second relation of "Ssidi Kur", a Calmuck romance.

An incident very similar to the blows with the rat's tail occurs in the story of the Brave Little Tailor, in Grimm; who outwits a giant in several ingenious ways, one of which may be described. On one occasion the giant wished to try the strength of the tailor, by challenging him to carry a tree. The latter said, "Very well, you carry the butt-end, while I will carry all the branches, by far the heaviest part of the tree." So the giant lifted the tree up on his shoulders, and the tailor very coolly sat on the branches while the giant carried the tree. At length he was so tired with his load, he was obliged to drop it, and the tailor, nimbly jumping off, made belief as if he had been carrying the branches all the time, and said: "A pretty fellow you are, that can't carry a tree!"

The edition of Jack the Giant-killer here used was printed at Newcastle-on-Tyne in 1711. The earliest in the British Museum is dated 1809, nor does the Bodleian, I believe, contain a copy of a more ancient type.

Jack and the Bean-stalk may be added to the series of English nursery tales derived from the Teutonic. The bean-stalk is a descendant of the wonderful ash in the Edda. The distich put into the mouth of the giant,

> Snouk but, snouk ben,
> I find the smell of earthly men,

is, says Scott, scarcely inferior to the keen-scented anthropophaginian in Jack the Giant-killer.]

In the reign of King Arthur, and in the county of Cornwall, near to the Land's End in England, there lived a wealthy farmer, who had an only son named Jack. He was brisk, and of a lively ready wit, so that whatever he could not perform by force and strength, he accomplished by ingenious wit and policy. Never was any person heard of that could worst him, and he very often even baffled the learned by his sharp and ready inventions.

In those days the Mount of Cornwall was kept by a huge and monstrous giant of eighteen feet in height, and about three yards in compass, of a fierce and grim countenance, the terror of all the neighbouring towns and villages. He inhabited a cave in the middle of the Mount, and he was such a selfish monster that he would not suffer any one to live near him. He fed on other men's cattle, which often became his prey, for whensoever he wanted food, he would

57

wade over to the main land, where he would furnish himself with whatever came in his way. The inhabitants, at his approach, forsook their habitations, while he seized on their cattle, making nothing of carrying half-a-dozen oxen on his back at a time; and as for their sheep and hogs, he would tie them round his waist like a bunch of bandoleers.* This course he had followed for many years, so that a great part of the country was impoverished by his depredations.

This was the state of affairs, when Jack, happening one day to be present at the town-hall when the authorities were consulting about the giant, had the curiosity to ask what reward would be given to the person who destroyed him. The giant's treasure was declared as the recompense, and Jack at once undertook the task.

In order to accomplish his purpose, he furnished himself with a horn, shovel, and pickaxe, and went over to the Mount in the beginning of a dark winter's evening, when he fell to work, and before morning had dug a pit twenty-two feet deep, and nearly as broad, covering it over with long sticks and straw. Then strewing a little mould upon it, it appeared like plain ground. This accomplished, Jack placed himself on the side of the pit which was furthest from the giant's lodging, and, just at the break of day, he put the horn to his mouth, and blew with all his might. Although Jack was a little fellow, and the powers of his voice are not described as being very great, he managed to make noise enough to arouse the giant, and excite his indignation. The monster accordingly rushed from his cave, exclaiming, "You incorrigible villain! Are you come to disturb my rest? You shall pay dearly for this. Satisfaction I will have, for I will take you whole and broil you for breakfast." He had no sooner uttered this cruel threat, than tumbling into the pit, he made the very foundations of the Mount ring again. "Oh, giant," said Jack, "where are you now? Oh, faith, you are gotten now into Lob's Pound,† where I will surely plague you for your threatening words: what do you think now of broiling me for your breakfast? will no other diet serve you but poor Jack?" Thus did little Jack tantalize the big giant, as a cat does a mouse when she knows it cannot escape, and when he had tired of that amusement, he gave him

---

* *Bandoleers* were little wooden cases covered with leather, each of them containing the charge of powder for a musket, and fastened to a broad band of leather, which the person who was to use them put round his neck.
† An old jocular term for a prison, or any place of confinement.

a heavy blow with his pickaxe on the very crown of his head, which "tumbled him down" and killed him on the spot. When Jack saw he was dead, he filled up the pit with earth, and went to search the cave, which he found contained much treasure. The magistrates, in the exuberance of their joy, did not add to Jack's gains from their own, but, after the best and cheapest mode of payment, made a declaration he should henceforth be termed *Jack the Giant-killer*, and presented him with a sword and embroidered belt, on the latter of which were inscribed these words in letters of gold:

> Here's the right valiant Cornish man,
> Who slew the giant Cormelian.

The news of Jack's victory, as might be expected, soon spread over all the West of England, so that another giant, named Thunderbore, hearing of it, and entertaining a partiality for his race, vowed to be revenged on the little hero, if ever it was his fortune to light on him. This giant was the lord of an enchanted castle, situated in the midst of a lonely wood. Now Jack, about four months after his last exploit, walking near this castle in his journey towards Wales, being weary, seated himself near a pleasant fountain in the wood, "o'ercanopied with luscious woodbine", and presently fell asleep. While he was enjoying his repose, the giant, coming to the fountain for water, of course discovered him, and recognised the hated individual by the lines written on the belt. He immediately took Jack on his shoulders, and carried him towards his enchanted castle. Now, as they passed through a thicket, the rustling of the boughs awakened Jack, who was uncomfortably surprised to find himself in the clutches of the giant. His terror was not diminished when, on entering the castle, he saw the courtyard strewed with human bones, the giant maliciously telling him his own would ere long increase the hateful pile. After this assurance, the cannibal locked poor Jack in an upper chamber, leaving him there while he went to fetch another giant living in the same wood to keep him company in the anticipated destruction of their enemy. While he was gone, dreadful shrieks and lamentations affrighted Jack, especially a voice which continually cried,

> Do what you can to get away,
> Or you'll become the giant's prey;

59

He's gone to fetch his brother, who
Will kill, and likewise torture you.

This warning, and the hideous tone in which it was delivered,
almost distracted poor Jack, who, going to the window, and open-
ing a casement, beheld afar off the two giants approaching towards
the castle. "Now," quoth Jack to himself, "my death or my
deliverance is at hand." The event proved that his anticipations
were well founded, for the giants of those days, however powerful,
were at best very stupid fellows, and readily conquered by stratagem,
were it of the humblest kind. There happened to be strong cords in
the room in which Jack was confined, two of which he took, and
made a strong noose at the end of each; and while the giant was un-
locking the iron gate of the castle, he threw the ropes over each of
their heads, and then, before the giants knew what he was about, he
drew the other ends across a beam, and, pulling with all his might,
throttled them till they were black in the face. Then, sliding down
the rope, he came to their heads, and as they could not defend
themselves, easily despatched them with his sword. This business so
adroitly accomplished, Jack released the fair prisoners in the castle,
delivered the keys to them, and, like a true knight-errant, continued
his journey without condescending to improve the condition of his
purse.

This plan, however honourable, was not without its disadvantages, and owing to his slender stock of money, he was obliged
to make the best of his way by travelling as hard as he could. At
length, losing his road, he was belated, and could not get to any
place of entertainment until, coming to a lonesome valley, he found
a large house, and by reason of his present necessity, took courage
to knock at the gate. But what was his astonishment, when there
came forth a monstrous giant with two heads; yet he did not appear
so fiery as the others were, for he was a Welsh giant, and what he
did was by private and secret malice under the false show of friendship. Jack having unfolded his condition to the giant, was shown
into a bedroom, where, in the dead of night, he heard his host in
another apartment uttering these formidable words:

Though here you lodge with me this night,
You shall not see the morning light:
My club shall dash your brains out quite!

60

"Say'st thou so," quoth Jack; "that is like one of your Welsh tricks, yet I hope to be cunning enough for you." He immediately got out of bed, and, feeling about in the dark, found a thick billet of wood, which he laid in the bed in his stead, and hid himself in a dark corner of the room. Shortly after he had done so, in came the Welsh giant, who thoroughly pummelled the billet with his club, thinking, naturally enough, he had broken every bone in Jack's skin. The next morning, however, to the inexpressible surprise of the giant, Jack came down stairs as if nothing had happened, and gave him thanks for his night's lodging. "How have you rested," quoth the giant; "did you not feel anything in the night?" Jack provokingly replied, "No, nothing but a rat which gave me two or three flaps with her tail." This reply was totally incomprehensible to the giant, who of course saw anything but a joke in it. However, concealing his amazement as well as he could, he took Jack in to breakfast, assigning to each a bowl containing four gallons of hasty pudding. One would have thought that the greater portion of so extravagant an allowance would have been declined by our hero, but he was unwilling the giant should imagine his incapability to eat it, and accordingly placed a large leather bag under his loose coat, in such a position that he could convey the pudding into it without the deception being perceived. Breakfast at length being finished, Jack excited the giant's curiosity by offering to show him an extraordinary sleight of hand; so taking a knife, he ripped the leather bag, and out of course descended on the ground all the hasty-pudding. The giant had not the slightest suspicion of the trick, veritably believing the pudding came from its natural receptacle; and having the same antipathy to being beaten, exclaimed in true Welsh, "Odds splutters, hur can do that trick hurself." The sequel may be readily guessed. The monster took the knife, and thinking to follow Jack's example with impunity, killed himself on the spot.*

King Arthur's only son requested his father to furnish him with a large sum of money, in order that he might go and seek his fortune in the principality of Wales, where lived a beautiful lady possessed with seven evil spirits. The king tried all he could do to

* The foregoing portion of this wonderful history is that most generally known; but the incidents now become more complicated, and after the introduction of Arthur's son upon the scene, we arrive at particulars which have long been banished from the nursery library.

persuade him to alter his determination, but it was all in vain; so at last he granted his request, and the prince set out with two horses, one loaded with money, the other for himself to ride upon. Now, after several days' travel, he came to a market-town in Wales, where he beheld a vast concourse of people gathered together. The prince demanded the reason of it, and was told that they had arrested a corpse for several large sums of money which the deceased owed when he died. The prince replied that it was a pity creditors should be so cruel, and said, "Go bury the dead, and let his creditors come to my lodging, and there their debts shall be discharged." They accordingly came, but in such great numbers, that before night he had almost left himself penniless.

Now Jack the Giant-killer happened to be in the town while these transactions took place, and he was so pleased with the generosity exhibited by the prince, that he offered to become his servant, an offer which was immediately accepted. The next morning they set forward on their journey, when, as they were just leaving the town, an old woman called after the prince, saying, "He has owed me twopence these seven years; pray pay me as well as the rest." So reasonable and urgent a demand could not be resisted, and the prince immediately discharged the debt, but it took the last penny he had to accomplish it. This event, though generally ridiculed by heroes, was one by no means overlooked by the prince, who required all Jack's assuring eloquence to console him. Jack himself, indeed, had a very poor exchequer, and after their day's refreshment, they were entirely without money. When night drew on, the prince was anxious to secure a lodging, but as they had no means to hire one, Jack said, "Never mind, master, we shall do well enough, for I have an uncle lives within two miles of this place; he is a huge and monstrous giant with three heads; he'll fight five hundred men in armour, and make them flee before him." "Alas!" quoth the prince, "What shall we do there? He'll certainly chop us up at a mouthful. Nay, we are scarce enough to fill his hollow tooth!" "It is no matter for that," quoth Jack; "I myself will go before, and prepare the way for you; therefore tarry, and wait till I return." Jack then rides off full speed, and coming to the gate of the castle, he knocked so loud that the neighbouring hills resounded like thunder. The giant, terribly vexed with the liberty taken by Jack, roared out, "Who's there?" He was answered, "None but your poor cousin Jack." Quoth he, "What news with my poor cousin Jack?" He replied, "Dear uncle, heavy news." "God wot," quoth the giant, "prithee what heavy news can come to me? I am a giant with three heads, and besides, thou knowest I can fight five hundred men in armour, and make them fly like chaff before the wind." "Oh, but," quoth Jack, "here's the prince a-coming with a thousand men in armour to kill you, and destroy all that you have!" "Oh, cousin Jack," said the giant, "this is heavy news indeed! I will immediately run and hide myself, and thou shalt lock, bolt, and bar me in, and keep the keys till the prince is gone." Jack joyfully complied with the giant's request, and fetching his master, they feasted and made themselves merry whilst the poor giant lay trembling in a vault under ground.

In the morning Jack furnished the prince with a fresh supply of gold and silver, and then sent him three miles forward on his journey, concluding, according to the story-book, "he was then pretty well out of the smell of the giant." Jack afterwards returned, and liberated the giant from the vault, who asked what he should give him for preserving the castle from destruction. "Why," quoth Jack, "I desire nothing but the old coat and cap, together with the old rusty sword and slippers, which are at your bed's head." Quoth the giant, "Thou shalt have them, and pray keep them for my sake, for they are things of excellent use; the coat will keep you invisible, the cap will furnish you with knowledge, the sword cuts asunder whatever you strike, and the shoes are of extraordinary swiftness. These may be serviceable to you: therefore take them with all my heart."

Jack was delighted with these presents, and having overtaken his master, they quickly arrived at the lady's house, who, finding the prince to be a suitor, prepared a splendid banquet for him. After the repast was concluded, she wiped his mouth with a handkerchief, and then concealed it in her dress, saying, "You must show me that handkerchief to-morrow morning, or else you will lose your head." The prince went to bed in great sorrow at this hard condition, but fortunately Jack's cap of knowledge instructed him how it was to be fulfilled. In the middle of the night she called upon her familiar* to carry her to the evil spirit. Jack immediately put on his coat of darkness, and his shoes of swiftness, and was there before her, his coat

* An attendant spirit.

rendering him invisible. When she entered the lower regions, she gave the handkerchief to the spirit, who laid it upon a shelf, whence Jack took it, and brought it to his master, who showed it to the lady the next day, and so saved his life. The next evening at supper she saluted the prince, telling him he must show her the lips to-morrow morning that she kissed last this night, or lose his head. He replied, "If you kiss none but mine, I will." "That is neither here nor there," said she, "if you do not, death is your portion!" At midnight she went below as before, and was angry with the spirit for letting the handkerchief go: "But now," quoth she, "I will be too hard for the prince, for I will kiss thee, and he is to show me thy lips." She did so, and Jack, who was standing by, cut off the spirit's head, and brought it under his invisible coat to his master, who produced it triumphantly the next morning before the lady. This feat destroyed the enchantment, the evil spirits immediately forsook her, and she appeared still more sweet and lovely, beautiful as she was before. They were married the next morning, and shortly afterwards went to the court of King Arthur, where Jack, for his eminent services, was created one of the knights of the Round Table.

Our hero, having been successful in all his undertakings, and resolving not to remain idle, but to perform what services he could for the honour of his country, humbly besought his majesty to fit him out with a horse and money to enable him to travel in search of new adventures; for, said he, "there are many giants yet living in the remote part of Wales, to the unspeakable damage of your majesty's subjects: wherefore, may it please you to encourage me, I do not doubt but in a short time to cut them off root and branch, and so rid all the realm of those giants and monsters in human shape." We need scarcely say that Jack's generous offer was at once accepted. The king furnished him with the necessary accoutrements, and Jack set out with his magical cap, sword, and shoes, the better to perform the dangerous enterprises which now lay before him.

After travelling over several hills and mountains, the country through which he passed offering many impediments to travellers, on the third day he arrived at a very large wood, which he had no sooner entered than his ears were assailed with piercing shrieks. Advancing softly towards the place where the cries appeared to proceed from, he was horror-struck at perceiving a huge giant dragging along a fair lady, and a knight her husband, by the hair of their heads, "with as much ease," says the original narrative, "as if they had been a pair of gloves." Jack shed tears of pity on the fate of this hapless couple, but not suffering his feelings to render him neglectful of action, he put on his invisible coat, and taking with him his infallible sword, succeeded, after considerable trouble, and many cuts, to despatch the monster, whose dying groans were so terrible, that they made the whole wood ring again. The courteous knight and his fair lady were overpowered with gratitude, and, after returning Jack their best thanks, they invited him to their residence, there to recruit his strength after the frightful encounter, and receive more substantial demonstrations of their obligations to him. Jack, however, declared that he would not rest until he had found out the giant's habitation. The knight, on hearing this determination, was very sorrowful, and replied, "Noble stranger, it is too much to run a second hazard: this monster lived in a den under yonder mountain, with a brother more fierce and cruel than himself. Therefore, if you should go thither, and perish in the attempt, it would be a heartbreaking to me and my lady: let me persuade you to go with us, and desist from any further pursuit." The knight's reasoning had the very opposite effect that was intended, for Jack, hearing of another giant, eagerly embraced the opportunity of displaying his skill, promising, however, to return to the knight when he had accomplished his second labour.

He had not ridden more than a mile and a half, when the cave mentioned by the knight appeared to view, near the entrance of which he beheld the giant, sitting upon a block of timber, with a knotted iron club by his side, waiting, as he supposed, for his brother's return with his barbarous prey. This giant is described as having "goggle eyes like flames of fire, a countenance grim and ugly, cheeks like a couple of large flitches of bacon, the bristles of his beard resembling rods of iron wire, and locks that hung down upon his brawny shoulders like curled snakes or hissing adders." Jack alighted from his horse, and putting on the invisible coat, approached near the giant, and said softly, "Oh! are you there? it will not be long ere I shall take you fast by the beard." The giant all this while could not see him, on account of his invisible coat, so that Jack, coming up close to the monster, struck a blow with his sword at his head, but unfortunately missing his aim, he cut off the nose instead. The giant, as we may suppose, "roared like claps of thunder", and began to lay about him in all directions with his iron club so desperately, that even Jack was frightened, but exercising his usual ingenuity, he soon despatched him. After this Jack cut off the giant's head, and sent it, together with that of his brother, to King Arthur, by a waggoner he hired for that purpose, who gave an account of all his wonderful proceedings.

The redoubtable Jack next proceeded to search the giant's cave in search of his treasure, and passing along through a great many winding passages, he came at length to a large room paved with freestone, at the upper end of which was a boiling caldron, and on the right hand a large table, at which the giants usually dined. After passing this dining-room, he came to a large and well-secured den filled with human captives, who were fattened and taken at intervals for food, as we do poultry. Jack set the poor prisoners at liberty, and, to compensate them for their sufferings and dreadful anticipations, shared the giant's treasure equally amongst them, and sent them to their homes overjoyed at their unexpected deliverance.

It was about sunrise when Jack, after the conclusion of this adventure, having had a good night's rest, mounted his horse to proceed on his journey, and by the help of directions reached the knight's house about noon. He was received with the most extraordinary demonstrations of joy, and his kind host, out of respect to Jack, prepared a feast which lasted many days, all the nobility and gentry in the neighbourhood being invited to it. The knight related the hero's adventures to his assembled guests, and presented him with a beautiful ring, on which was engraved a representation of the giant dragging the distressed knight and his lady, with this motto:

> We were in sad distress you see,
> Under the giant's fierce command,
> But gain'd our lives and liberty
> By valiant Jack's victorious hand.

But earthly happiness is not generally of long duration, and so in some respects it proved on the present occasion, for in the midst of the festivities arrived a messenger with the dismal intelligence that one Thunderdell, a giant with two heads, having heard of the death of his two kinsmen, came from the north to be revenged on Jack, and was already within a mile of the knight's house, the country people flying before him in all directions. The intelligence had no effect on the dauntless Jack, who immediately said, "Let him come! I have a tool to pick his teeth;" and with this elegant assertion, he invited the guests to witness his performance from a high terrace in the garden of the castle.

It is now necessary to inform the reader that the knight's house or castle was situated in an island encompassed with a moat thirty feet deep, and twenty feet wide passable by a drawbridge. Now Jack, intending to accomplish his purpose by a clever stratagem, employed men to cut through this drawbridge on both sides nearly to the middle; and then, dressing himself in his invisible coat, he marched against the giant with his well-tried sword. As he approached his adversary, although invisible, the giant, being, as it appears, an epicure in such matters, was aware of his approach, and exclaimed, in a fearful tone of voice—

Fi, fee, fo, fum!*
I smell the blood of an English man!
Be he alive or be he dead,
I'll grind his bones to make me bread!

"Say you so," said Jack; "then you are a monstrous miller indeed." The giant, deeply incensed, replied, "Art thou that villain who killed my kinsman? then I will tear thee with my teeth, and grind thy bones to powder." "But," says Jack, still provoking him, "you must catch me first, if you please:" so putting aside his invisible coat, so that the giant might see him, and putting on his wonderful shoes, he enticed him into a chase by just approaching near enough to give him an apparent chance of capture. The giant, we are told, "following like a walking castle, so that the very foundations of the earth seemed to shake at every step". Jack led him a good distance, in order that the wondering guests at the castle might see him to advantage, but at last, to end the matter, he ran over the drawbridge, the giant pursuing him with his club; but coming to the place where the bridge was cut, the giant's great weight burst it asunder, and he was precipitated into the moat, where he rolled about, says the author, "like a vast whale". While the monster was in this condition, Jack sadly bantered him about the boast he had made of grinding his bones to powder, but at length, having teased him sufficiently, a cart-rope was cast over the two heads of the

* These lines are quoted by Edgar in the tragedy of King Lear.

giant, and he was drawn ashore by a team of horses, where Jack served him as he had done his relatives—cut off his heads, and sent them to King Arthur.

It would seem that the giant-killer rested a short time after this adventure, but he was soon tired of inactivity, and again went in search of another giant, the last whose head he was destined to chop off. After passing a long distance, he came at length to a large mountain, at the foot of which was a very lonely house. Knocking at the door, it was opened by "an ancient* man, with a head as white as snow", who received Jack very courteously, and at once consented to his request for a lodging. Whilst they were at supper, the old man, who appears to have known more than was suspected, thus addressed the hero: "Son, I am sensible you are a conqueror of giants, and I therefore inform you that on the top of this mountain is an enchanted castle, maintained by a giant named Galligantus, who, by the help of a conjuror, gets many knights into his castle, where they are transformed into sundry shapes and forms: but, above all, I especially lament a duke's daughter, whom they took from her father's garden, bringing her through the air in a chariot drawn by fiery dragons, and securing her within the castle walls, transformed her into the shape of a hind. Now, though a great many knights have endeavoured to break the enchantment, and work her deliverance, yet no one has been able to accomplish it, on account of two fiery griffins which are placed at the gate, and which destroyed them at their approach; but you, my son, being furnished with an invisible coat, may pass by them undiscovered, and on the gates of the castle you will find engraven in large characters by what means the enchantment may be broken." The undaunted Jack at once accepted the commission, and pledged his faith to the old man to proceed early in the morning on this new adventure.

In the morning, as soon as it was daylight, Jack put on his invisible coat, and prepared himself for the enterprise. When he had reached the top of the mountain, he discovered the two fiery griffins, but, being invisible, he passed them without the slightest danger. When he had reached the gate of the castle, he noticed a golden trumpet attached to it, under which were written in large characters the following lines:

* An old man.

68

Whoever doth this trumpet blow,*
Shall soon the giant overthrow,
And break the black enchantment straight,
So all shall be in happy state.

Jack at once accepted the challenge, and putting the trumpet to his mouth, gave a blast that made the hills re-echo. The castle trembled to its foundations, and the giant and conjuror were over-stricken with fear, knowing that the reign of their enchantments was at an end. The former was speedily slain by Jack, but the conjuror, mounting up into the air, was carried away in a whirl-wind, and never heard of more. The enchantments were immediately broken, and all the lords and ladies, who had so long been cruelly transformed, were standing on the native earth in their natural shapes, the castle having vanished with the conjuror.

The only relic of the giant which was left was the head, which Jack cut off in the first instance, and which we must suppose rolled away from the influence of the enchanted castle, or it would have "vanished into thin air" with the body. It was fortunate that it did so, for it proved an inestimable trophy at the court of King Arthur, where Jack the Giant-killer was shortly afterwards united to the duke's daughter whom he had freed from enchantment, "not only to the joy of the court, but of all the kingdom". To complete his happiness, he was endowed with a noble house and estates, and his *penchant* for giant-killing having subsided, or, what is more probable, no more monsters appearing to interrupt his tranquillity, he accomplished the usual conclusion to these romantic narratives, by passing the remainder of his life in the enjoyment of every domestic felicity.

[I have alluded to the quotation from this primitive romance made by Shakespeare in "King Lear", but if the story of Rowland, published by Mr. Jamieson, is to be trusted, it would seem that the great dramatist was indebted to a ballad of the time. This position would, however, compel us to adopt the belief that the words of the giant are also taken from the ballad; a supposition to which I am most unwilling to assent. In fact, I believe that Edgar quotes from two different compositions, the first line from a ballad on Rowland,

---

* Variations of this incident are found in romances of all nations.

the second from Jack and the Giants. "And Rowland into the castle came" is a line in the second ballad of Rosmer Hafmand, or the Merman Rosmer, in the Danish "Kæmpe Viser", p. 165. The story alluded to above may be briefly given as follows.

The sons of King Arthur were playing at ball in the merry town of Carlisle, and their sister, "Burd* Ellen", in the midst of them. Now it happened that Child Rowland gave the ball such a powerful kick with his foot that "o'er the kirk he gar'd it flee". Burd Ellen went round about in search of the ball, but what was the consternation of her brothers when they found that she did not return, although "they bade lang and ay langer",

> They sought her east, they sought her west,
> They sought her up and down;
> And wae were the hearts in merry Carlisle,
> For she was nae gait found.

At last her eldest brother went to the Warlock or Wizard Merlin, and asked him if he knew where his sister, the fair Burd Ellen, was. "The fair Burd Ellen," said the Warlock Merlin, "is carried away by the fairies, and is now in the castle of the King of Elfland; and it were too bold an undertaking for the stoutest knight in Christendom to bring her back." The brother, however, insisted upon undertaking the enterprise, and after receiving proper instructions from Merlin, which he failed in observing, he set out on his perilous expedition and was never more seen.

The other brothers took the same course, and shared a similar fate, till it came to the turn of Child Rowland, who with great difficulty obtained the consent of his mother, for Queen Guinever began to be afraid of losing all her children. Rowland, having received her blessing, girt on his father's celebrated sword Excaliber, that never struck in vain, and repaired to Merlin's cave. The wizard gave him all necessary instructions for his journey and conduct, the most important of which were that he should kill every person he met with after entering the land of Faerie, and should neither eat nor drink of what was offered him in that country, whatever his hunger or thirst might be; for if he tasted or touched in Elfland, he must remain in the power of the elves, and never see middle-earth again.

* It is almost unnecessary to observe that *burd* was an ancient term for *lady*.

Child Rowland faithfully promised to observe the instructions of Merlin, and he accordingly went to Elfland, where he found, as the wizard had foretold, the king's horseherd feeding his horses. "Canst thou tell me," said Rowland, "where the castle of the king of Elfland is?" "I cannot not," replied the horseherd, "but go a little farther, and thou wilt come to a cowherd, and perhaps he will know." When he had made this answer, Rowland, remembering his instructions, took his good sword, and cut off the head of the horseherd. He then went a little farther, and met with a cowherd, to whom he repeated the same question, and obtained the same answer. Child Rowland then cut off the cowherd's head, and having pursued exactly the same course with a shepherd, goatherd, and swineherd, he is referred by the last to a hen-wife, who, in reply to his question, said, "Go on yet a little farther till you come to a round green hill, surrounded with terraces from the bottom to the top: go round it three times widershins,* and every time say, 'Open door, open door, and let me come in!' and the third time the door will open, and you may go in." Child Rowland immmediately cut off the hen-wife's head in return for her intelligence, and following her directions, a door in the hill opened, and he went in. As soon as he entered, the door closed behind him, and he traversed a long passage, which was dimly but pleasantly lighted by crystallized rock, till he came to two wide and lofty folding-doors, which stood ajar. He opened them, and entered an immense hall, which seemed nearly as big as the hill itself. It was the most magnificent apartment in all the land of Faerie, for the pillars were of gold and silver, and the keystones ornamented with clusters of diamonds. A gold chain hung from the middle of the roof, supporting an enormous lamp composed of one hollowed transparent pearl, in the midst of which was a large magical carbuncle that beautifully illumined the whole of the hall.

At the upper end of the hall, seated on a splendid sofa, under a rich canopy, was his sister the Burd Ellen, "kembing her yellow hair wi' a silver kemb", who immediately perceiving him, was sorrow-struck at the anticipation of his being destroyed by the king of Elfland,

> And hear ye this, my youngest brither,
> Why badena ye not at hame?

* The contrary way to the course of the sun.

> Had ye a hunder and thousand lives,
> Ye canna brook ane o' them.

And she informs him that he will certainly lose his life if the king finds him in the hall. A long conversation then took place, and Rowland tells her all his adventures, concluding his narrative with the observation that, after his long journey, he is *very hungry*.

On this the Burd Ellen shook her head, and looked sorrowfully at him; but, impelled by her enchantment, she rose up, and procured him a golden bowl full of bread and milk. It was then that the Child Rowland remembered the instructions of the Warlock Merlin, and he passionately exclaimed, "Burd Ellen, I will neither eat nor drink till I set thee free!" Immediately this speech was uttered, the folding-doors of the hall burst open with tremendous violence, and in came the king of Elfland,—With

> Fe, fi, fo, fum,
> I smell the blood of a Christian man!
> Be he dead, be he living, wi' my brand
> I'll clash his harns frae his harn-pan!*

"Strike, then, Bogle, if thou darest," exclaimed the undaunted Child Rowland, and a furious combat ensued, but Rowland, by the help of his good sword, conquered the elf-king, sparing his life on condition that he would restore to him his two brothers and sister. The king joyfully consented, and having disenchanted them by the anointment of a bright red liquor, they all four returned in triumph to merry Carlisle.]

TOM HICKATHRIFT

[Tom Hickathrift belongs to the same series as Jack the Giant-killer, one of the popular corruptions of old northern romances. It seems to allude to some of the insurrections in the Isle of Ely, such as that of Hereward, described in Wright's Essays, ii. 91. Spelman, however, describes a tradition, which he says was credited by the inhabitants of Tylney, in which Hickifric appears as the assertor of the rights of their ancestors, and the means he employed on the occasion correspond with incidents in the following tale. The entire

* Literally, "I will dash his brains from his skull with my sword".

passage is worth transcription. "In Marslandia sitæ sunt Walsoka, Waltona, et Walpola. In viciniis jacent Terrington et St. Maries— adjacet Tylney veteris utique Tylneiorum familiæ radix. Hic se expandit insignis area quæ a planicie nuncupatur *Tylney Smeeth*, pinguis adeo et luxurians ut Paduana pascua videatur superasse. Tuentur eam indigenæ velut aras et focos, fabellamque recitant longa petitam vetustate de Hickifrico (nescio quo) Haii illius instar in Scotorum Chronicis qui civium suorum dedignatus fuga, aratrum quod agebat solvit; arreptoque temone furibundus insiliit in hostes victoriamque ademit exultantibus. Sic cum de agri istius possessione acriter olim dimicatum esset, inter fundi dominum et villarum in-colas, nec valerent hi adversus eum consistere, redeuntibus occurrit Hickifrickus, *axemque excutiens a curru quem agebat, eo vice gladii usus; rota, clypei;* invasores repulit ad ipsos quibus nunc funguntur terminos. Ostendunt in cœmeterio Tilniensi sepulchrum sui pugilis, axem cum rota insculptum exhibens."—Icenia, "Descriptio Norfolciæ", p. 138. Hearne mentions this gravestone, and perhaps some Norfolk topographer will tell us if it now exists.]

The author of the renowned "History of Tom Hickathrift" prefaces his narrative with the following consolatory exordium:

> And if thou dost buy this book,
> Be sure that you do on it look,
> And read it o'er, then thou wilt say
> Thy money is not thrown away.

In the reign before William the Conqueror, I have read in ancient history that there dwelt a man in the parish of the Isle of Ely, in the county of Cambridge, named Thomas Hickathrift, a poor labouring man, but so strong that he was able to do in one day the ordinary work of two. He had an only son, whom he christened Thomas, after his own name. The old man put his son "to good learning", but he would take none, for he was, as we call them in this age, none of the wisest, but something soft, and had no docility at all in him. God calling this good man, the father, to his rest, his mother, being tender of him, maintained him by her hard labour as well as she could; but this was no easy matter, for Tom would sit all day in the chimney-corner, instead of doing anything to assist her; and although at the period we are speaking of he was only ten years old, he would eat more than four or five ordinary men, and was five feet and a half in height, and two feet and a half broad. His hand was more like a shoulder of mutton than a boy's hand, and he was altogether like a little monster, "but yet his great strength was not known".

Tom's strength came to be known in this manner. His mother, it appears, as well as himself, for they lived in the primitive days of merry old England, slept upon straw. This was in character with the wretched mud hovels then occupied by the labouring population, not half so good as many pigsties are nowadays. Now being a tidy old creature, she must every now and then replenish her homely couch, and one day, having been promised a "bottle" of straw by a neighbouring farmer, after considerable entreaty, she prevailed on her son to go to fetch it. Tom, however, made her borrow a cart-rope first, before he would budge a step, without condescending to enter into any explanation respecting the use he intended it for; and the poor woman, too glad to obtain his assistance on any terms, readily complied with his singular request. Tom, swinging the rope round his shoulders, went to the farmer's, and found him with two men, thrashing in a barn. Having mentioned the object of his visit, the farmer somewhat inconsiderately told him he might take as much straw as he could carry. Tom immediately took him at his word, and, placing the rope in a right position, rapidly made up a bundle containing at least a cartload, the men jeering him on the absurdity of raising a pile they imagined no man could carry, and maliciously asking him if his rope was long enough. Their merriment, however, was not of long duration, for Tom flung the enormous bundle over his shoulders, and walked away with it without any apparent exertion, much to the astonishment and dismay of the master and his men.

After this exploit, Tom was no longer suffered to enjoy his idle humours. Everyone was endeavouring to secure his services, and we are told many remarkable tales of his extraordinary strength, still more wonderful than the one just related. On one occasion, having been offered as great a bundle of firewood as he could carry, he marched off with one of the largest trees in the forest! Tom was also extremely fond of attending fairs; and in cudgelling, wrestling, or throwing the hammer, there was no one who could compete with him. He thought nothing of flinging a huge hammer into the middle of a river a mile off, and in fact performed such extraordinary feats, that it was currently reported throughout the country he had dealings with the Evil One.

Tom Hickathrift, too, was a very care-for-nothing fellow, and there were very few persons in all the Isle of Ely who dared to give him an ill word. Those who did paid very dearly for their impertinence, and Tom was, in fact, paramount over his companions. His great strength, however, caused him to be much sought after by those who were in want of efficient labour, and at length a brewer at Lynn, who required a strong, lusty fellow to carry his beer to the Marsh and to Wisbech, after much persuasion, and promising him a new suit of clothes and as much as he liked to eat and drink, secured Tom for this purpose. The distance he daily travelled with the beer was upwards of twenty miles, for although there was a shorter cut through the Marsh, no one durst go that way for fear of a monstrous giant, who was lord of a portion of the district, and who killed or made slaves of every one he could lay his hands upon.

Now in the course of time Tom was thoroughly tired of going such a roundabout way, and without communicating his purpose to any one, he was resolved to pass through the giant's domain, or lose his life in the attempt. This was a bold undertaking, but good living had so increased Tom's strength and courage, that, venturesome as he was before, his hardiness was so much increased that he would have faced a still greater danger. He accordingly drove his cart in the forbidden direction, flinging the gates wide open, as if for the purpose of making his daring more conspicuous. At length he was espied by the giant, who was indignant at his boldness, but consoled himself with the reflection that Tom and the beer would soon become his prey. "Sirrah," said the monster, "who gave you permission to come this way? Do you not know how I make all stand in fear of me? and you, like an impudent rogue, must come and fling my gates open at your pleasure! How dare you presume to do so? Are you careless of your life? Do not you care what you do? But I will make you an example for all rogues under the sun! Dost thou not see how many thousand heads hang upon yonder tree, heads of those who have offended against my laws? but thy head shall hang higher than all the rest for an example!" But Tom made him this impudent answer, "A dishclout in your teeth for your news, for you shall not find me to be one of them!" "No!" said the giant, in astonishment and indignation; "and what a fool you must be if you come to fight with such a one as I am, and bring never a weapon to defend yourself!" Quoth Tom, "I have a weapon here will make you know you are a traitorly rogue." This impertinent speech highly incensed the giant, who immediately ran to his cave for his club, intending to dash out Tom's brains at one blow. Tom was now much distressed for a weapon, that necessary accoutrement in his expedition having by some means escaped his memory, and he began to reflect how very little his whip would avail him against a monster twelve feet in height, and six feet round the waist, small dimensions certainly for a giant, but sufficient to be formidable. But while the giant was gone for his club, Tom bethought himself, and turning his cart upside down, adroitly takes out the axletree, which would serve him for a staff, and removing a wheel, adapts it to his arm in lieu of a shield; very good weapons indeed in time of trouble, and worthy of Tom's ingenuity. When the monster returned with his club, he was amazed to see the weapons with which Tom had armed himself, but uttering a word of defiance, he bore down upon the poor fellow with such heavy strokes, that it was as much as Tom could do to defend himself with his wheel. Tom, however, at length managed to give the giant* a heavy blow with the axletree on the side of his head, that he nearly reeled over. "What!" said Tom, "are you tipsy with my strong beer already?" This inquiry did not, as we may suppose, mollify the giant, who laid on his blows so sharply and heavily that Tom was obliged to act on the defensive. By and by, not making any impression on the wheel, he got almost tired out, and was obliged to ask Tom if he would let him drink a little, and then he would fight again. "No," said Tom, "my mother did not teach me that wit; who would be fool then?" The sequel may readily be imagined, and Tom having beaten the giant, and, disregarding his supplications for mercy, cut off his head, entered the cave, which he found completely filled with gold and silver.

The news of this celebrated victory rapidly spread throughout the country, for the giant had been a common enemy to the inhabitants. They made bonfires for joy, and testified their respect to Tom by every means in their power. A few days afterwards,

* In the original it is *lent the giant*, the term *lent* being old English or Saxon for *gave*. The expression sufficiently proves the antiquity of the version.

Tom took possession of the cave and all the giant's treasure. He pulled down the former, and built a magnificent house on the spot; but with respect to the land forcibly obtained by the giant, part of it he gave to the poor for their common, merely reserving enough to maintain himself and his good old mother, Jane Hickathrift. His treasure, we may suppose, notwithstanding this great liberality, enabled him to maintain a noble establishment, for he is represented as having numbers of servants, and a magnificent park of deer. He also built a famous church, which was called St. James's, because it was on that saint's day that he had killed the giant. And, what was as good and better than all this, he was no longer called Tom Hickathrift by the people, but "Mr. Hickathrift", a title then implying a greater advancement in social position than can now scarcely be imagined.

Like many other persons who have become suddenly possessed of great wealth, Tom was sadly at a loss to know what to do with his money; nor does this sage history condescend to inform us in what manner he expended it. He seems, however, to have amused himself rarely, attending every sport he could hear of for miles round, cracking skulls at cudgel-playing, bear-baiting, and all the gentlemanly recreations current in those days. At football he could scarcely have been a welcome addition to the company, for one kick from his foot, if he caught it in the middle, was sure to send the ball so great a distance over hedges and trees that it was never seen again. Tom was, also, one evening attacked by four robbers; but they sadly mistook the person they had to deal with, for he quickly killed two of them, made the others sue for mercy, and carried off their booty, which amounted to the large sum of two hundred pounds. One would have thought the Hickathrifts were wealthy enough before, but this addition to their store was, somehow or other, a source of great delight and merriment to Tom's aged mother.

Tom was a long time before he found anyone that could match him; but, one day, going through his woods, he met with a lusty tinker, who had a great staff on his shoulder, and a large dog to carry his bag and tools. Tom was not particularly courteous; it may readily be supposed that his unvarying successes had made him rather overbearing; and he somewhat rudely asked the tinker what was his business there. But the tinker was no man to succumb, and as rudely answered, "What's that to you? Fools must needs be meddling!" A quarrel was soon raised, and the two laid on in good earnest, blow for blow, till the wood re-echoed with their strokes. The issue of the contest was long doubtful, but, the tinker was so persevering, that Tom confessed he was fairly vanquished; and they then went home together, and were sworn brothers in arms ever afterwards. It happened, from the events that followed, to be a fortunate occurrence.

In and about the Isle of Ely, many disaffected persons, to the number of ten thousand and upwards, drew themselves up in a body, presuming to contend for their ancient rights and liberties, insomuch that the gentry and civil magistrates of the county were in great danger. The danger was so great, that the sheriff was obliged to come to Tom Hickathrift, under cover of the night, for shelter and protection, and gave him a full account of the rebellion. The tinker and Tom immediately promised their assistance, and they went out as soon as it was day, armed with their clubs, the sheriff conducting them to the rendezvous of the rebels. When they arrived there, Tom and the tinker marched up to the leaders of the multitude, and asked them the reason of their disturbing the government. To this they answered loudly, "Our will is our law, and by that alone will we be governed." "Nay," quoth Tom, "if it be so, these trusty clubs are our weapons, and by them alone you shall be chastised." These words were no sooner uttered, than they madly rushed on the immense multitude, bearing all before them, laying twenty or thirty sprawling with every blow. It is also related, as something remarkable, that the tinker struck a tall man on the nape of the neck with such immense force that his head flew off, and was carried forty feet from the body with such violence that it knocked down one of the chief ringleaders, killing him on the spot. The feats of Tom were no less wonderful; for, after having slain hundreds, and at length broke his club, he seized upon "a lusty rawboned miller" as a subtitute, and made use of him as a weapon, till he had quite cleared the field.

The king of course received intelligence of these extraordinary exploits, and sent for the two heroes to his palace, where a royal banquet was prepared for their honour and entertainment, most of the nobility being present. Now after the banquet was over, the king made a speech, neither too short nor too long, but having the extraordinary merit of being much to the purpose. We cannot omit so remarkable a specimen of royal eloquence. "These, my guests," said the king, "are my trusty and well-beloved subjects, men of approved courage and valour; they are the men that overcame and conquered ten thousand rebels who were combined for the purpose of disturbing the peace of my realm. According to the character I have received of Thomas Hickathrift and Henry Nonsuch, my two worthy guests here present, they cannot be matched in any other kingdom in the world. Were it possible to have an army of twenty thousand such as these, I dare venture to assert I would act the part of Alexander the Great over again. In the meanwhile, as a proof of my royal favour, kneel down, Thomas Hickathrift, and receive the ancient order of knighthood. And with respect to Henry Nonsuch, I will settle upon him, as a reward for his great services, the sum of forty shillings a year for life." After the delivery of this excellent address, the king retired, and Tom and Henry shortly afterwards took their departure, attended for many miles by a portion of the court.

When Sir Thomas Hickathrift returned home, he found, to his great sorrow, that his mother had died during his stay at the court. It can scarcely be said that he was inconsolable for her loss, but being "left alone in a large and spacious house, he found himself strange and uncouth". He therefore began to consider whether it would not be advisable to seek out for a wife, and hearing of a wealthy young widow not far from Cambridge, he went and paid his addresses to her. At his first coming, she appeared to favour his suit, but, before he paid her a second visit, her fancy had been attracted by a more elegant wooer, and Sir Thomas actually found him at her feet. The young spark, relying on the lady's favour, was vehemently abusive to the knight, calling him a great lubberly whelp, a brewer's servant, and a person altogether unfitted to make love to a lady. Sir Thomas was not a likely man to allow such an affront to go unpunished, so going out in the courtyard with the dandy to settle the matter, he gave him a kick which sent him over the tops of the houses into a pond some distance off, where he would have been drowned, had not a poor shepherd, passing by, pulled him out with his crook.

The gallant studied every means of being revenged upon the knight, and for this purpose engaged two troopers to lie in ambush for him. Tom, however, according to the story, "crushed them like cucumbers".* Even when he was going to church with his bride to be married, he was set upon by one-and-twenty ruffians in armour; but, borrowing a backsword from one of the company, he laid about him with such dexterity, that, purposely desiring not to kill anyone, at every blow he chopped off a leg or an arm, the ground being strewed with the relics, "as it is with the tiles from the tops of the houses, after a dreadful storm". His intended and friends were mightily amused at all this, and the fair one jokingly observed, "What a splendid lot of cripples he had made in the twinkling of an eye!" Sir Thomas only received a slight scratch, and he consoled himself for the trifling misfortune by the conviction that he had only lost a drop of blood for every limb he had chopped off.

The marriage ceremony took place without any further adventure, and Sir Thomas gave a great feast on the occasion, to which all the poor widows for miles round were invited in honour of his deceased mother, and it lasted for four days, in memory of the four last victories he had obtained. The only occurrence at this feast worth mentioning was the theft of a silver cup, which was traced to the possession of an old woman of the name Stumbelup,† and the others were so disgusted at her ingratitude to their kind host, that she would have been hanged on the spot, had not Sir Thomas interfered and undertaken the appointment of the punishment. Nor was it otherwise than comical, for she was condemned to be drawn through all the streets and lanes of Cambridge on a wheelbarrow, holding a placard in her hands, which informed the public,

I am the naughty Stumbelup,
Who tried to steal the silver cup.

The news of Tom's wedding soon reached the court, and the king, remembering his eminent services, immediately invited him and his lady, who visited their sovereign immediately, and were received by him most affectionately. While they were on this visit, intelligence arrived that an extraordinary invasion had taken place in the county of Kent. A huge giant riding on a dragon, and

* The author is not very particular in his similes, but this appears to be quite peculiar to this history.
† This incident has been slightly altered, the original narrative being of a nature that will not bear an exact transcription.

accompanied with a large number of bears and lions, had landed on the coast of that unfortunate county, and was ravaging it in all directions. The king, says the history, was "a little startled", and well he might be, at such a visitation; but, taking advantage of the opportune presence of Tom Hickathrift, he solved the difficulty by creating him governor of the Isle of Thanet,* and thus making him responsible for the protection of the inhabitants from this terrible monster.

There was a castle in the island, from which the country was visible for miles round, and this was the governor's abode. He had not been there long before he caught a view of the giant, who is described as "mounted upon a dreadful dragon, with an iron club upon his shoulders, having but one eye, the which was placed in his forehead; this eye was larger in compass than a barber's bason, and appeared like a flame of fire; his visage was dreadful to behold, grim and tawny; the hair of his head hung down his back and shoulders like snakes of an enormous length; and the bristles of his beard were like rusty wire"! It is difficult to imagine a being more terrible than this, but Tom was only surprised, not frightened, when he saw one day the giant making his way to the castle on his formidable dragon. After he had well viewed the edifice with his glaring eye, he tied the dragon to a tree, and went up to the castle as if he had intended to thrust it down with his shoulder. But somehow or other he managed to slip down, so that he could not extricate himself; and Tom, advancing with his two-handed sword, cut off the giant's head at one blow, and the dragon's at four, and sent them up in a "waggon" to the court of his sovereign.

The news of Tom's victories reached the ears of his old companion, the tinker, who became desirous of sharing in his glory, and accordingly joined him at his castle. After mutual congratulations, Tom informed him of his wish to destroy, without delay, the beasts of prey that infested the island. They started for this purpose in company, Tom armed with his two-handed sword, and the tinker with his long pikestaff. After they had travelled about four or five hours, it was their fortune to meet with the whole knot of wild beasts together, being in number fourteen, six bears and eight lions.

---

* In the heading of the chapter in the original it is *East Angles, now called the Isle of Thanet*, an error which favours the supposition of the story having been adapted from a much older original.

The two heroes waited for them with their backs against a tree, and whenever they came "within cutting distance" they cut their heads off, and in this manner killed all but one lion, who, unfortunately, by an inconsiderate movement on the part of Tom, crushed the poor tinker to death. The animal was, however, ultimately slain by Sir Thomas.

Sir Thomas Hickathrift had killed the giants, dragon, and lions, and he had conquered the rebels, but his happiness was by no means completed, for he was inconsolate for the loss of his friend. He, however, returned home to his lady, and made a grand feast in commemoration of his important victories. The history terminates with the following brilliant metrical speech he made on this festive occasion:

> My friends, while I have strength to stand,
>   Most manfully I will pursue
> All dangers, till I clear this land
>   Of lions, bears, and tigers too.
>
> This you'll find true, or I'm to blame.
>   Let it remain upon record,—
> Tom Hickathrift's most glorious fame,
>   Who never yet has broke his word!

TOM THUMB

[Thumb stories are common in German and Danish, and the English tale comprises much that is found in the Northern versions. A writer in the "Quarterly Review", xxi. 100, enters into some speculations respecting the mythological origin of Tom Thumb and records his persuasion, in which we agree, that several of our common nursery tales are remnants of ancient μυθοι. Sir W. Scott mentions the Danish popular history of Svend Tomling, analysed by Nierup, "a man no bigger than a thumb, who would be married to a woman three ells and three quarters long". This personage is probably commemorated in the nursery rhyme—

> I had a little husband
> No bigger than my thumb:

I put him in a pint-pot,
And there I bid him drum.

According to popular tradition, Tom Thumb died at Lincoln, and a little blue flagstone in the pavement of the cathedral used to be pointed out as his monument.

"It was my good fortune," says Dr. Wagstaffe, "some time ago, to have the library of a schoolboy committed to my charge, where, among other discovered valuable authors, I pitched upon Tom Thumb and Tom Hickathrift, authors indeed more proper to adorn the shelves of Bodley or the Vatican, than to be confined to the retirement and obscurity of a private study. I have perused the first of these with an infinite pleasure and a more than ordinary application, and have made some observations on it, which may not, I hope, prove unacceptable to the public; and however it may have been ridiculed and looked upon as an entertainment only for children and those of younger years, may be found perhaps a performance not unworthy the perusal of the judicious, and the model superior to either of those incomparable poems of Chevy Chase or the Children in the Wood. The design was undoubtedly to recommend virtue, and to show, that however anyone may labour under the disadvantages of stature and deformity, or the meanness of parentage, yet if his mind and actions are above the ordinary level, those very disadvantages that seem to depress him add a lustre to his character."—A Comment upon the History of Tom Thumb, 1711, p. 4.]

In the merry days of good King Arthur, there lived in one of the counties of England a ploughman and his wife. They were poor, but as the husband was a strong workman, and his partner an able assistant in all matters pertaining to the farmhouse, the dairy, and poultry, they managed to make a very good living, and would have been contented and happy, had Nature blessed them with any offspring. But although they had been married several years, no olive-branch had yet appeared, and the worthy couple sadly lamented their hard lot.

There lived at this period, at the court of Arthur, a celebrated conjuror and magician, whose name was Merlin, the astonishment of the whole world, for he knew the past, present, and future, and nothing appeared impossible to him. Persons of all classes solicited his assistance and advice, and he was perfectly accessible to the humblest applicant. Aware of this, the ploughman, after a long consultation with his "better half", determined to consult him, and for this purpose travelled to the court, and with tears in his eyes, beseeched Merlin that he might have a child, "even though it should be no bigger than his thumb".

Now Merlin had a strange knack of taking people exactly at their words, and without waiting for any more explicit declaration of the ploughman's wishes, at once granted his request. What was the poor countryman's astonishment to find, when he reached home, that his wife had given birth to a gentleman so diminutive, that it required a strong exercise of the vision to see him. His growth was equally wonderful, for—

> In four minutes he grew so fast,
> That he became as tall
> As was the ploughman's thumb in length,
> And so she did him call.

The christening of this little fellow was a matter of much ceremony, for the fairy queen, attended by all her company of elves, was present at the rite, and he formally received the name of Tom Thumb. Her majesty and attendants attired him with their choicest weeds, and his costume is worth a brief notice. His hat was made of a beautiful oak-leaf; his shirt was composed of a fine spider's web, and his hose and doublet of thistle-down. His stockings were made with the rind of a delicate green apple, and the garters were two of the finest little hairs one can imagine, plucked from his mother's eyebrows. Shoes made of the skin of a little mouse, "and tanned most curiously", complete his fairy-like accoutrement.

It may easily be imagined that Tom was an object of astonishment and ridicule amongst the other children of the village, but they soon discovered that, notwithstanding his diminutive size, he was more than a match for them. It was a matter of very little consequence to Tom whether he lost or won, for if he found his stock of counters or cherrystones run low, he soon crept into the pockets of his companions, and replenished his store. It happened, on one occasion, that he was detected, and the aggrieved party punished Tom by shutting him up in a pin-box. The fairy boy was sadly annoyed at his imprisonment, but the next day he amply revenged himself; for hanging a row of glasses on a sunbeam, his companions thought they would follow his example, and, not possessing Tom's fairy gifts, broke the glasses, and were severely whipped, whilst the little imp was overjoyed at their misfortune, standing by and laughing till the tears ran down his face.

The boys were so irritated with the trick that had been played upon them, that Tom's mother was afraid to trust him any longer in their company. She accordingly kept him at home, and made him assist her in any light work suitable for so small a child. One day, while she was making a batter-pudding, Tom stood on the edge of the bowl, with a lighted candle in his hand, so that she might see it was properly made. Unfortunately, however, when her back was turned, Tom accidentally fell in the bowl, and his mother not missing him, stirred him up in the pudding "instead of minced fat", and put the pudding in the kettle with Tom in it. The poor woman paid dearly for her mistake, for Tom had no sooner felt the warm water, than he danced about like mad, and the pudding jumped about till she was nearly frightened out of her wits, and was glad to give it to a tinker who happened to be passing that way. He was thankful for a present so acceptable, and anticipated the pleasure of eating a better dinner than he had enjoyed for many a long day. But his joy was of short duration, for as he was getting over a stile, he happened to sneeze very hard, and Tom, who had hitherto remained silent, cried out, "Hollo, Pickens!" which so terrified the tinker that he threw the pudding into the field, and scampered away as fast as ever he could go. The pudding tumbled to pieces with the fall, and Tom, creeping out, went home to his mother, who had been in great affliction on account of his absence.

A few days after this adventure, Tom accompanied his mother when she went into the fields to milk the cows, and for fear he should be blown away by the wind, she tied him to a thistle with a small piece of thread. While in this position, a cow came by, and swallowed him up:

> But, being missed, his mother went,
>   Calling him everywhere:
> "Where art thou, Tom? where art thou, Tom?"
>   Quoth he, "Here, mother, here!

85

> Within the red cow's stomach, here
>   Your son is swallowed up;"
> All which within her fearful heart
>   Much woful dolour put.

The cow, however, was soon tired of her subject, for Tom kicked and scratched till the poor animal was nearly mad, and at length tumbled him out of her mouth, when he was caught by his mother and carried safely home.

A succession of untoward accidents followed. One day, Tom's father took him to the fields a-ploughing, and gave him "a whip made of a barley straw" to drive the oxen with, but the dwarf was soon lost in a furrow. While he was there, a great raven came and carried him an immense distance to the top of a giant's castle. The giant soon swallowed him up, but he made such a disturbance when he got inside, that the monster was soon glad to get rid of him, and threw the mischievous little imp full three miles into the sea. But he was not drowned, for he had scarcely reached the water before he was swallowed by a huge fish, which was shortly after captured, and sent to King Arthur by the fisherman for a new-year's gift. Tom was now discovered, and at once adopted by the king as his dwarf:

> Long time he lived in jollity,
>   Beloved of the court,
> And none like Tom was so esteem'd
>   Amongst the better sort.

The queen was delighted with the little dwarf, and made him dance a galliard on her left hand. His performance was so satisfactory, that King Arthur gave him a ring, which he wore about his middle like a girdle; and he literally "crept up the royal sleeve", requesting leave to visit his parents, and take them as much money as he could carry:

> And so away goes lusty Tom
>   With threepence at his back,
> A heavy burthen, which did make
>   His very bones to crack.

Tom remained three days with the old couple, and feasted upon a hazel-nut so extravagantly that he grew ill. His indisposition was not of long continuance, and Arthur was so anxious for the return of his dwarf, that his mother took a birding-trunk, and blew him to the court. He was received by the king with every demonstration of affection and delight, and tournaments were immediately proclaimed:

> Thus he at tilt and tournament
> Was entertained so,
> That all the rest of Arthur's knights
> Did him much pleasure show.

> And good Sir Launcelot du Lake,
> Sir Tristram and Sir Guy,
> Yet none compared to brave Tom Thumb
> In acts of chivalry.

Tom, however, paid dearly for his victories, for the exertions he made upon this celebrated occasion threw him into an illness which ultimately occasioned his death. But the hero was carried away by his godmother, the fairy queen, into the land of Faerie, and after the lapse of two centuries, he was suffered to return to earth, and again amuse men by his comical adventures. On one occasion, after his return from fairy-land, he jumped down a miller's throat, and played all manners of pranks on the poor fellow, telling him of all his misdeeds, for millers in former days were the greatest rogues, as everybody knows, that ever lived. A short time afterwards, Tom a second time is swallowed by a fish, which is caught, and set for sale at the town of Rye, where a steward haggles for it,

> Amongst the rest the steward came,
> Who would the salmon buy,
> And other fish that he did name,
> But he would not comply.

> The steward said, You are so stout,
> If so, I'll not buy any.
> So then bespoke Tom Thumb aloud,
> "Sir, give the other penny!"

At this they all began to stare,
    To hear this sudden joke:
Nay, some were frighted to the heart,
    And thought the dead fish spoke.

So the steward made no more ado,
    But bid a penny more;
Because, he said, I never heard
    A fish to speak before.

The remainder of the history, which details Tom's adventures with the queen, his coach drawn by six beautiful white mice, his escaping on the back of a butterfly, and his death in a spider's web, is undoubtedly a later addition to the original, and may therefore be omitted in this analysis. It is, in fact, a very poor imitation of the first part of the tale.

THREE

Game Rhymes

The most obvious method of arranging the rhymes employed in the amusements of children is to commence with the simple lines used by the nurse in the infantine toe, finger, and face-games, then proceeding to bo-peep, and concluding with the more complicated games, many of the latter possessing a dramatic character.

TOE GAMES

> Harry Whistle, Tommy Thistle,
> Harry Whible, Tommy Thible,
> And little Oker-bell.

A game with the five toes, each toe being touched in succession as these names are cried. "This song affords a proof of the connection between the English and Scandinavian rhymes. The last line, as it now stands, appears to mean nothing. The word *oker*, however, is the A.-S. æcer, Icel, akr, Dan. ager, and Swed. åker, pronounced *oker*, a field, and a flower is the field-bell."—(Mr. Stephens's MS.) The following lines are also used in a play with the toes,

> Shoe the colt, shoe!
> Shoe the wild mare!

Put a sack on her back,
　　See if she'll bear.
If she'll bear,
　　We'll give her some grains;
If she won't bear,
　　We'll dash out her brains.

There are many various versions of this song in English, and it also exists in Danish (Thiele, iii. 133).

Skoe min hest!
Hvem kan bedst?
Det kan vor Præst!
Nei mæn kan han ej!
For det kan vor smed,
Som boer ved Leed.

(Shoe my horse!
Who can best?
Why, our priest!
Not he, indeed!
But our smith can,
He lives at Leed.)

Perhaps, however, this will be considered more like the common rhyme, "Robert Barnes, fellow fine," printed in the "Nursery Rhymes of England". An analogous verse is found in nursery anthology of Berlin (Kuhn, Kinderlieder, 229), and in that of Sweden (Lilja, p. 14),

Sko, sko min lille häst,
I morgon frosten blir' vår gäst,
Då bli' hästskorna dyra,
Två styfver fōr fyra.

(Shoe, shoe my little horse,
To-morrow it will be frosty;
Then will horse-shoes be dear,
Two will cost a stiver.)

English nurses use the following lines, when a child's shoe is tight, and they pat the foot to induce him to allow it to be tried on,

> Cobbler, cobbler, mend my shoe,
> Give it a stitch and that will do.
> Here's a nail, and there's a prod,
> And now my shoe is well shod.

Or, occasionally, these lines,

> This pig went to market,
>   Squeak, mouse, mouse, mousey;
> Shoe, shoe, shoe the wild colt,
>   And here's my own doll dowsy.

The following lines are said by the nurse when moving the child's foot up and down,

> The dog of the kill,*
> He went to the mill
>   To lick mill-dust:
> The miller he came
> With a stick on his back,—
>   Home, dog, home!
> The foot behind,
>   The foot before:
> When he came to a stile,
>   Thus he jumped o'er.

THE FIVE FINGERS

I do not recollect to have seen anywhere noticed the somewhat singular fact, that our ancestors had distinct names for each of the five fingers—the thumb being generally called a finger in old works. Yet such was the case; and it may not displease the reader to have these cognominations duly set forth in order, viz., *thumb, toucher, longman, lecheman, littleman*. This information is derived from a very curious MS. quoted in my "Dictionary of Archaisms", p. 357;

* A north-country term for *kiln*.

and the reasons for the names are thus set forth: The first finger was called *toucher*, because "therewith men touch i-wis"; the second finger *longman*, "for longest finger it is" (this, I beg to say, is intended for rhyme). The third finger was called *lecheman*, because a leche or doctor tasted everything by means of it. This is very curious; though we find elsewhere another reason for this appellation, on account of the pulsation in it, which was at one time supposed to communicate directly with the heart. The other finger was, of course, called *littleman*, because it was the least of all. It is rather curious that some of these names should have survived the wrecks of time, and be still preserved in a nursery rhyme; yet such is the fact; for one thus commences, the fingers being kept in corresponding movements:

> Dance, thumbkin, dance,
> Dance, thumbkin, dance;
> Dance, ye merry men all around:
> But thumbkin he can dance alone;
> But thumbkin he can dance alone.

> Dance, foreman, dance,
> Dance, foreman, dance;
> Dance, ye merry men all around:
> But thumbkin he can dance alone;
> But thumbkin he can dance alone.

And so on, substituting in succession *middleone*, *longman*, or *middleman*, *ringman* and *littleman*, and each verse terminating with "thumbkin he can dance alone". In some instances the original name for the third finger, *lecheman*, is preserved in the rhyme, but *ringman* is most generally adopted.

It is worthy of remark, too, that there is, even at the present day, amongst many of the old women of the Peak of Derbyshire, a strong belief in the superiority of *lecheman* over *foreman* in all matters of taste. They say that the forefinger is *venomous*, and that the superiority of the third is to be ascribed to its being possessed of a *nerve*; and as they appear to pay a most superstitious reverence to a nerve, whether in the finger, the tooth, or the ear, they do not fail to impress upon their daughters the importance of tasting any-thing of consequence with the third finger.

The names given to the fingers vary considerably in the different counties. In Essex they call them,

> Tom Thumbkin,
> Bess Bumpkin,
> Bill Wilkin,
> Long Linkin,
> And little Dick!

And in some parts of Yorkshire,

> Tom Thumbkins,
> Bill Wilkins,
> Long Daniel,
> Bessy Bobtail,
> And little Dick.

Similar appellations for the fingers are common in Denmark. Thus (Thiele iii. 136),

> Tommeltot,
> Slikkepot,
> Langemand,
> Guldbrand,
> Lille Peer Spilleman.

"Lille Peer Spilleman" is "little Peter the fiddler", not a bad name for the little finger. A slight variation of this is current in Sweden,

> Tomme tott,
> Slicke pott;
> Långe man,
> Hjertlig hand;
> Lille, lille, lille, gullvive!

The following song for the four fingers is obtained from Lancashire:

> This broke the barn,
> This stole the corn,
> This got none:
> This went pinky-winky
> All the way home!

FACE SONGS

Bo Peeper,
Nose dreeper,
Chin chopper,
White lopper,
Red rag,
And little gap.

These lines are said to a very young child, touching successively for each line the eye, nose, chin, tooth, tongue, and mouth. Sometimes the following version is used:

Brow brinky,
Eye winky,
Chin choppy,
Nose noppy,
Cheek cherry,
Mouth merry.

The most pleasing amusement of this kind is the game of "face-tapping", the nurse tapping each feature as she sings these lines,

Here sits the lord mayor (*forehead*),
Here sit his two men (*eyes*);
Here sits the cock (*right cheek*),
Here sits the hen (*left cheek*).
Here sit the little chickens (*tip of nose*),
Here they run in (*mouth*);
Chinchopper, chinchopper,
Chinchopper, chin! (*chucking the chin.*)

Similar songs are common in the North of Europe. A Danish one is given by Thiele, iii. 130:

Pandebeen,
Oisteen,
Næsebeen,
Mundelip,
Hagetip,
Dikke, dikke, dik.

(Brow-bone,
Eye-stone,
Nose-bone,
Mouth-lip,
Chin-tip,
Dikke, dikke, dik!)

The nurse, while repeating the last line, tickles the child under the chin. A German version now common at Berlin, is printed by M. Kuhn, in his article on Kinderlieder, p. 237 (a separate sheet sent me from Germany, part of a book):

Kinnewippchen,
Rothlippchen,
Nasendrippchen,
Augenthränechen,
Ziep ziep Maränechen.

The following lines are repeated by the nurse when sliding her hand down the child's face:

My mother and your mother
Went over the way:
Said my mother to your mother,
It's chop-a-nose day!

KNEE-SONGS

This is the way the ladies ride;
Tri, tre, tre, tree,
Tri, tre, tre, tree!
This is the way the ladies ride,
Tri, tre, tre, tri-tre-tre-tree!

This is the way the gentlemen ride;
Gallop-a-trot,
Gallop-a-trot!
This is the way the gentlemen ride,
Gallop-a-gallop-a-trot!

This is the way the farmers ride,
  Hobbledy-hoy,
  Hobbledy-hoy!
This is the way the farmers ride,
  Hobbledy hobbledy-hoy!

This is a famous song for a young child, the nurse dancing it on her
knee, and gradually increasing the ascent of the foot. Similar songs,
but differing considerably from the above, are given in the Swedish
nursery ballads of Arwidsson, iii. 489–91; the Danish of Thiele,
iii. 130–2, iv. 176–7; and the German Wunderhorn, iii. 60–1. The
following pretty Swedish version is given from Mr. Stephens's
MS. collections:

        Hvem är det som rider?
        Det är en fröken som rider:
        Det går i sakta traf,
            I sakta traf!

        Hvem är det som rider?
        Det är en Herre som rider:
        Det går jo i galopp,
            I galopp!

        Hvem är det som rider?
        Det är en Bonde som rider:
        Det går så lunka på,
            Lunka på!

        (And pray, who now is riding?
        A lady it is that's riding:
        And she goes with a gentle trot,
            A gentle trot!

        And pray, who now is riding?
        A gentleman it is that's riding:
        And he goes with a gallop-away,
            A gallop-away!

And pray, who now is riding?
A farmer it is that's riding:
And he goes with a jog along,
    A jog along!)

There are a great number of English variations of the above
song, differing very materially from one another. A second version
may be worth giving:

Here goes my lord,
A trot! a trot! a trot! a trot!

Here goes my lady,
A canter! a canter! a canter! a canter!

Here goes my young master,
Jockey-hitch! jockey-hitch! jockey-hitch! jockey-hitch!

Here goes my young miss,
An amble! an amble! an amble! an amble!

The footman lags behind to tipple ale and wine,
And goes gallop, a gallop, a gallop, to make up his time.

Here are other Knee Songs:

Little Shon a Morgan,
   Shentleman of Wales,
Came riding on a nanny-goat,
   Selling of pigs' tails.

Chicky, cuckoo, my little duck,
   See-saw, sickna downy;
Gallop a trot, trot, trot,
   And hey for Dublin towny!

BO-PEEP

The children's game of Bo-peep is as old as the hills, hiding from
each other, and saying,

> Bo-Peep, Little Bo-Peep:
> Now's the time for hide and seek.

But in ancient times the amusement appears to have been even of a simpler character, and adopted by nurses before children are capable of seeking recreation for themselves. Sherwood describes bo-peep as a child's game, in which the nurse conceals the head of the infant for an instant, and then removes the covering quickly. The Italians say *far bau bau*, or *baco, baco*, which Douce thinks is sufficient to show a connection between the nurse's *boggle* or *buggy-bo*, and the present expression. Shakespeare has condescended to notice the game, unless, indeed, we suppose the term to have passed into a proverb. The reader will recollect what Butler says of Sir Edward Kelly, the celebrated conjuror,

> Kelly did all his feats upon
> The devil's looking-glass, a stone:
> Where, *playing with him at bo-peep*,
> He solved all problems ne'er so deep.

The term bo-peep appears to have been connected at a very early period with sheep. Thus in an old ballad of the time of Queen Elizabeth, in a MS. in the library of Corpus Christi College, Cambridge,

> Halfe Englande ys nowght now but shepe,
> In everye corner they playe boe-pepe;
> Lorde, them confownde by twentye and ten,
> And fyll their places with Cristen men.

And every one is acquainted with the nursery rhyme which details the adventures of "Little Bo-peep",

> Little Bo-peep has lost her sheep,
>   And can't tell where to find them:
> Leave them alone, and they'll come home,
>   And bring their tails behind them.
>
> Little Bo-peep fell fast asleep,
>   And dreamt she heard them bleating:

But when she awoke, she found it a joke,
For they were still all fleeting.

Minsheu gives us a funny derivation of the word, which he says is no other than the noise which chickens make when they come out of the shell! I regret I have nothing better, certainly nothing so ingenious, to offer to my philological readers. Letting that pass, I take the opportunity of giving an anecdote respecting Ben Jonson and Randolph, which affords another illustration of the analogy above mentioned. It is taken from a manuscript of the seventeenth century, in the possession of Mr. Stephens of Stockholm, who considers the volume to have been transcribed before the year 1650:

"Randolph havinge not soe much as ferry money, sought out Ben Jonson, and comminge to a place in London where he and three more were drinkinge, peeps in att the chamber doore. Ben Jonson, espyinge him, said, 'Come in, Jack Bo-peepe.' Randolph, beinge very thirsty, it beeing then summer, and willinge to quench his thirst, willingly obeyed his command. The company dranke untill it came to five shillings: every man drawinge his money, Randolph made this motion, viz. that he that made the first coppy of verses upon the reckoninge should goe scot-free. Ben and all the rest, beeinge poetts, readily consented. Randolph, surpassinge them in acutenesse, utter'd forthwith these followinge,

I, Jack Bo-peep,
And you foure sheep,
Lett every one yeeld his fleece:
Here's five shillinge,
If you are willinge,
That will be fifteen pence a-peece.
Et sic impune evasit inops."

We conclude in the words of Shakespeare,

They then for sudden joy did weep,
And I for sorrow sung,
That such a king should play *bo-peep*,
And go the fools among.

99

MISCELLANEOUS PUERILE AMUSEMENTS

I went to the sea,
And saw twentee
  Geese all in a row:
My glove I would give
Full of gold, if my wife
  Was as white as those.

These lines are to be repeated rapidly and correctly, inserting the word *cother* after *every* word, under pain of a forfeit.

It's time, I believe,
For us to get leave:
The little dog says
It isn't, it is; it isn't, it is, &c.

Said by a schoolboy, who places his book between his knees. His two forefingers are then placed together, and the breadth of each is measured alternately along the length of the book. The time to get leave (to be dismissed) is supposed to have arrived or not according as one finger or the other fills up the last space.

A duck and a drake,
And a white penny cake.
It's time to go home,
It isn't, it is, &c.

So going on with the fingers one over the other along the edge of a book or desk, till the last finger determines the question.

Put your finger in foxy's hole,
  Foxy is not at home:
Foxy is at the back door,
  Picking of a bone.

Holding the fist in such a way that if a child puts its finger in, you can secure it, still leaving the hole at top open.

Jack's alive and in very good health,
If he dies in your hand you must look to yourself.

Played with a stick, one end burnt red-hot: it is passed round a
circle from one to the other, the one who passes it saying this and
the one whose hand it goes out in paying a forfeit.

SEE-SAW

A common game, children vacillating on either end of a plank
supported on its centre. While enjoying this recreation, they have a
song of appropriate cadence, the burden of which is,

> Titty cum tawtay,
>   The ducks in the water:
> Titty cum tawtay,
>   The geese follow after.

HITTY-TITTY

> Hitty-titty in doors,
>   Hitty-titty out;
> You touch Hitty-titty,
>   And Hitty-titty will bite you.

These lines are said by children when one of them has hid herself.
They then run away, and the one who is bitten (caught) becomes
Hitty-titty, and hides in her turn. A variation of the above lines
occurs in MS. Harl. 1962, as a riddle, the solution of which is *a nettle*.

BEANS AND BUTTER

So the game of *hide-and-seek* is called in some parts of Oxfordshire.
Children hide from each other, and when it is time to commence
the search, the cry is,

> Hot boil'd beans and very good butter,
> If you please to come to supper!

DROP-CAP

In the game where the following lines are used, one person goes round inside a ring of children, clapping a cap between his hands. When he drops it at the foot of any one, that one leaves his position and gives chase, and is obliged to thread the very same course among the children till the first is caught. The first then stands with his back towards the centre of the ring, the one called out takes his place, and thus they continue till nearly all are "turned".

> My hand burns hot, hot hot,
> And whoever I love best, I'll drop this at his foot!

MY SOW HAS PIGGED

A game at cards, played now only by children. It is alluded to by Taylor the Water-poet, in his "Motto", 12mo. Lond. 1622, and it is also mentioned in Poor Robin's Almanac for 1734. The following distich is used in this game:

> Higgory, diggory, digg'd,
> My sow has pigg'd.

NIDDY-NODDY

A simple but very amusing game at cards, at which any number can play. The cards are dealt round, and one person commences the game by placing down a card, and the persons next in succession who hold the same card in the various suits place them down upon it, the holder of the last winning the trick. The four persons who hold the cards say, when they put them down.

1. There's a good card for thee.
2. There's a still better than he!
3. There's the best of all three.
4. And there is Niddy-noddee!

The person who is first *out*, receives a fish for each card unplayed.

SLATE GAMES

Entertaining puzzles or exercises upon the slate are generally great favourites with children. A great variety of these are current in the nursery, or rather were so some years ago. The story of the four rich men, the four poor men, and the pond, was one of these; the difficulty merely requiring a zig-zag inclosure to enable it to be satisfactorily solved.

Once upon a time there was a pond lying upon common land, which was extremely commodious for fishing, bathing, and various other purposes. Not far from it lived four poor men, to whom it was of great service; and farther off there lived four rich men. The latter envied the poor men the use of the pond, and, as inclosure bills had not then come into fashion, they wished to invent an inclosure-wall which should shut out the poor men from the pond, although they lived so near it, and still gave free access to the rich men, who resided at a greater distance. How was this done?

THE GAME OF THE CAT

This is another slate game, in which, by means of a tale and appropriate indications on the slate, a rude figure of a cat is delineated. It requires, however, some little ingenuity to accomplish it.

Tommy would once go to see his cousin Charles. [Here one draws T for Tommy, and C for Charles, forming the forehead, nose, and mouth of the cat.] But before he went, he would make walls to his house. [Here he draws lines from the arms of the T to its foot, forming the cheeks of the cat.] But then it smoked, and he would put chimneys to it. [Here he inserts two narrow triangles on each arm of the T, forming the ears of the cat.] But then it was so dark, he would put windows into it. [Here he draws a small circle under each arm of the T, forming the eyes.] Then to make it pretty, he would spread grass at the door. [Here he scratches lines at the foot of the T, representing the cat's whiskers.] Then away he went on his journey, but after a little while, down he fell. [Here he draws down a line a little way from the foot of the T.] But he soon climbed up again. [Here he draws a zig-zag horizontally from the foot of the last line, and draws one up, forming with the last movement the first foot of the cat.] Then he walks along again, but soon falls down once more. [Here he draws a short horizontal line, and one downwards.] He soon, however, got up again, as before, &c. [The second leg is then formed, and by similar movements the four legs of the cat appear.] After thus falling down four times, Tommy determined to proceed more firmly, and climbing up, he walks along [the back of the cat] another way round till he comes to C. His journey is now accomplished, and an animal, called by courtesy a cat, appears on the slate, "the admiration of all beholders".

HANDY-DANDY

This game is now played as follows: A child hides something in one hand, and then places both fists endways on each other, crying,

> Handy-dandy riddledy ro,
> Which will you have, high or low?

Or, sometimes, the following distich,

> Handy-dandy, Jack-a-dandy,
> Which good hand will you have?

The party addressed either touches one hand, or guesses in which one the article (whatever it may be) is placed. If he guesses rightly, he wins its contents; if wrongly, he loses an equivalent.

Some versions read *handy-pandy* in the first of these, with another variation, that would not now be tolerated. This is one of the oldest English games in existence, and appears to be alluded to in Piers Ploughman, ed. Wright, p. 69:

> Thanne wowede Wrong
> Wisdom ful yerne,
> To maken pees with his pens,
> Handy-dandy played.

Florio, in his "World of Words", ed. 1611, p. 57, translates *bazziciáre*, "to shake between two hands, to play handie-dandie". Miege, in his Great French Dictionary, 1688, says, "Handy-dandy,

a kind of play with the hands, *sorte de jeu de main*"; and Douce, ii.
167, quotes an early MS., which thus curiously mentions the game:
"They hould safe your children's patrymony, and play with your
majestie, as men play with little children at *handye-dandye which
hand will you have*? when they are disposed to keep anything from
them." Some of the commentators on Shakespeare have mistaken
the character of the game, from having adopted Coles's erroneous
interpretation of *micare digitis*. Sometimes the game is played by a
sort of sleight of hand, changing the article rapidly from one hand
to the other, so that the looker-on is often deceived, and induced to
name the hand into which it is apparently thrown. This is what
Shakespeare alludes to by changing places.

Pope, in his "Memoirs of Martinus Scriblerus", says that the
game of handy-dandy is mentioned by Plato; but if, as I suppose,
he refers to a well-known passage in the Lysis, the allusion appears
somewhat too indistinct to warrant such an assertion: αστρα γαλιζοντας
τε δη και κεκοσμημενους ἁπαντας. οἱ μεν ουν πολλοι εν τη αυλη επαιζον εξω.
οἱ δε τινες τον αποδυτηριου εν γωνιᾳ ἡρτιαζον αστραγαλοις παμπολλοις, εκ
φορμισκων τινων προαιρουμενοι. A passage, however, in Julius Pollux,
ix. 101, referring to this, is rather more distinct, and may allude to
one form of the game: Και μην και αρτιαζειν, αστραγαλους εκ φορμισκων
καθαιρομενους εν τῳ αποδυτηριῳ τους παιδας, ὁ Πλατων εφη. το δε αρτιαζειν
εν αστραγαλων πληθει κεκρυμμενων ὑπο ταιν χεροιν, μαντειαν ειχε των αρτιων
η και περιττων. ταυτο δε τουτο και κυαμοις, η καρυοις τε και αμυγδαλαις, οἱ
δε και αργυριῳ πραττειν ηξιουν, a passage which Meursius, "De Ludis
Græcorum," ed. 1625, p. 5, thus partially translates, "Nempe
ludentes sumptis in manu talis, fabis, nucibus, amygdalis, interdum
etiam nummis, interrogantes alterum divinare jubebant." Here we
have the exact game of handy-dandy, which is after all the simple
form of the odd and even of children.

Browne has a curious allusion to this game in "Britannia's
Pastorals", i. 5:

> Who so hath sene yong lads, to sport themselves,
> Run in a low ebbe to the sandy shelves,
> Where seriously they worke in digging wels,
> Or building childish sorts of cockle-shels;
> Or liquid water each to other bandy,
> Or with the pibbles play at handy-dandy.

BARLEY-BRIDGE

A string of boys and girls, each holding by his predecessor's skirts, approaches two others, who, with joined and elevated hands, form a double arch. After the dialogue is concluded, the line passes through the arch, and the last is caught, if possible, by the sudden lowering of the arms.

> "How many miles to Barley-bridge?"
> "Three score and ten."
> "Can I get there by candle-light?"
> "Yes, if your legs be long."
> "A courtesy to you, and a courtesy to you,
> If you please will you let the king's horses through?"
> Through and through shall they go,
> For the king's sake;
> But the one that is hindmost
> Will meet with a great mistake.

THE TOWN LOVERS

A game played by boys and girls. A girl is placed in the middle of a ring, and says the following lines, the names being altered to suit the party. She points to each one named, and at the last line, the party selected immediately runs away, and if the girl catches him, he pays a forfeit, or the game is commenced again, the boy being placed in the middle, and the lines, *mutatis mutandis*, serve for a reversed amusement:

> There is a girl of our town,
> She often wears a flowered gown:
> Tommy loves her night and day,
> And Richard when he may,
> And Johnny when he can:
> I think Sam will be the man!

MARY BROWN. FAIR GUNDELA

A slightly dramatic character may be observed in this game, which was obtained from Essex. Children form a ring, one girl kneeling in the centre, and sorrowfully hiding her face with her hands. One in the ring then says,

> Here we all stand round the ring,
> And now we shut poor Mary in;
> Rise up, rise up, poor Mary Brown,
> And see your poor mother go through the town.

To this she answers,

> I will not stand up upon my feet,
> To see my poor mother go through the street.

The children then cry,

> Rise up, rise up, poor Mary Brown,
> And see your poor father go through the town.

Mary

I will not stand up upon my feet.
To see my poor father go through the street.

Children

Rise up, rise up, poor Mary Brown,
To see your poor brother go through the town.

Mary

I will not stand up upon my feet.
To see my poor brother go through the street.

Children

Rise up, rise up, poor Mary Brown,
To see your poor sister go through the town.

Mary

I will not stand up upon my feet,
To see my poor sister go through the street.

Children

Rise up, rise up, poor Mary Brown,
To see the poor beggars go through the town.

Mary

I will not stand up upon my feet,
To see the poor beggars go through the street.

One would have thought that this tiresome repetition had been continued quite long enough, but two other verses are sometimes added, introducing *gentlemen* and *ladies* with the same questions, to both of which it is unnecessary to say that the callous and hard-hearted Mary Brown replies with perfect indifference and want of curiosity. All versions, however, conclude with the girls saying,

Rise up, rise up, poor Mary Brown,
And see your poor sweetheart go through the town.

The chord is at last touched, and Mary, frantically replying,

I will get up upon my feet,
To see my sweetheart go through the street,

rushes with impetuosity to break the ring, and generally succeeds in escaping the bonds that detain her from her imaginary love.

The Swedish ballad of the "Maiden that was sold into Slavery", has a similar dramatic character. (See an article by Mr. Stephens, on the Popular Ballads and Songs of Sweden, in the "Foreign Quarterly Review" for 1840.) Another Swedish ballad, or ring-dance song, entitled, "Fair Gundela", is, however, more analogous to the above. A girl sits on a stool or chair within a ring of dancers; and, with something in her hands, imitates the action of rowing. She should have a veil on her head, and at the news of her sweetheart's death, let it fall over her face, and sink down, overwhelmed with sorrow. The ring of girls dance round her, singing and pausing, and she sings in reply. The dialogue is conducted in the following manner:

The Ring

Why row ye so, why row ye so?
Fair Gundela!

Gundela

Sure I may row, ay sure may I row,
While groweth the grass,
All summer through.

The Ring

But now I've speir'd that your father's dead,
Fair Gundela!

Gundela

What matters my father? My mother lives still.
Ah, thank heaven for that!

The Ring

But now I've speir'd that your mother's dead,
Fair Gundela!

Gundela

What matters my mother? My brother lives still.
Ah, thank heaven for that!

The Ring

But now I've speir'd that your brother's dead,
Fair Gundela!

Gundela

What matters my brother? My sister lives still.
Ah, thank heaven for that!

The Ring

But now I've speir'd that your sister's dead,
   Fair Gundela!

Gundela

What matters my sister? My sweetheart lives still.
   Ah, thank heaven for that!

The Ring

But now I've speir'd that your sweetheart's dead,
   Fair Gundela!

[*Here she sinks down overwhelmed with grief.*]

Gundela

  Say! can it be true,
   Which ye tell now to me,
  That my sweetheart's no more?
   Ah, God pity me!

The Ring

But now I've speir'd that your father lives still,
   Fair Gundela!

Gundela

What matters my father? My sweetheart's no more!
   Ah, God pity me!

The Ring

But now I've speir'd that your mother lives still,
   Fair Gundela!

Gundela

What matters my mother? My sweetheart's no more!
   Ah, God pity me!

The Ring

But now I've speir'd that your brother lives still,
        Fair Gundela!

Gundela

What matters my brother? My sweetheart's no more!
        Ah, God pity me!

The Ring

But now I've speir'd that your sister lives still,
        Fair Gundela!

Gundela

What matters my sister? My sweetheart's no more!
        Ah God, pity me!

The Ring

But now I've speir'd that your sweetheart lives still,
        Fair Gundela!

Gundela

    Say! can it be true
      Which ye tell now to me,
    That my sweetheart lives still?
    Thank God, thank God for that!

The veil is thrown on one side, her face beams with joy, the circle is broken, and the juvenile drama concludes with merriment and noise. It is difficult to say whether this is the real prototype of the English game, or whether they are both indebted to a still more primitive original. There is a poetical sweetness, an absolute and dramatic fervour in the Swedish ballad we vainly try to discover in the English version. In the latter, all is vulgar, common-place, and phlegmatic. Cannot we trace in both the national character? Do we not see in the last that poetic simplicity which has made the works of Andersen so popular and irresistibly charming? It may be that the style pleases by contrast, and that we appreciate its genuine chasteness the more, because we have nothing similar to it in our own vernacular literature.

MY DAUGHTER JANE

Eccleshall version, played as a game by the schoolgirls. See the "Nursery Rhymes of England".

Suitors. Here come two dukes all out of Spain,
A courting to your daughter Jane.

Mother. My daughter Jane, she is so young,
She can't abide your flattering tongue.

Suitor. Let her be young or let her be old,
It is the price, she must be sold,
Either for silver or for gold.
So, fare you well, my lady gay,
For I must turn another way.

Mother. Turn back, turn back, you Spanish knight,
And rub your spurs till they be bright.

Suitor. My spurs they are of a costliest wrought,
And in this town they were not bought;
Nor in this town they won't be sold,
Neither for silver nor for gold.
So, fare you well, my lady gay,
For I must turn another way.

Through the kitchen, and through the hall,
And take the fairest of them all;
The fairest is, as I can see,
Pretty Jane—come here to me.

Now I've got my pretty fair maid,
Now I've got my pretty fair maid
To dance along with me—
To dance along with me!

There is a different version in Cambridgeshire, but the girl recollects it so imperfectly, and only two stanzas, that I cannot depend upon their being correct.

> Here come three lords dressed all in green,
> For the sake of your daughter Jane.
> My daughter Jane she is so young,
> She learns to talk with a flattering tongue.
>
> Let her be young, or let her be old,
> For her beauty she must be sold.
> My mead's not made, my cake's not baked,
> And you cannot have my daughter Jane.

HEWLEY-PULEY

The children are seated and the following questions put by one of the party, holding a twisted handkerchief or something of the sort in the hand. The handkerchief was called hewley-puley, and the questions are asked by the child who holds it. If one answered wrongly, a box on the ear with the handkerchief was the consequence; but if they all replied correctly, then the one who broke silence first had that punishment.

> Take this! What's this?—Hewley-puley.
> Where's my share?—About the kite's neck.
> Where's the kite?—Flown to the wood.
> Where's the wood?—The fire has burned it.
> Where's the fire?—The water has quenched it.
> Where's the water?—The ox has drunk it.
> Where's the ox?—The butcher has killed it.
> Where's the butcher?—The rope has hanged him.
> Where's the rope?—The rat has gnawed it.
> Where's the rat?—The cat has killed it.
> Where's the cat?—Behind the door, cracking pebble-stones and marrow-bones for yours and my supper, and the one who speaks first shall have a box on the ear.

THE DIAMOND RING

Children sit in a ring or in a line, with their hands placed together palm to palm, and held straight, the little fingers down-most between the knees. One of them is then chosen to represent a servant, who takes a ring, or some other small article as a substitute, between her two palms, which are pressed flat together like those of the rest, and goes round the circle or line, placing her hands into the hands of every player, so that she is enabled to let the ring fall wherever she pleases without detection. After this, she returns to the first child she touched, and with her hands behind her exclaims,

> My lady's lost her diamond ring:
> I pitch upon you to find it!

The child who is thus addressed must guess who has the ring, and the servant performs the same ceremony with each of the party. They who guess right, escape; but the rest forfeit. Should anyone in the ring exclaim, "I have it", she also forfeits; nor must the servant make known who has the ring, until all have guessed, under the same penalty. The forfeits are afterwards cried as usual.

THE POOR SOLDIER

Children form a half-circle, first choosing one of their number to represent the poor soldier. The chief regulation is that none of the players may use the words *yes*, *no*, *black*, *white*, or *grey*. The poor soldier traverses the semicircle, thus addressing each player,

> Here's a poor soldier come to town!
> Have you aught to give him?

The answer must of course be evasive, else there is a fine. He continues, "Have you a pair of trousers [or old coat, shoes, cap, &c.] to give me?" The answer must again be evasive, or else another forfeit. The old soldier then asks: "Well, what colour is it?" The reply must avoid the forbidden colours, or another forfeit is the penalty. Great ingenuity may be exhibited in the manner in which the questions and answers are constructed, and, in the hands of some children, this is a most amusing recreation. The forfeits are of course cried at the end of the game.

THE BRAMBLE-BUSH

A ring-dance imitation-play, the metrical portion of which is not without a little melody. The bramble-bush is often imaginative, but sometimes represented by a child in the centre of the ring. All join hands, and dance round in a circle, singing,

> Here we go round the bramble-bush,
> The bramble-bush, the bramble-bush:
> Here we go round the bramble-bush
> On a cold frosty morning!

After the chanting of this verse is ended, all the children commence an imitation of washing clothes, making appropriate movements with their hands, and saying,

> This is the way we wash our clothes,
> Wash our clothes, wash our clothes:
> This is the way we wash our clothes
> On a cold frosty morning!

They then dance round, repeating the first stanza, after which the operation of drying the clothes is commenced with a similar verse, "This is the way we dry our clothes", &c. The game may be continued almost *ad infinitum* by increasing the number of duties to be performed. They are, however, generally satisfied with mangling, *smoothing* or ironing, the clothes, and then putting them away. Sometimes they conclude with a general cleaning, which may well be necessary after the large quantity of work that has been done:

> This is the way we clean our rooms,
> Clean our rooms, clean our rooms:
> This is the way we clean our rooms
> On a cold frosty morning!

And like good merry washing-women, they are not exhausted with their labours, but conclude with the song, "Here we go round the bramble-bush," having had sufficient exercise to warm themselves on any "cold frosty morning", which was doubtlessly the result, we may observe *en passant*, as a matter of domestic economy, aimed at by the author. It is not so easy to give a similar explanation to the game of the mulberry-bush, conducted in the same manner:

> Here we go round the mulberry-bush,
> The mulberry-bush, the mulberry-bush:
> Here we go round the mulberry-bush
>   On a sunshiny morning.

In this game, the motion-cries are usually "This is the way we wash our clothes", "This is the way we dry our clothes", "This is the way we make our shoes", "This is the way we mend our shoes", "This is the way the gentlemen walk", "This is the way the ladies walk", &c. As in other cases, the dance may be continued by the addition of cries and motions, which may be rendered pretty and characteristic in the hands of judicious actors. This game, however, requires too much exercise to render it so appropriate to the season as the other.

THE GAME OF DUMP

A boys' amusement in Yorkshire, in vogue about half a century ago, but now, I believe, nearly obsolete. It is played in this manner. The lads crowd round, and place their fists end-ways the one on the other, till they form a high pile of hands. Then a boy who has one hand free, knocks the piled fists off one by one, saying to every boy, as he strikes his fist away, "What's there, Dump?" He continues this process till he comes to the last fist, when he exclaims:

> What's there?
> Cheese and bread, and a mouldy halfpenny!
>   Where's my share?
> I put it on the shelf, and the cat got it.
>   Where's the cat?
> She's run nine miles through the wood.

Where's the wood?
T' fire burnt it.
Where's the fire?
T' water sleckt (extinguished) it.
Where's the water?
T' oxen drunk it.
Where's the oxen?
T' butcher kill'd 'em.
Where's the butcher?

Upon the church-top cracking nuts, and you may go and eat the shells; and *them as* speak first shall have nine nips, nine scratches, and nine boxes over the lug!

Every one then endeavours to refrain from speaking, in spite of mutual nudges and grimaces, and he who first allows a word to escape is punished by the others in the various methods adopted by schoolboys. In some places the game is played differently. The children pile their fists in the manner described above; then one, or sometimes all of them sing,

I've built my house, I've built my wall;
I don't care where my chimneys fall!

The merriment consists in the bustle and confusion occasioned by the rapid withdrawal of the hands.

DANCING LOOBY

Now we dance looby, looby, looby,
Now we dance looby, looby, light.
Shake your right hand a little
And turn you round about.

Now we dance looby, looby, looby.
Shake your right hand a little,
Shake your left hand a little,
And turn you round about.

Now we dance looby, looby, looby.
Shake your right hand a little,
Shake your left hand a little,
Shake your right foot a little,
And turn you round about.

Now we dance looby, looby, looby.
Shake your right hand a little,
Shake your left hand a little,
Shake your right foot a little,
Shake your left foot a little,
And turn you round about.

Now we dance looby, looby, looby.
Shake your right hand a little,
Shake your left hand a little,
Shake your right foot a little,
Shake your left foot a little,
Shake your head a little,
And turn you round about.

Children dance round first, then stop and shake the hand, &c.,
then turn slowly round, and then dance in a ring again.

DROP-GLOVE

Children stand round in a circle, leaving a space between each.
One walks round the outside, and carries a glove in her hand, saying,

I've a glove in my hand,
        Hittity hot!
Another in my other hand,
        Hotter than that!
So I sow beans, and so they come up,
Some in a mug, and some in a cup.
I sent a letter to my love,
I lost it, I lost it!
I found it, I found it!
It burns, it scalds!

Repeating the last words very rapidly, till she drops the glove behind one of them, and whoever has the glove must overtake her, following her exactly in and out till she catches her. If the pursuer makes a mistake in the pursuit, she loses, and the game is over; otherwise she continues the game with the glove.

NETTLES GROW IN AN ANGRY BUSH

Nettles grow in an angry bush,
    An angry bush, an angry bush;
Nettles grow in an angry bush,
    With my High, Ho, Ham!
This is the way the lady goes,
    The lady goes, the lady goes;
This is the way the lady goes,
    With my High, Ho, Ham!

The children dance round, singing the first three lines, turning round and clapping hands for the fourth line. They curtsey while saying, "This is the way the lady goes", and again turn round and clap hands for the last line. The same process is followed in every verse, only varying what they act—thus, in the third verse, they *bow* for the gentleman,

Nettles grow in an angry bush, &c.
This is the way the gentleman goes, &c.

Nettles grow in an angry bush, &c.
This is the way the tailor goes, &c.

And so the amusement is protracted *ad libitum*, with shoemaking, washing the clothes, ironing, churning, milking, making up butter, &c.

GAME OF THE GIPSY

One child is selected for Gipsy, one for Mother, and one for Daughter Sue. The Mother says,

I charge my daughters every one
To keep good house while I am gone.
You and *you* (*points*) but specially *you*,
[*Or sometimes*, but specially *Sue*.]
Or else I'll beat you black and blue.

During the Mother's absence, the Gipsy comes in, entices a child away, and hides her. This process is repeated till all the children are hidden, when the Mother has to find them.

THE GAME OF THE FOX

One child is Fox. He has a knotted handkerchief, and a home to which he may go whenever he is tired, but while out of home he must always hop on one leg. The other children are geese, and have no home. When the Fox is coming out he says,

> The Fox gives warning
> It's a cold frosty morning.

After he has said these words he is at liberty to hop out, and use his knotted handkerchief. Whoever he can touch is Fox instead, but the geese run on two legs, and if the Fox puts his other leg down, he is hunted back to his home.

THE OLD DAME

One child, called the Old Dame, sits on the floor, and the rest, joining hands, form a circle round her, and dancing, sing the following lines:

> *Children.* To Beccles; to Beccles!
> To buy a bunch of nettles!
> Pray, Old Dame, what's o'clock?
> *Dame.* One, going for two,
> *Children.* To Beccles! to Beccles!
> To buy a bunch of nettles!
> Pray, Old Dame, what's o'clock?
> *Dame.* Two, going for three.

And so on till she reaches, "Eleven, going for twelve". After this the following questions are asked, with the replies: C. Where have you been? D. To the wood. C. What for? D. To pick up sticks. C. What for? D. To light my fire. C. What for? D. To boil my kettle. C. What for? D. To cook some of your chickens. The children then all run away as fast as they can, and the Old Dame tries to catch one of them. Whoever is caught is the next to personate the Dame.

THE POOR WOMAN OF BABYLON

One child stands in the middle of a ring formed by the other children joining hands round her. They sing,

> Here comes a poor woman from Babylon,
> With three small children all alone:
> One can brew, and one can bake,
> The other can make a pretty round cake.
>
> One can sit in the arbour and spin,
> Another can make a fine bed for the king.
> Choose the one and leave the rest,
> And take the one you love the best.

The child in the middle having chosen one in the ring of the opposite sex, the rest say,

> Now you're married, we wish you joy;
> Father and mother you must obey:
> Love one another like sister and brother,
> And now, good people, kiss each other!

They then kiss, and the process is repeated till all the children are in the ring. Another game, played in the same way, begins with this verse:

> Sally, Sally Waters, why are you so sad?
> You shall have a husband either good or bad:
> Then rise, Sally Waters, and sprinkle your pan,
> For you're just the young woman to get a nice man.

The partner being chosen, the two kneel down, and the rest sing,

> Now you're married we wish you joy,
> Father and mother and little boy!
> Love one another like sister and brother,
> And now, good people, kiss each other.

QUEEN ANNE

> Queen Anne, Queen Anne, who sits on her throne,
> As fair as a lily, as white as a swan;
> The king sends you three letters,
> And begs you'll read one.

This is said by all the children but one, who represents the Queen, they having previously hid a ball upon one of their number. The Queen answers,

> I cannot read one unless I read all,
> So pray, ——, deliver the ball.

Naming any child she pleases. If she guesses rightly the child who has the ball takes her place as Queen. If wrongly, the child who has the ball says,

> The ball is mine, and none of thine,
> So you, proud Queen, may sit on your throne,
> While we, your messengers, go and come.

Or, sometimes, these lines,

> The ball is mine, and none of thine,
> You are the fair lady to sit on:
> And we're the black gipsies to go and come.

COUNTING-OUT RHYMES

The operation of counting out is a very important mystery in many puerile games. The boys or girls stand in a row, and the operator begins with the counting-out rhyme, appropriating a word to each, till he comes to the person who receives the last word, and who is accordingly "out". This operation is continued till there is only one left, who is the individual chosen for the hero of the game, whatever

it may be. The following verses are selected from a host of rhymes
employed for this purpose:

> One–ery, two–ery,
>   Tick–ery, tee–vy;
> Hollow–bone, crack–a–bone,
>   Pen and eevy;
> Ink, pink,
>   Pen and ink;
> A study, a stive,
>   A stove, and a sink!
>
> One–ery, two–ery,
>   Tickery, teven;
> Alabo, crackabo,
>   Ten and eleven:
> Spin, spon,
>   Must be gone;
> Alabo, crackabo,
>   Twenty-*one*!
> O–U–T spells out.

[Something similar to this is found in Swedish, Arwidsson, iii. 492:

> Apala, mesala,
> Mesinka, meso,
> Sebedei, sebedo!
> Extra, lara,
> Kajsa, Sara!
> Heck, veck,
> Vällingsäck,
> Gack du din länge man veck,
> Ut!]

> Igdum, digdum, didum, dest,
> Cot–lo, we–lo, wi–lo, west;
> Cot pan, must be done,
> Twiddledum, twaddledum, twenty-one!
>
> Hytum, skytum,
> Perridi styxum,
> Perriwerri wyxum,
> A bomun D.

FOUR

Alphabet Rhymes

Amongst the various devices to establish a royal road to infantine learning, none are more ancient or useful than the rhymes which serve to impress the letters of the alphabet upon the attention and memory of children. As early as the fifteenth century, "Mayster Benet", who was rector of Sandon, in Essex, in 1440, and afterwards a prebend of St. Paul's, composed or translated an alphabet-rhyme, which not only professed to recall the memory of the letters, but, at a time when the benefit of clergy was in vogue, held out the inducement of providing means for avoiding the punishment of death. The following copy is taken from two versions in MS. Harl. 541, compared with each other:

"Who so wyll be wyse and worshyp to wynne, leern he on lettur and loke upon another of the A. B. C. of Arystotle. Noon argument agaynst that, ffor it is counselle for clerkes and knightes a thowsand; and also it myght amend a meane man fulle oft the lernyng of a lettur, and his lyf save. It shal not greve a good man, though gylt be amend. Rede on this ragment, and rule the theraftur, and whoso be grevid yn his goost governe the bettur. Herkyn and here every man and child how that I begynne:

A. to Amerous, to Aventurous, ne Angre the not to moche.
B. to Bold, to Besy, and Bourde not to large.
C. to Curtes, to Cruel, and Care not to sore.

D. to Dulle, to Dredefulle, and Drynk not to oft.
E. to Ellynge, to Excellent, ne to Ernstfulle neyther.
F. to Ferse, ne to Familier, but Frendely of chere.
G. to Glad, to Gloryous, and Gelowsy thow hate.
H. to Hasty, to Hardy, ne to Hevy yn thyne herte.
J. to Jettyng, to Janglyng, and Jape not to oft.
K. to Keping, to Kynd, and ware Knaves tatches among.
L. to Lothe, to Lovyng, to Lyberalle of goodes.
M. to Medlus, to Mery, but as Maner asketh.
N. to Noyous, to Nyce, nor yet to Newefangle.
O. to Orpyd, to Ovyrthwarte and Othes thou hate.
P. to Preysyng, to Privy, with Prynces ne with dukes.
Q. to Queynt, to Querelous, to Quesytife of questions.
R. to Ryetous, to Revelyng, ne Rage not to meche.
S. to Straunge, ne to Steryng, nor Stare not to brode.
T. to Taylous, to Talewyse, for Temperaunce ys best.
V. to Venemous, to Vengeable, and Wast not to myche.
W. to Wyld, to Wrothfulle, and Wade not to depe,
    A mesurabulle meane Way is best for us alle."

A. APPLE-PIE

Eachard, a learned clergyman of the Church of England, published
a work in 1671,* in which he condescends to illustrate his argument
by a reference to this celebrated history. Talking of the various
modes of preaching adopted by different sects, he proceeds in this
manner: "And whereas it has been observed that some of our
clergie are sometimes over nice in taking notice of the meer words
that they find in texts, so these are so accurate as to go to the very
letters. As suppose, sir, you are to give an exhortation to repentance
upon that of St. Matthew, 'Repent ye, for the kingdom of heaven
is at hand': you must observe that *Repent* is a rich word, wherein
every letter exhorts us to our duty,—Repent, R. readily, E.
earnestly, P. presently, E. effectually, N. nationally, T. thoroughly.
Again, Repent Roaringly, Eagerly, Plentifully, Heavily (because of
h), Notably, Terribly. And why not Repent Rarely, Evenly, Prettily,
Elegantly, Neatly, Tightly? And also, why not, A apple-pasty, B

* Observations, &c., 8vo. Lond. 1671, p. 160.

bak'd it, C cut it, D divided it, E eat it, F fought for it, G got it,
&c. ? I had not time, sir, to look any further into their way of preaching; but if I had, I am sure I should have found that they have no
reason to despise our church upon that account." The worthy
divine would have censured the sermon on Malt attributed to the
elder Dodd.

We thus find this nursery romance descending in all its purity
for nearly two centuries. It may be even older than the time of
Charles II, for it does not appear as a novelty in the quotation we
have just given. Be this as it may, the oldest edition I know of was
printed some half century since by Marshall in Aldermary Churchyard, entitled "The Tragical Death of A. Apple-pye, who was cut
in pieces and eat by twenty-five gentlemen, with whom all little
people ought to be very well acquainted", which runs as follows:

> A. apple-pye, B. bit it,
> C. cut it, D. dealt it,
> E. eat it, F. fought for it,
> G. got it, H. had it,*
> J. join'd for it, K. kept it,
> L. long'd for it, M. mourn'd for it,
> N. nodded at it, O. open'd it,
> P. peep'd in it, Q. quarter'd it,
> R. ran for it, S. stole it,
> T. took it, V. viewed it, W. wanted it;
> X. Y. Z. and Ampersy-and,
> They all wish'd for a piece in hand.
>
> At last they every one agreed
> Upon the apple-pye to feed;
> But as there seem'd to be so many,
> Those who were last might not have any,
> Unless some method there was taken,
> That every one might save their bacon,
> They all agreed to stand in order
> Around the apple-pye's fine border,

---

* Some copies say "H. halv'd it, I. ey'd it", and afterwards, "U. hew'd it, . . . X.
crossed it, Y. yearn'd for it, and Z. put it in his pocket, and said, Well done!"

Take turn as they in hornbook stand,
From great A down to &,
In equal parts the pye divide,
As you may see on t'other side.

Then follows a woodcut of the pye, surrounded by a square of the letters, though it is not very easy to perceive how the conditions of the problem are to be fulfilled. The remainder of the book, a small 32mo., is occupied with "A Curious Discourse that passed between the twenty-five letters at dinnertime",

Says A, give me a good large slice.
Says B, a little bit, but nice.
Says C, cut me a piece of crust.
Take it, says D, it's dry as dust.
Says E, I'll eat now fast, who will.
Says F, I vow I'll have my fill.
Says G, give it me good and great.
Says H, a little bit I hate.
Says I, I love the juice the best,
And K the very same confest.
Says L, there's nothing more I love.
Says M, it makes your teeth to move.
N noticed what the others said.
O others' plates with grief survey'd.
P praised the cook up to the life.
Q quarrel'd 'cause he'd a bad knife.
Says R, it runs short, I'm afraid.
S silent sat, and nothing said.
T thought that talking might lose time;
U understood it at meals a crime.
W wish'd there had been a quince in;
Says X, those cooks there's no convincing.
Says Y, I'll eat, let others wish.
Z sat as mute as any fish,
While Ampersy-and he lick'd the dish.

The manner in which a practical moral good was to be inferred from this doggerel is not very apparent, but Mr. Marshall had a way of his own in settling the difficulty. The finale must not be omitted: "Having concluded their discourse and dinner together, I have nothing more to add, but that, if my little readers are pleased with what they have found in this book, they have nothing to do but to run to Mr. Marshall's at No. 4, in Aldermary Churchyard, where they may have several books, not less entertaining than this, of the same size and price. But that you may not think I leave you too abruptly, I here present you with the picture of the old woman who made the apple-pye you have been reading about. She has several more in her basket, and she promises, if you are good children, you shall never go supperless to bed while she has one left. But as good people always ask a blessing of God before meals, therefore, as a token that you are good, and deserve a pye, you must learn the two following graces, the one to be said before the meals, the other after; and the Lord's Prayer every night and morning." Two graces and the Lord's Prayer conclude the tract.

The following alphabet or literal rhyme refers to Carr, Earl of Somerset, the favourite of James I:

> J. C. U. R.
> Good Mounseir Car
>   About to fall;
> U. R. A. K.
> As most men say,
>   Yet that's not all.
> U. O. K. P.
> With a nullytye,
>   That shamelesse packe!
> S. X. his yf (*wife*),
> Whos shamelesse lyfe
>   Hath broke your backe.
>
>   *MS. Sloane*, 1489, f. 9, v°.

> A. B. C.
> D. E. F. G.
> H. I. J. K., if you look you'll see;
> L. M. N. O. P. Q.
> R. S. T. U. V. W.
> X. Y. Z.

Heigh ho! my heart is low,
My mind is all on one;
It's W for I know who,
And T for my love, Tom!

Riddle Rhymes

A very favourite class of rhymes with children, though the solutions are often most difficult to guess. Nursery riddle rhymes are extremely numerous, and a volume might be filled with them without much difficulty. Many of the most common ones are found in manuscript collections of the sixteenth and seventeenth centuries.

> I'm in every one's way,
>   But no one I stop;
>   My four horns every day
>   In every way play,
> And my head is nailed on at the top!

—A turnstile.

> There was a king met a king
>   In a straight lane;
> Says the king to the king,
>   Where have you been?
> I've been in the wood,
>   Hunting the doe:
> Pray lend me your dog,
>   That I may do so?

> Call him, call him!
> What must I call him?
> Call him as you and I,
> We've done both.

—The dog's name was *Been*, and the name of the persons who met each other was King. This riddle was obtained recently from oral tradition. I observe, however, a version of it in MS. Harl. 1962, of the seventeenth century.

> The cuckoo and the gowk,
> The laverock and the lark,
> The twire-snipe, the weather-bleak;
> How many birds is that?

—Three, for the second name in each line is a synonyme. The cuckoo is called a *gowk* in the North of England; the lark, a *laverock*; and the twire-snipe and weather-bleak, or weather-bleater, are the same birds.

> Hoddy-doddy,
> With a round black body!
> Three feet and a wooden hat:
> What's that?

—An iron pot. In the country, an iron pot with three legs, and a wooden cover, the latter raised or put on by means of a peg at the top, is used for suspending over a fire, or to place on the hearth with a wood fire.

> Riddle me, riddle me, what is that
> Over the head and under the hat?

—Hair. From Kent.

> The fiddler and his wife,
> The piper and his mother,
> Ate three half-cakes, three whole cakes,
> And three quarters of another.
> How much did each get?

—The fiddler's wife was the piper's mother. Each one therefore got $\frac{1}{2} + 1 + \frac{1}{4}$, or $1\frac{3}{4}$.

There was a little green house,
And in the little green house
There was a little brown house,
And in the little brown house
There was a little yellow house,
And in the little yellow house
There was a little white house,
And in the little white house
There was a little heart.

—A walnut.

A flock of white sheep
    On a red hill;
Here they go, there they go,
    Now they stand still!

—The teeth and gums.

Old Father Greybeard,
    Without tooth or tongue,
If you'll give me your finger,
    I'll give you my thumb.

—Greybeard, says Moor, "Suffolk Words", p. 155, was the appropriate name for a fine large handsome stone bottle, holding perhaps three or four, or more gallons, having its handle terminating in a venerable Druidic face. This riddle appears to be alluded to in MS. Harl. 7316, p. 61:

I'm a dull senseless blockhead, 'tis true, when I'm young,
And like old grandsire Greybeard without tooth or tongue,
But by the kind help and assistance of arts
I sometimes attain to politeness of parts.

What God never sees,
What the king seldom sees;
What we see every day;
Read my riddle,—I pray.

—An equal. This riddle is well known in Sweden. The following version was given me by Mr. Stephens:

133

Jag ser det dagligen;
Kungen ser det sällan;
Gud ser det aldrig.

"I see it daily;
The king sees it seldom;
God sees it never."

As white as milk,
And not milk;
As green as grass,
And not grass;
As red as blood,
And not blood;
As black as soot,
And not soot!

—A bramble-blossom.

The land was white,
The seed was black;
It'll take a good scholar
To riddle me that.

—Paper and writing.

As high as a castle,
As weak as a wastle;
And all the king's horses
Cannot pull it down.

—Smoke. A wastle is a North country term for a twig or withy,
possibly connected with A.-S. wædl.

I've seen you where you never was,
And where you ne'er will be;
And yet you in that very same place
May still be seen by me.

—The reflection of a face in a looking-glass.

Banks full, braes full,
Though ye gather all day,
Ye'll not gather your hands full.

—The mist. From Northumberland. Sometimes thus:

> A hill full, a hole full,
> Ye cannot catch a bowl full.

A young man and a young woman quarrelled, and the former, in his anger, exclaimed,

> Three words I know to be true,
> All which begin with W.

The young woman immediately guessed the enigma, and replied in a similar strain,

> I too know them,
> And eke three which begin with M.

—Woman wants wit. Man much more.

> The calf, the goose, the bee,
> The world is ruled by these three.

—Parchment, pens, and wax.

> A house full, a yard full,
> And ye can't catch a bowl full.

—Smoke.

> As I was going o'er London bridge,
> I heard something crack;
> Not a man in all England
> Can mend that!

—Ice.

> I had a little sister,
> They called her Pretty Peep;
> She wades in the waters,
> Deep, deep, deep!
> She climbs up the mountains,
> High, high, high;
> My poor little sister,
> She has but one eye.

—A star. This charming little riddle is always a great favourite with children.

As I was going o'er yon moor of moss,
I met a man on a grey horse;
He whipp'd and he wail'd.
I ask'd him what he ail'd;
He said he was going to his father's funeral,
Who died seven years before he was born!

—His father was a dyer.

As I look'd out of my chamber window,
I heard something fall;
I sent my maid to pick it up,
But she couldn't pick it all.

—Snuff. From Yorkshire.

Black within, and red without,
Four corners round about.

—A chimney. From Yorkshire.

As I was going o'er London bridge,
I met a drove of guinea pigs;
They were nick'd and they were nack'd,
And they were all yellow back'd.

—A swarm of bees; not a very likely family to meet in that neighbourhood, at least nowadays, but some of the authors of these
poems seem to have been continually traversing London bridge.

Higher than a house, higher than a tree;
Oh! whatever can that be?

—A star. From Yorkshire.

Which weighs heavier—
A stone of lead
Or a stone of feathers?

—They both weigh alike.

Lilly low, lilly low, set up on an end,
See little baby go out at town end.

—A candle. Lillylow is a North country term for the flame of a
candle. Low, A.-S. lig, is universal.

At the end of my yard there is a vat,
Four-and-twenty ladies dancing in that:
Some in green gowns, and some with blue hat:
He is a wise man who can tell me that.

—A field of flax.

Jackatawad ran over the moor,
Never behind, but always before!

—The ignus fatuus, or Will o' the Wisp. *Jackatawad* is a provincial
term for this phenomenon.

Black'm, saut'm, rough'm, glower'm, saw,
Click'm, gatt'm flaug'm into girnigaw.

—Eating a sloe. A North country riddle, given by Brockett.
Girnigaw is the cavity of the mouth.

There was a man rode through our town,
    Grey Grizzle was his name;
His saddle-bow was gilt with gold;
    Three times I've named his name.

—Gaffer Was. From Yorkshire.

There was a man went over the Wash,
Grizzle grey was his horse;
Bent was his saddle-bow:
I've told you his name three times,
And yet you don't know!

—The same as the last. From Norfolk.

I am become of flesh and blood,
    As other creatures be;
Yet there's neither flesh nor blood
    Doth remain in me.
I make kings that they fall out,
    I make them agree;
And yet there's neither flesh nor blood
    Doth remain in me.

—A pen. Riddles similar to this are current in most languages. Mr.

Stephens has kindly furnished me with the following one obtained in Sweden:

Af kött och blod är jag upprunnen,
Men ingen blod är i mig funnen;
Många herrar de mig bära,
Med hvassa knifvar de mig skära.
Mången har jag gifvit ära,
Mången har jag tagit af,
Mången har jag lagt i graf.

(Of flesh and blood sprung am I ever;
But blood in me that find ye never.
Many great lords bear me proudly,
With sharp knives cutting me loudly.
Many I've graced right honourably:
Rich ones many I've humble made;
Many within their grave I've laid!)

The pen has been a fertile subject for the modern riddle-writer. The best production of the kind was printed some years ago in the *Times* newspaper, contributed by Miss Agnes Strickland.

Into my house came neighbour John,
With three legs and a wooden one;
If one be taken from the same,
Then just five there will remain.

—He had a IV-legged stool with him, and taking away the left-hand numeral, there remains V.

Link lank, on a bank,
Ten against four.

—A milkmaid.

Two legs sat upon three legs,
With four legs standing by;
Four then were drawn by ten:
Read my riddle ye can't,
However much ye try.

—An amplification of the above, the milkmaid of course sitting on a three-legged stool.

Over the water,
And under the water,
And always with its head down!

—A nail in the bottom of a ship.

As straight as a maypole,
As little as a pin,
As bent as a bucker,
And as round as a ring.

I do not know the solution of this riddle. A bucker is a bent piece of wood by which slaughtered sheep are hung up by their expanded hind legs, before being cut out.

Hitty Pitty within the wall,
Hitty Pitty without the wall:
If you touch Hitty Pitty,
Hitty Pitty will bite you.

—A nettle. MS. Harl. 1962, xvii. cent.

The first letter of our fore-fadyr,
A worker of wax,
An I and an N;
The colour of an ass:
And what have you then?

—Abindon, or Abingdon, in Berks. An ancient rebus given in "Lelandi Itin", ed. 1744, ii. 136.

I saw a fight the other day;
A damsel did begin the fray.
She with her daily friend did meet,
Then standing in the open street;
She gave such hard and sturdy blows,
He bled ten gallons at the nose;
Yet neither seemed to faint nor fall,
Nor gave her any abuse at all.

—A pump. MS. Harl. 1962, xvij. cent.

A water there is I must pass,
A broader water never was;
And yet of all waters I ever did see,
To pass over with less jeopardy.

—The dew. From the same MS.

There is a bird of great renown,
Useful in city and in town;
None work like unto him can do;
He's yellow, black, red, and green,
A very pretty bird I mean;
Yet he's both fierce and fell:
I count him wise that can this tell.

—A bee. From the same MS.

As I went over Hottery Tottery,
I looked into Harbora Lilly;
I spied a cutterell
Playing with her cambril.
I cryed, Ho, neighbour, ho!
Lend me your cue and your goe,
To shoot at yonder cutterell
Playing with her cambril,
And you shall have the curle of her loe.

—A man calling to his neighbour for a gun to shoot a deer, and he should have her humbles. MS. ibid.

As I went through my houter touter,
Houter touter, verly;
I see one Mr. Higamgige
Come over the hill of Parley.
But if I had my carly verly,
Carly verly verly;
I would have bine met with Mr. Higamgige
Come over the hill of Parley.

—A man going over a hill, and a fly lighting on his head. MS. ibid.

THE FOUR SISTERS

I have four sisters beyond the sea,
    Para-mara, dictum, domine!
And they did send four presents to me,
    Partum, quartum, paradise, tempum,
    Para-mara, dictum, domine!

The first it was a bird without e'er a bone;
    Para-mara, dictum, &c.
The second was a cherry without e'er a stone;
    Partum, quartum, &c.

The third it was a blanket without e'er a thread;
    Para-mara, dictum, &c.
The fourth it was a book which no man could read;
    Partum, quartum, &c.

How can there be a bird without e'er a bone?
    Para-mara, dictum, &c.
How can there be a cherry without e'er a stone?
    Partum, quartum, &c.

How can there be a blanket without e'er a thread?
    Para-mara, dictum, &c.
How can there be a book which no man can read?
    Partum, quartum, &c.

When the bird's in the shell, there is no bone;
    Para-mara, dictum, &c.
When the cherry's in the bud, there is no stone;
    Partum, quartum &c.

When the blanket's in the fleece, there is no thread;
    Para-mara, dictum, &c.
When the book's in the press, no man can read;
    Partum, quartum, &c.

Several versions of this metrical riddle are common in the North of
England, and an ingenious antiquary has suggested that it is a

parody on the old monkish songs! It will remind the reader of the Scottish ballad of Captain Wedderburn's Courtship,

O hold away from me, kind sir,
   I pray you let me be;
For I will not go to your bed,
   Till you dress me dishes three:
Dishes three you must dress to me,
   And I must have them a'
Before that I lie in your bed,
   Either at stock or wa'.

O I must have to my supper
   A cherry without a stone;
And I must have to my supper
   A chicken without a bone:
And I must have to my supper
   A bird without a ga',
Before I lie into your bed,
   Either at stock or wa'.

When the cherry is in the bloom,
   I'm sure it hath no stone;
And when the chicken is in its shell,
   I'm sure it hath no bone:
The dove it is a gentle bird,
   It flies without a ga',
And we shall both lie in ae bed,
   And thou's lie next the wa'.

The belief that a pigeon or dove has no gall forms the subject of a chapter in Browne's "Vulgar and Common Errors", iii. 3. The gall-bladder does not exist in the dove.

THE DEMANDS JOYOUS

It is not generally known that many of our popular riddles are centuries old. Yet such is the fact, and those whose course of reading has made them acquainted with ancient collections are not infrequently startled by observing a quibble of the fifteenth or sixteenth century go the round of modern newspapers as a new invention, or perhaps as an importation from America. An instance of this species of resuscitation took place in the publication some years ago of the question, "Which were made first, elbows or knees?" This was an enigma current in England in the time of Queen Elizabeth, and is found in a manuscript in the British Museum written before the close of the sixteenth century.

The earliest collection of riddles printed in this country came from the press of Wynkyn de Worde in the year 1511, in black letter, under the title of "The Demaundes Joyous". Only one copy of this tract, which was "imprynted at London, in Flete Strete, at the sygne of the Sonne", is known to exist, and it is now preserved in the public library at Cambridge. It is chiefly a compilation from an early French tract under a similar title, but which is far more remarkable for its grossness. The reader may be amused with the following specimens, and perhaps recognize some of them as old favourites:

"*Demand.* Who bore the best burden that ever was borne?— *R.* The ass on which our Lady rode when she fled with our Lord into Egypt. *D.* What became of that ass?—*R.* Adam's mother did eat her. *D.* Who is Adam's mother?—*R.* The earth.

Demand. What space is from the surface of the sea to its greatest depth?—*R.* A stone's cast.

Demand. How many calves' tails behoveth to reach from the earth to the sky?—*R.* No more but one, an it be long enough.

Demand. Which is the most profitable beast, and that which men eat least of?—*R.* Bees.

Demand. Which is the broadest water, and the least jeopardy to pass over?—*R.* The dew.

Demand. What thing is that which never was nor never will be? —*R.* A mouse making her nest in a cat's ear.

Demand. Why doth a dog turn himself thrice round before he lieth down?—*R.* Because he knoweth not the bed's head from its foot.

Demand. Why do men make an oven in the town?—*R.* For because they cannot make the town in the oven.

Demand. How may a man know or perceive a cow in a flock of sheep?—*R.* By sight.

Demand. What alms are worst bestowed that men give?—*R.* Alms to a blind man, for he would willingly see him hanged by the neck that gave it him.

Demand. What thing is that which hath no end?—*R.* A bowl.

Demand. What people be they that never go a-procession?—*R.* Those that ring the bells in the mean time.

Demand. What is that that freezeth never?—*R.* Hot water.

Demand. What thing is that that is most likest unto a horse?—*R.* That is a mare.

Demand. What thing is that which is more frightful the smaller it is?—*R.* A bridge.

Demand. Why doth an ox lie down?—*R.* Because he cannot sit.

Demand. How many straws go to a goose's nest?—*R.* None, for lack of feet.

Demand. Who slew the fourth part of the world?—*R.* Cain, when he killed his brother Abel.

Demand. What man is he that getteth his living backwards?—*R.* A ropemaker."

The reader will please to recollect the antiquity of these, and their curiosity, before he condemns their triviality. Let the worst be said of them, they are certainly as good as some of Shakespeare's jokes, which no doubt elicited peals of laughter from an Elizabethan audience. This may be said to be only a negative kind of recommendation, and, indeed, when we reflect on the apparent poverty of verbal humour in those days, the wonder is that it could have been so well relished. The fact must be that we often do not understand the greater part of the meaning intended to be conveyed.

To revert to the lengthened transmission of jokes, I may mention my discovery of the following in MS. Addit. 5008, in the British Museum, a journal of the time of Queen Elizabeth. The anecdote, by some means, went the round of the provincial press in 1843, as of modern composition. "On a very rainy day, a man, entering his house, was accosted by his wife in the following manner: 'Now, my dear, while you are wet, go and fetch me a bucket of water.' He obeyed, brought the water and threw it all over her, saying at the same time, 'Now, my dear, while you are wet, go and fetch another!'"

Nature Songs

Rhymes upon natural objects and rural sayings are perhaps more generally interesting than any other relics of the popular anthology. They not unfrequently contain scientific truths, and have been considered worthy of examination by the philosopher; while the unlearned are often contented to use them as substitutes for the barometer or Nautical Almanac. We all recollect the story of Dr. Johnson and the boy who prophesied a shower when not a speck was to be seen in the sky. The doctor, drenched with rain, hastened back to the lad, and offered him a shilling if he would divulge the data of this prediction. "Why, you zee, zur, when that black ram holds its tail up, it be sure to rain!" The story loses none of its force when we find it in the "Hundred Merry Tales", printed nearly two centuries before Dr. Johnson was born.

THE RAINBOW

Rainbow i' th' morning
Shipper's warning;
Rainbow at night
Shipper's delight.

This, in one form or other, is a most common weather proverb. The present version was heard in Essex.

If there be a rainbow in the eve,
It will rain and leave;
But if there be a rainbow in the morrow,
It will neither lend nor borrow.

WEATHER RHYMES

The ev'ning red, and the morning gray,
Are the tokens of a bonny day.

Winter's thunder
Is the world's wonder.
—From Lancashire.

As the days grow longer,
The storms grow stronger;
As the days lengthen,
So the storms strengthen.

No weather is ill,
If the wind be still.

When clouds appear like rocks and towers,
The earth's refresh'd by frequent showers.

This proverb is sufficiently homely, yet the first line reminds us of the description of the clouds in "Antony and Cleopatra", act iv. sc. 12; but the commonest observer must have seen the "tower'd citadel", and the "pendent rock".

A northern har
Brings drought from far.

A har is a mist or thick fog.

First comes David, next comes Chad,
Then comes Whinwall as if he was mad.

Alluding to the storms about the day of St. Winwaloe, March 3rd, called St. Whinwall by the country people.

> Rain, rain, go to Spain;
> Come again another day:
> When I brew and when I bake,
> I'll give you a figgy cake.

This appears to be a child's address to rain, a kind of charm or entreaty for its disappearance. A plum-cake is always called a figgy cake in Devonshire, where raisins are denominated *figs*, and hence the term. Other versions are given by Chambers, p. 155, who remarks that it was the practice among the children of Greece, when the sun happened to be obscured by a cloud, to exclaim, *Ἔξεχ' ὦ, φίλ' ἥλιε*!—Come forth, beloved sun! Howell, in his Proverbs, 1659, p. 20, has,

> Rain, rain, go to Spain;
> Fair weather, come again.

"Little children have a custome, when it raines, to sing or charme away the raine; they all joine in a chorus, and sing thus, viz:

> Raine, raine, goe away,
> Come againe a Saterday.

I have a conceit that this childish custome is of great antiquity, and that it is derived from the gentiles." (Aubrey, MS. Lansd. 231.)

> If Candlemas day be fair and bright,
> Winter will have another flight.

It is generally the case that fine weather continues if it is mild at Candlemas. A somewhat similar proverb is given by M. Kuhn, "Gebräuche und Aberglauben", ii. 12.

> It is time to cock your hay and corn
> When the old donkey blows his horn.

The braying of the ass is said to be an indication of rain or hail.

SNOW

In Yorkshire, when it begins to snow, the boys exclaim,

> Snow, snow faster,
> The cow's in the pasture.

When the storm is concluding, or when they wish it to give over, they sing,

> Snow, snow, give over,
> The cow's in the clover!

White is the rural generic term for snow, and *black* for rain. Thus, in the well-known proverb,

> February fill the dyke,
> Be it black or be it white;
> But if it be white,
> It's the better to like.

The Anglo-Saxon and Northern literatures are full of similar poetical synonymes. A common nursery riddle conceals the term snow by the image of a white glove, and another in the same manner designates rain as a black glove,

> Round the house, and round the house,
> And there lies a white glove in the window.*
> Round the house, and round the house,
> And there lies a black glove in the window.

THE WIND

> When the wind is in the east,
> Then the fishes do bite least;
> When the wind is in the west,
> Then the fishes bite the best;
> When the wind is in the north,
> Then the fishes do come forth;
> When the wind is in the south,
> It blows the bait in the fish's mouth.

This weather-wise advice to anglers was obtained from Oxfordshire. It is found in a variety of versions throughout Great Britain.

The Lincolnshire shepherds say,

* A copy of this riddle occurs in MS. Harl. 1962, of the seventeenth century.

When the wind is in the east,
'Tis neither good for man nor beast:
When the wind is in the south,
It is in the rain's mouth.

March winds are proverbial, and the following distich is not uncommon in Yorkshire:

March winds and April showers,
Bring forth May flowers.

To which we may add,

The south wind brings wet weather,
The north wind wet and cold together;
The west wind always brings us rain,
The east wind blows it back again.

The solution of the following pretty nursery riddle is a hurricane of wind:

Arthur o' Bower has broken his band,
He comes roaring up the land:
The King of Scots, with all his power,
Cannot turn Arthur of the Bower.

THE MOON

The inhabitants of most of our rural districts still retain the old dislike to a new moon on Friday, and perpetuate it by the saying,

Friday's moon,
Come when it wool,
It comes too soon.

Or by the following,

Friday's moon,
Once in seven year comes too soon.

Some persons, however, contend that Saturday is the unlucky day for the new, and Sunday equally so for the full moon. So runs the distich,

Saturday's new, and Sunday's full,
Was never fine, nor never wool.

The moon anciently occupied an important place in love-divinations. The following invocation to the planet is used by young women throughout the country:

> New moon, new moon, declare to me,
> Shall I this night my true love see?
> Not in his best, but in the array
> As he walks in every day.

Or, sometimes, the following:

> New moon, new moon, I hail thee!
> By all the virtue in thy body,
> Grant this night that I may see
> He who my true love is to be.

Aubrey, in his "Miscellanies", ed. 1696, p. 105, gives the following lines, used in Yorkshire for charming the moon to cause a dream of a future husband:

> All hail to the moon, all hail to thee!
> I prithee, good moon, reveal to me
> This night who my husband must be!

THE CUCKOO

We are usefully reminded of the season of the cuckoo by the following homely proverbial lines:

> In April,
> The cuckoo shows his bill;
> In May,
> He sings all day;
> In June,
> He alters his tune;
> In July,
> Away he'll fly;
> Come August,
> Away he must!

In some dialects thus:

> In April,
> 'A shake 'as bill;
> In May,
> 'A pipe all day;
> In June,
> 'A change 'as tune;
> In July,
> Away 'a fly;
> Else in August,
> Away 'a must.

Of the "change of tune" alluded to in these verses, it has been remarked (Trans. Linn. Soc.) that in early season the cuckoo begins with the interval of a minor third, proceeds to a major third, then to a fourth, then to a fifth; after which his voice breaks, never attaining a minor sixth. This was observed by old John Heywood, Workes, 1576, vi. 95:

> In April the koo-coo can sing her note by rote,
> In June of tune she cannot sing a note;
> At first, koo-koo, koo-coo, sing shrill can she do;
> At last, kooke, kooke, kooke, six kookes to one coo.

The following proverbial verses relating to this bird are current in the North of England:

> The cuckoo comes in April,
> Stops all the month of May,
> Sings a song at Midsummer,
> And then he goes away.

> When the cuckoo comes to the bare thorn,
> Sell your cow and buy your corn;
> But when she comes to the full bit,
> Sell your corn and buy your sheep.

The following "tokens of love and marriage by hearing the cuckow, or seeing other birds first in the morning", are extracted from an old chapbook entitled, "The Golden Cabinet; or, The Compleat Fortune-teller", n. d.: "When you walk out in the soon as you hear the cuckow, sit down on a bank or other convenient place, and pull your stockings off, saying,

> May this to me,
> Now happy be.

Then look between your great toe and the next, you'll find a hair that will easily come off. Take and look at it, and of the same colour will that of your lover be; wrap it in a piece of paper, and keep it ten days carefully; then, if it has not changed, the person will be constant: but if it dies, you are flattered." Gay alludes to this method of divination in his Fourth Pastoral, ed. 1742, p. 32.

THE ROBIN AND THE WREN

The superstitious reverence with which these birds are almost universally regarded takes its origin from a pretty belief that they undertake the delicate office of covering the dead bodies of any of the human race with moss or leaves, if by any means left exposed to the heavens. This opinion is alluded to by Shakespeare and many writers of his time, as by Drayton, for example:

> Cov'ring with moss the dead's unclosed eye,
> The little red-breast teacheth charitie.

Webster, in his tragedy of "Vittoria Corombona", 1612, couples the wren with the robin as coadjutors in this friendly office:

> Call for the robin red-breast and the wren,
> Since o'er shady groves they hover,
> And with leaves and flowers do cover
> The friendless bodies of unburied men.

Notwithstanding the beautiful passage in Shakespeare to which we have alluded, it is nevertheless undeniable that, even to this day, the ancient belief attached to these birds is perpetuated chiefly by the simple ballad of the Babes in the Wood. Early in the last century, Addison was infatuated with that primitive song. "Admitting," he says, "there is even a despicable simplicity in the verse, yet because the sentiments appear genuine and unaffected, they are able to move the mind of the most polite reader with inward meltings of humanity and compassion." Exactly so; but this result arises from the extraordinary influence of early association over the mind, not from the pathos of the ballad itself, which is infinitely inferior to the following beautiful little nursery song I have the pleasure of transcribing into these pages:

My dear, do you know
How a long time ago
    Two poor little children,
Whose names I don't know,
Were stolen away
On a fine summer's day,
    And left in a wood,
As I've heard people say.

And when it was night,
So sad was their plight,
    The sun it went down,
And the moon gave no light!
They sobb'd and they sigh'd,
And they bitterly cried,
    And the poor little things
They lay down and died.

And when they were dead,
The robins so red
    Brought strawberry leaves,
And over them spread;
And all the day long,
They sang them this song,—
Poor babes in the wood!
Poor babes in the wood!
    And don't you remember
The babes in the wood?

Adages respecting the robin and the wren, generally including the martin and swallow, are common in all parts of the country. In giving the following, it should be premised it is a popular notion that the wren is the wife of the robin: and Mr. Chambers mentions an extraordinary addition to this belief current in Scotland, that the wren is the paramour of the tom-tit!

> The robin red-breast and the wren
> Are God Almighty's cock and hen;*
> The martin and the swallow
> Are the two next birds that follow.

The next was obtained from Essex:

> A robin and a titter-wren
> Are God Almighty's cock and hen;
> A martin and a swallow
> Are God Almighty's shirt and collar!

And the following from Warwickshire:

> The robin and the wren
> Are God Almighty's cock and hen;
> The martin and the swallow
> Are God Almighty's bow and arrow!†

The latter part of this stanza is thus occasionally varied:

> The martin and the swallow
> Are God Almighty's birds to hollow;

where the word *hollow* is most probably a corruption of the verb *hallow*, to keep holy.‡ If this conjecture be correct, it exhibits the antiquity of the rhyme.

Nor let it be thought there is any impiety in giving these verses in the form in which they are cherished, for the humble recorders of them dream of no irreverence. On the contrary, the sanctification

---

* The wren was also called *our Lady's hen*. See Cotgrave, in v. *Berchot*.
† In Cheshire the last line is, "Are God's mate and marrow", *marrow* being a provincial term for a companion. See Wilbraham's Chesh. Gloss. p. 105.
‡ Parker, in his poem of "The Nightingale", published in 1632, speaking of swallows, says:
> And if in any's hand she chance to dye,
> 'Tis counted ominous, I know not why.

of these harmless birds is no unpoetical or objectionable fragment of the old popular mythology; and when we reflect that not even a sparrow "is forgotten before God", can we blame a persuasion which protects more innocent members of the feathered tribes from the intrusion of the wanton destroyer?

It is exceedingly unlucky to molest the nests of any of these birds. This belief is very prevalent, and it was acted upon in a case which came under my observation, where, misfortune having twice followed the destruction of a swallow's nest, the birds were afterwards freely permitted to enjoy the corner of a portico, where their works were certainly not very ornamental. The following verses were obtained from Essex:

> The robin and the red-breast,
>   The robin and the wren;
> If ye take out o' their nest,
>   Ye'll never thrive agen!

> The robin and the red-breast,
>   The martin and the swallow;
> If ye touch one o' their eggs,
>   Bad luck will sure to follow!

The Irish call the wren the king of birds; and they have a story that, when the birds wanted to choose a king, they determined that the one which could fly highest should have the crown. The wren, being small, very cunningly hid itself under the wing of the eagle; and when that bird could fly no higher, the wren slipped from its hiding-place, and easily gained the victory. In Cotgrave's Dictionarie, 1632, we find the wren called *roitelet*, and in another dictionary, quoted by Mr. Wright, it is called *roi des oiseaux*, so it is probable a similar superstition prevailed in France. The ceremony of hunting the wren on St. Stephen's day has been so frequently described, that it is not necessary to do more than allude to it, and to mention that the late Mr. Crofton Croker possessed a proclamation issued by the mayor of Cork forbidding the custom, with the intent "to prevent cruelty to animals", as the document is headed. This custom was also prevalent in France. An analogous ceremony is still observed in Pembrokeshire on Twelfth-day, where it is customary to carry about a wren, termed *the king*, inclosed in a box with glass windows, surmounted by a wheel, from which are appended various coloured ribands. It is attended by men and boys, who visit the farm-houses, and sing a song, the following fragments of which are all that have come under my observation:

> For we are come here,
> To taste your good cheer,
> And the king is well dressed
> In silks of the best.
>
> He is from a cottager's stall,
> To a fine gilded hall.

The poor bird often dies under the ceremony, which tradition connects with the death of an ancient British king at the time of the Saxon invasion. The rhyme used in Ireland runs thus:

> The wren, the wren, the king of all birds,
> Was caught St. Stephen's day in the furze;
> Although he's little his family's great.
> Then pray, gentlefolks, give him a treat.

THE OWL

> To-whoo—to-whoo!
> Cold toe—toe!

expresses the hooting of the owl. This bird, according to old ballads and legends, was of exalted parentage. A rural ballad, cited in Waterton's "Essays on Natural History", 1838, p. 8, says:

> Once I was a monarch's daughter,
>   And sat on a lady's knee;
> But am now a nightly rover,
>   Banished to the ivy-tree.
>
> Crying hoo, hoo, hoo, hoo, hoo, hoo,
> Hoo, hoo, hoo, my feet are cold.

Pity me, for here you see me
Persecuted, poor, and old.

An anonymous writer, in the "Gentleman's Magazine", vol. lxxiv. p. 1003, mentions an old fairy tale respecting the owl, which, he says, is well known to the nurses of Herefordshire. A certain fairy, disguised as an old distressed woman, went to a baker's shop, and begged some dough of his daughter, of whom she obtained a very small piece. This she farther requested leave to bake in the oven, where it swelling to the size of a large loaf, the baker's daughter refused to let her have it. She, however, gave the pretended beggar another piece of dough, but still smaller than the first; this swelled in the oven even more than the other, and was in like manner retained. A third and still smaller piece of dough came out of the oven the largest of all, and shared the same fate. The disguised fairy, convinced of the woman's covetousness by these repeated experiments, no longer restrained her indignation. She resumed her proper form and struck the culprit with her wand, who immediately flew out of the window in the shape of an owl. This story may be a version of the legend alluded to by Ophelia in "Hamlet", iv. 5: "They say the owl was a baker's daughter. Lord, we know what we are, but know not what we may be."

MAGPIES

Wide-spread is the superstition that it is unlucky to see magpies under certain conditions, but these vary considerably in different localities. Thus, in some counties, two bring sorrow, in others joy; while, in some places, we are instructed that one magpie is a signal of misfortune, which can, however, be obviated by pulling off your hat, and making a very polite bow to the knowing bird. This operation I have more than once seen quite seriously performed. In Lancashire they say:

One for anger,
Two for mirth,
Three for a wedding,
Four for a birth,
Five for rich,
Six for poor,

Seven for a witch:
I can tell you no more.

But in Tim Bobbin it is expressly said that two are indicative of ill fortune: "I saigh two rott'n pynots, hongum, that wur a sign o' bad fashin; for I heard my gronny say hoode os leef o seen two owd harries os two pynots." The same belief obtains in Scotland. In the North they thus address the bird:

Magpie, magpie, chatter and flee,
Turn up thy tail, and good luck fall me.

The half-nest of the magpie is accounted for by a rural ornithological legend. Once on a time, when the world was very young, the magpie, by some accident or another, although she was quite as cunning as she is at present, was the only bird that was unable to build a nest. In this perplexity, she applied to the other members of the feathered race, who kindly undertook to instruct her. So, on a day appointed, they assembled for that purpose, and, the materials having been collected, the blackbird said, "Place that stick there", suiting the action to the word, as she commenced the work. "Ah!" said the magpie, "I knew that afore." The other birds followed with their suggestions, but to every piece of advice the magpie kept saying, "Ah! I knew that afore." At length, when the birdal habitation was half-finished, the patience of the company was fairly exhausted by the pertinacious conceit of the pye, so they all left her with the united exclamation, "Well, Mistress Mag, as you seem to know all about it, you may e'en finish the nest yourself." Their resolution was obdurate and final, and to this day the magpie exhibits the effects of partial instruction by her miserably incomplete abode.

The magpie is always called Madge, and the Christian names given to birds deserve a notice. Thus we have Jack Snipe, Jenny Wren, Jack Daw, Tom Tit, Robin Redbreast, Poll Parrot, Jill Hooter, Jack Curlew, Jack Nicker, and King Harry for the goldfinch, and the list might be widely extended. A starling is always Jacob, a sparrow is Philip, a raven is Ralph, and the consort of the Tom Tit rejoices in the euphonic name of Betty! Children give the name of Dick to all small birds, which, in nursery parlance are universally Dicky-birds.

WHO KILL'D COCK ROBIN?

Who kill'd Cock Robin?
  I, said the sparrow,
  With my bow and arrow,
I kill'd Cock Robin.

Who see him die?
  I, said the fly,
  With my little eye,
And I see him die.

Who catch'd his blood?
  I, said the fish,
  With my little dish,
And I catch'd his blood.

Who made his shroud?
  I, said the beadle,
  With my little needle,
And I made his shroud.

Who shall dig his grave?
  I, said the owl,
  With my spade and showl,*
And I'll dig his grave.

Who'll be the parson?
  I, said the rook,
  With my little book,
And I'll be the parson.

Who'll be the clerk?
  I, said the lark,
  If 'tis not in the dark,
And I'll be the clerk.

Who'll carry him to the grave?
  I, said the kite,
  If 'tis not in the night,
And I'll carry him to his grave.

* Shovel. An archaism.

Who'll carry the link?
    I, said the linnet,
    I'll fetch it in a minute,
And I'll carry the link.

Who'll be chief mourner?
    I said the dove,
    I mourn for my love,
And I'll be chief mourner.

Who'll bear the pall?
    We, said the wren,
    Both the cock and the hen,
And we'll bear the pall.

Who'll sing a psalm?
    I, said the thrush,
    As she sat in a bush,
And I'll sing a psalm.

And who'll toll the bell?
    I, said the bull,
    Because I can pull:
And so, Cock Robin, farewell!

All the birds in the air,
    Fell to sighing and sobbing,
When they heard the bell toll
    For poor Cock Robin!

The above version of this widely-extended poem is taken from a copy printed many years ago in Aldermary Churchyard, entitled, "Cock Robin, a pretty gilded *toy* for either girl or *boy*, suited to children of all ages", 18mo. It is reprinted even at the present day with a few immaterial variations.

In Eccardi "Historia Studii Etymologici", 8vo. Han. 1711, p. 269, is an old Wendic nursery ballad of a somewhat similar character. Perhaps the first verse will be sufficient to give the reader an idea of its composition:

Katy mês Ninka beyt?
Teelka mês Ninka beyt:
Teelka rîtzi
Wapakka neimo ka dwemo:
Gos giss wiltge grîsna Sena,
Nemik Ninka beyt;
Gos nemik Ninka beyt.

(Who, who, the bride will be?
The owl she the bride shall be.
  The owl quoth,
   Again to them both,
I am sure a grim ladye;
Not I the bride can be,
I not the bride can be!)

CROWS

In Essex they have a rhyme respecting crows very similar to that above quoted regarding magpies. The following lines are said to be true, if crows fly *towards* you:

One's unlucky,
Two's lucky;
Three is health,
Four is wealth;
Five is sickness,
And six is death!

PIGEONS

Pigeons never do know woe,
Till they do a benting go.

This means that pigeons are never short of food except when they are obliged to live on the seeds of the grass, which ripen before the crops of grain. The seed-stalk of grass is called the *bent*, and hence the term *benting*.

LAPWING AND RINGDOVE

The common people in the North Riding of Yorkshire, says Brockett, ii. 71, believe that at one period the cushat, or ring-dove, laid its eggs upon the ground, and that the peewit, or lapwing, made its nest on high; but that some time or other an amicable arrangement took place between these birds, exchanging their localities for building. The peewit accordingly expresses its disappointment at the bargain as follows:

> Pee-wit, pee-wit,
> I coup'd my nest and I rue it.

While the cushat rejoices that she is out of the reach of mischievous boys,

> Coo, coo, come now,
> Little lad
> With thy gad,
> Come not thou!

THE WOOD-PIGEON

An Isle of Wight legend respecting this bird tells us that, soon after the creation of the world, all the birds were assembled for the purpose of learning to build their nests, and the magpie being very sagacious and cunning, was chosen to teach them. Those birds that were most industrious, such as the wren and the long-tailed capon, or pie-finch, he instructed to make whole nests in the shape of a cocoa-nut, with a small hole on one side; others, not so diligent, he taught to make half-nests, shaped something like a teacup. Having thus instructed a great variety of birds according to their capacity, it came to the turn of the wood-pigeon, who, being a careless and lazy bird, was very indifferent about the matter, and while the magpie was directing him how to place the little twigs, &c., he kept exclaiming, "What, athurt and across! what zoo! what zoo!— athurt and across! what zoo! what zoo!" At length the magpie was so irritated with his stupidity and indolence, that he flew away, and the wood-pigeon, having had no more instruction, to this day builds the worst nest of any of the feathered tribe, consisting merely of layers of cross-twigs.

Montagu gives a Suffolk version of the tale, which differs considerably from the above. "The magpie, it is said, once undertook to teach the pigeon how to build a more substantial and commodious dwelling; but, instead of being a docile pupil, the pigeon kept on her old cry of 'Take two, Taffy! take two!' The magpie insisted that this was a very unworkmanlike manner of proceeding, one stick at a time being as much as could be managed to advantage; but the pigeon reiterated her 'Two, take two', till Mag, in a violent passion, gave up the task, exclaiming, 'I say that one at a time's enough; and, if you think otherwise, you may set about the work yourself, for I will have no more to do with it!' Since that time, the wood-pigeon has built her slight platform of sticks, which certainly suffers much in comparison with the strong substantial structure of the magpie." The cooing of the wood-pigeon produces, it is said—

Take two-o coo, Taffy!
Take two-o coo, Taffy!

alluding, says Mr. Chambers, to the story of a Welshman who thus interpreted the note, and acted upon the recommendation by stealing two of his neighbour's cows.

DOMESTIC POULTRY

The clucking conversation of poultry, the cackling of the hen, and the replying chuckle of the cock, is represented by the following dialogue:

Hen.   Cock, cock, I have la-a-a-yed!
Cock.   Hen, hen, that's well sa-a-a-yed!
Hen.   Although I have to go barefooted every d-a-ay!
Cock (*con spirito*). Sell your eggs, and buy shoes.
      Sell your eggs, and buy shoes!

Mr. Chambers, p. 167, has given a very different version of this current in Scotland. In Galloway the hen's song is:

The cock gaed to Rome, seeking shoon, seeking shoon,
The cock gaed to Rome, seeking shoon,
      And yet I aye gang barefit, barefit!

The following proverb is current in the North of England:

> If the cock moult before the hen,
> We shall have weather thick and thin;
> But if the hen moult before the cock,
> We shall have weather hard as a block.

DRAGON-FLIES

In some parts of the Isle of Wight, these insects are found of a peculiarly large size, and their colours are extremely beautiful. There is an old legend respecting them which is still current. It is supposed by the country people that their sting or bite is venomous, as bad as that of a snake or adder, and perhaps from this belief their provincial name of snake-stanger or snake-stang is derived. It is said that these insects can distinguish the good children from the bad when they go fishing: if the latter go too near the water, they are almost sure to be bitten; but when the good boys go, the dragon-flies point out the places where the fish are, by settling on the banks, or flags, in the proper direction. This curious myth is commemorated by the following song:

> Snakestanger! snakestanger! vlee aal about the brooks;
> Sting aal the bad bwoys that vor the vish looks,
> But lat the good bwoys ketch aal the vish they can,
> And car'm awaay whooam* to vry'em in a pan;
> Bred and butter they shall yeat at zupper wi' their vish,
> While aal the littul bad bwoys shall only lick the dish.

This has of late years been introduced into the nursery, but in a different suit of clothes:

> Dragon fly! dragon fly! fly about the brook;
> Sting all the bad boys who for the fish look;
> But let the good boys catch all that they can,
> And then take them home to be fried in a pan;
> With nice bread and butter they shall sup upon their fish,
> While all the little naughty boys shall only lick the dish.

*Carry them away home.

THE SNAIL

In Yorkshire, in evenings when the dew falls heavily, the boys hunt the large black snails, and sing:

> Snail, snail, put out your horn,
> Or I'll kill your father and mother i' thi' morn.

Another version runs thus:

> Snail, snail, put out your horns,
> I'll give you bread and barleycorns.

And sometimes the following song is shouted on this occasion:

> Sneel, snaul,
> Robbers are coming to pull down your wall.
> Sneel, snaul,
> Put out your horn,
> Robbers are coming to steal your corn,
> Coming at four o'clock in the morn.

The version generally heard in the southern counties differs very considerably from the above, and the original use and meaning are very seldom practised or understood.—"In places where snails abound, children amuse themselves by charming them with a chant to put forth their horns, of which I have only heard the following couplet, which is repeated until it has the desired effect, to the great amusement of the charmer:

> Snail, snail, come out of your hole,
> Or else I'll beat you as black as a coal.

It is pleasant to find that this charm is not peculiar to English children, but prevails in places as remote from each other as Naples and Silesia. The Silesian rhyme is:

> Schnecke, schnecke, schnürre!
> Zeig mir dein viere,
> Wenn mir dein viere nicht zeigst,
> Schmeisz ich dich in den Graben,
> Fressen dich die Raben:

which may be thus paraphrased:

> Snail, snail, slug-slow,
> To me thy four horns show;
> If thou dost not show me thy four,
> I will throw thee out of the door,
> For the crow in the gutter,
> To eat for bread and butter.

In that amusing Folks'-book of Neapolitan childish tales, the 'Pentamerone' of the noble Count-Palatine Cavalier Giovan-Battista Basile, in the seventeenth tale, entitled 'La Palomma', we have a similar rhyme:

> Jesce, jesce, corna;
> Ca mammata te scorna,
> Te scorna 'ncoppa lastrico,
> Che fa lo figlio mascolo:

of which the sense may probably be:

> Peer out! peer out! put forth your horns!
> At you your mother mocks and scorns;
> Another son is on the stocks,
> And you she scorns, at you she mocks."*

Mr. Chambers gives some very interesting observations on these lines. "In England," he says, "the snail scoops out hollows, little rotund chambers, in limestone, for its residence. This habit of the animal is so important in its effects, as to have attracted the attention of geologists; one of the most distinguished of whom (Dr. Buckland) alluded to it at the meeting of the British Association at Plymouth in 1841." The above rhyme is a boy's invocation to the snail to come out of such holes or any other places of retreat resorted to by it. Mr. Chambers also informs us that in some districts of Scotland it is supposed that it is an indication of good weather if the snail obeys the injunction of putting out its horn:

> Snailie, snailie, shoot out your horn,
> And tell us if it will be a bonnie day the morn.

* Notes and Queries.

It appears from Gay's "Shepherd's Week", ed. 1742, p. 34, that snails were formerly used in rural love-divinations. It was the custom* to place the little animal on the soft ashes, and to form an opinion respecting the initial of the name of a future lover by the fancied letter made by the crawling of the snail on the ashes:

> Last May-day fair I search'd to find a snail,
> That might my secret lover's name reveal;
> Upon a gooseberry bush a snail I found,
> For always snails near sweetest fruit abound.
> I seized the vermin, home I quickly sped,
> And on the hearth the milk-white embers spread.
> Slow crawl'd the snail, and if I right can spell,
> In the soft ashes mark'd a curious L.
> Oh, may this wondrous omen lucky prove,
> For L is found in Lubberkin and Love!

Verses on the snail, similar to those given above, are current over many parts of Europe. In Denmark, the children say (Thiele, iii. 138)—

> Snegl! snegl! kom herud!
> Her er en Mand, som vil kjöbe dit Huus,
> For en Skjæppe Penge!
>
> (Snail! snail! come out here!
> Here is a man thy house will buy,
> For a measure of white money.)

A similar idea is preserved in Germany, the children saying ("Das Knaben Wunderhorn," iii. 81)—

> Klosterfrau im Schneckenhäussle,
> Sie meint, sie sey verborgen.
> Kommt der Pater Guardian,
> Wünscht ihr guten Morgen!
>
> (Cloister-dame, in house of shell,
> Ye think ye are hidden well.
> Father Guardian will come,
> And wish you good morning.)

* A similar practice is common in Ireland. See Croker's "Fairy Legends", i. 215.

The following lines are given by M. Kuhn, "Gebräuche und Aberglauben", 398, as current in Stendal:

> Schneckhûs, peckhûs,
> Stäk du dîn vêr hörner rût,
> Süst schmît ick dî in'n gråven,
> Då frêten dî de råven.

APPLES

Children in the North of England, when they eat apples, or similar fruit, delight in throwing away the pippin, exclaiming—

> Pippin, pippin, fly away,
> Get me one another day!

THE WALNUT-TREE

There is a common persuasion amongst country people that whipping a walnut-tree tends to increase the produce, and improve the flavour of the fruit. This belief is embodied in the following distich:

> A woman, a spaniel, and a walnut-tree,
> The more you whip them the better they be.

And also in this quatrain:

> Three things by beating better prove,
> A nut, an ass, a woman;
> The cudgel from their back remove,
> And they'll be good for no man.

THE ASH

> Burn ash-wood green,
> 'Tis a fire for a queen:
> Burn ash-wood sear,
> 'Twill make a man swear.

Ash, when green, makes good fire-wood, and, contrary perhaps to all other sorts of wood, is bad for that purpose when *sear*, or dry, withered. The old Anglo-Saxon term *sear* is well illustrated by this homely proverb. The reader will remember Macbeth:

> I have lived long enough:
> My way of life is fallen into the *sear* and yellow leaf.

PEAS

Children get the pods of a pea, and flinging them at each other, cry,

> Pea-pod hucks,
> Twenty for a pin!
> If you don't like them,
> I'll take them agin.

The *hucks* are the shells or pods, and *agin* the provincial pronunciation of *again*.

PIMPERNELL

> No heart can think, no tongue can tell,
> The virtues of the pimpernell.

Gerard enumerates several complaints for which this plant was considered useful, and he adds, that country people prognosticated fine or bad weather by observing in the morning whether its flowers were spread out or shut up.—("Herbal", first ed., p. 494.) According to a MS. on magic, preserved in the Chetham Library at Manchester, "the herb pimpernell is good to prevent witchcraft, as Mother Bumby doth affirme"; and the following lines must be used when it is gathered:

> Herbe pimpernell, I have thee found
> Growing upon Christ Jesus' ground:
> The same guift the Lord Jesus gave unto thee,
> When he shed His blood on the tree.
> Arise up, pimpernell, and goe with me,
> And God blesse me,
> And all that shall were thee.   Amen.

"Say this fifteen dayes together, twice a day, morning earlye fasting, and in the evening full."—MS. ibid.

MARUM

If you set it,
The cats will eat it;
If you sow it,
The cats will know it.

BIRD-SHOOER'S SONG

Awa', birds, awa',
Take a peck
And leave a seck,
And come no more to-day:

This is the universal *bird-shooer's* song in the midland counties.

THE GNAT

In the eastern counties of England, and perhaps in other parts of the country, children chant the following lines when they are pursuing this insect:

Gnat, gnat, fly into my hat,
And I'll give you a slice of bacon!

THE TROUT

In Herefordshire the alder is called the *aul,* and the country people use the following proverbial lines:

When the bud of the *aul* is as big as the trout's eye,
Then that fish is in season in the river Wye.

TOBACCO

Tobacco hic,
Will make you well
If you be sick.

Tobacco was formerly held in great esteem as a medicine. Sickness was the old term for illness of any kind, and is no doubt the more correct expression.

It may just be worth a passing notice to observe, that Shakespeare never mentions *tobacco*, nor alludes to it even indirectly. What a brilliant subject for a critic! A treatise might be written to prove from this circumstance that the great poet was not in the habit of smoking; or, on the contrary, that he was so great an admirer of the pernicious weed, that, being unable to allude to it without a panegyric, he very wisely eschewed the subject for fear of giving offence to his royal master, the author of the "Counterblast". The discussion, at all events, would be productive of as much utility as the disputes which have occasioned so many learned letters respecting the orthography of the poet's name.

JACK-A-DANDY

Boys have a very curious saying respecting the reflection of the sun's beams from the surface of water upon a ceiling, which they call "Jack-a-dandy beating his wife with a stick of silver". If a mischievous boy with a bit of looking-glass, or similar material, threw the reflection into the eye of a neighbour, the latter would complain, "He's throwing Jack-a-dandy in my eyes."

SEVEN

Proverb Rhymes

Metrical proverbs are so numerous, that a large volume might be filled with them without much difficulty; and it is, therefore, unnecessary to say that nothing beyond a very small selection is here attempted. We may refer the curious reader to the collections of Howell, Ray, and Denham, the last of which chiefly relates to natural objects and the weather, for other examples; but the subject is so diffuse, that these writers have gone a very short way towards the compilation of a complete series.

> Give a thing and take again,
> And you shall ride in hell's wain!

Said by children when one wishes a gift to be returned, a system naturally much disliked. So says Plato, των ορθως δοθεντων αφαιρεσις ουκ εστι. (Ray, p. 113, ed. 1768). Ben Jonson appears to allude to this proverb in the "Sad Shepherd", where Maudlin says—"Do you give a thing and take a thing, madam?" Cotgrave, "Dictionarie of the French and English Tongues", 1632, in v. *Retirer*, mentions "a triviall proverb":

> Give a thing,
> And take a thing,
> To weare the divell's gold-ring.

173

And it is alluded to in a little work entitled "Homer à la Mode", a mock poem upon the First and Second Books of Homer's Iliad, 12mo. Oxford, 1665, p. 34:

> Prethee for my sake let him have her,
> Because to him the Græcians gave her;
> To give a thing, and take a thing,
> You know is the devil's gold-ring!

The proverb sometimes runs thus:

> Give a thing, take a thing,
> That's an old man's play-thing.

"A lee with a hatchet", as they say in the North, is a circumstantial self-evident falsehood, and so runs the proverb:

> That's a lie with a latchet,
> All the dogs in the town cannot match it.

Children say the following when one has been detected in any misrepresentation of a mischievous character:

> Liar, liar, lick spit,
> Your tongue shall be slit,
> And all the dogs in the town
> Shall have a little bit.

The following versions of the former rhyme are current in the North of England:

> That's a lee wi' a latchet,
> You may shut the door and catch it.

> That's a lee wi' a lid on,
> And a brass handle to tak houd on.

In Yorkshire a tell-tale is termed a *pleen-pie*, and there is a proverb current which is very similar to that given above:

> A pleen-pie tit,
> Thy tongue sal be slit,
> An iv'ry dog i' th' town
> Sal hev a bit.

> Left and right
> Brings good at night.

When your right eye itches, it is a sign of good luck; when the left, a sign of bad luck. When both itch, the above distich expresses the popular belief.

> He got out of the muxy,
> And fell into the pucksy.

A muxy is a dunghill, and the pucksy a quagmire. This is a variation of the old saying of falling out of the dripping-pan into the fire:

> Incidit in Scyllam cupiens vitare Charybdini.

> Those that made me were uncivil,
> For they made me harder than the devil!
> Knives won't cut me, fire won't sweat me,
> Dogs bark at me, but can't eat me!

These proverbial lines are supposed to be spoken by Suffolk cheese, which is so hard that a myth tells us gate-pegs in that county are made of it. The proverb has been long true, and Pepys, writing in 1661, says: "I found my wife vexed at her people for grumbling to eate Suffolk cheese, which I also am vexed at."

> Speak of a person and he will appear,
> Then talk of the dule, and he'll draw near.

Said of a person who makes his appearance unexpectedly, when he is spoken of.

> When Easter falls in our Lady's lap,
> Then let England beware a rap.

That is, when Easter falls on Lady-day, March 25, which happens when the Sunday Letter is G, and the Golden Number 5, 13, or 16. See Aubrey's Miscellanies, ed. 1696, p. 21.

> In July
> Some reap rye,
> In August,
> If one won't, the other must.

From Hertfordshire and Bedfordshire, given in Hone's "Year-Book", col. 1595.

In March
The birds begin to search;
In April
The corn begins to fill;
In May
The birds begin to lay.

From Lancashire. This resembles in its character the cuckoo song we have given at p. 150.

Friday night's dream
   On the Saturday told,
Is sure to come true,
   Be it never so old.

When it gangs up i' sops,
It'll fau down i' drops.

A North country proverb, the *sops* being the small detached clouds hanging on the sides of a mountain. Carr, ii. 147.

To-morrow come never,
When two Sundays come together.

This is sometimes addressed to one who promises something "to-morrow", but who is often in the habit of making similar engagements, and not remembering them.

TIT FOR TAT

The proverb of *tit for tat* may perhaps be said to be going out of fashion, but it is still a universal favourite with children. When any one is ill-natured, and the sufferer wishes to hint his intention of retaliating at the first convenient opportunity, he cries out—

Tit for tat,
If you kill my dog
I'll kill your cat.

LAZY LAWRENCE

Lazy Lawrence, let me go,
Don't me hold summer and winter too.

This distich is said by a boy who feels very lazy, yet wishes to exert himself. Lazy Lawrence is a proverbial expression for an idle person: and I possess an old chap-book, entitled "The History of Lawrence Lazy, containing his birth and slothful breeding; how he served the schoolmaster, his wife, the squire's cook, and the farmer, which, by the laws of Lubberland, was accounted high treason". A West country proverb, relating to a disciple of this hero, runs thus:

> Sluggardy guise,
> Loth to go to bed,
> And loth to rise.

> March will search, April will try,
> May will tell ye if ye'll live or die.

> Sow in the sop,
> 'Twill be heavy a-top.

That is, land in a soppy or wet state is in a favourable condition for receiving seed; a statement, however, somewhat questionable.

> A cat may look at a king,
> And surely I may look at an ugly thing.

Said in derision by one child to another, who complains of being stared at.

> He that hath it and will not keep it,
> He that wanteth it and will not seek it;
> He that drinketh and is not dry,
> Shall want money as well as I.

From Howell's "English Proverbs", 1659, p. 21.

> Gray's Inn for walks,
>   Lincoln's Inn for a wall;
> The Inner-Temple for a garden,
>   And the Middle for a hall.

A proverb no doubt true in former times, but now only partially correct.

> In time of prosperity friends will be plenty.
> In time of adversity not one amongst twenty.

177

From Howell's "English Proverbs", p. 20. The expression *not one amongst twenty* is a generic one for not one out of a large number. It occurs in Shakespeare's "Much Ado About Nothing", v.2.

> Trim tram,
> Like master like man.

From an old manuscript political treatise, dated 1652, entitled "A Cat may look at a King".

> Beer a bumble,
> 'Twill kill you
> Afore 'twill make ye tumble.

A proverbial phrase applied to very small beer, implying that no quantity of it will cause intoxication.

> Lancashire law,
> No stakes, no draw!

A saying by which a person, who has lost a verbal wager, avoids payment on the plea of no stakes having been deposited.

> As foolish as monkeys till twenty and more,
> As bold as a lion till forty-and-four;
> As cunning as foxes till three-score-and-ten,
> We then become asses, and are no more men.

These proverbial lines were obtained from Lancashire. An early version occurs in Tusser, p. 199.

> They that wash on Monday
> Have a whole week to dry:
> They that wash on Tuesday
> Are not so much agye;
> They that wash on Wednesday
> May get their clothes clean;
> They that wash on Thursday
> Are not so much to mean;
> They that wash on Friday
> Wash for their need;

But they that wash on Saturday,
  Are clarty-paps indeed!

A North country version of these common proverbial lines, given
by Mr. Denham, p. 16. *Clarty-paps* are dirty sluts.

  The children of Holland
    Take pleasure in making
  What the children of England
    Take pleasure in breaking.

Alluding to toys, a great number of which are imported into this
country from Holland.

EIGHT

Places and Families

This division, like the last, might be greatly extended by references to Ray and Grose.

ELTON

The following lines are still remembered by the members of the Elton family:

Upon Sir Abraham Elt being knighted, and taking the name of Elton.

> In days of yore old Abraham Elt,
> When living, had nor sword nor belt;
> But now his son, Sir Abraham Elton,
> Being knighted, has both sword and belt on.

MS. Harl. Brit. Mus. 7318, p. 206.

NOEL

> N. for a word of deniance,
> E. with a figure of L. fiftie,
> Spelleth his name that never
> Will be thriftie.

MS. Sloane 2497, of the sixteenth century.

COLLINGWOOD

The Collingwoods have borne the name,
Since in the bush the buck was ta'en;
But when the bush shall hold the buck,
Then welcome faith, and farewell luck.

Alluding to the Collingwood crest of a stag beneath an oak tree.

THE CAULD LAD OF HILTON

This fairy or goblin was seldom seen, but his gambols were heard nightly in the hall of the great house. He overturned everything in the kitchen after the servants had gone to bed, and was, in short, one of the most mischievous sprites you could imagine. One night, however, the kitchen happened to be left in great confusion, and the goblin, who did everything by contraries, set it completely to rights; and the next morning it was in perfect apple-pie order. We may be quite sure that, after this occurrence, the kitchen was not again made orderly by the servants.

Notwithstanding, however, the service thus nightly rendered by the Cauld Lad, the servants did not like it. They preferred to do their own work without preternatural agency, and accordingly resolved to do their best to drive him from their haunts. The goblin soon understood what was going on, and he was heard in the dead of night to warble the following lines in a melancholy strain:

> Wae's me! wae's me!
> The acorn is not yet
> Fallen from the tree,
> That's to grow the wood,
> That's to make the cradle,
> That's to rock the bairn,
> That's to grow to a man,
> That's to lay me.

He was, however, deceived in this prediction; for one night, being colder than usual, he complained in moving verse of his condition. Accordingly, on the following evening, a cloak and hood were placed for him near the fire. The servants had unconsciously accomplished their deliverance, for present gifts to fairies, and they for ever disappear. On the next morning the following lines were found inscribed on the wall:

> I've taken your cloak, I've taken your hood;
> The Cauld Lad of Hilton will do no more good!

A great variety of stories in which fairies are frightened away by presents, are still to be heard in the rural districts of England. Another narrative, by Mr. Longstaffe, relates that on one occasion a woman found her washing and ironing regularly performed for her every night by the fairies. In gratitude to the "good people", she placed green mantles for their acceptance, and the next night the fairies departed, exclaiming—

> Now the pixies' work is done!
> We take our clothes, and off we run.

Mrs. Bray tells a similar story of a Devonshire pixy, who helped an old woman to spin. One evening she spied the fairy jumping out of her door, and observed that it was very raggedly dressed; so the next day she thought to win the services of the elf further by placing some smart new clothes, as big as those made for a doll, by the side of her wheel. The pixy came, put on the clothes, and clapping its hands with delight, vanished, saying these lines:

> Pixy fine, pixy gay,
> Pixy now will run away.

Fairies always talk in rhyme. Mr. Allies mentions a Worcestershire fairy legend which says that, upon one occasion, a pixy came to a ploughman in a field, and exclaimed:

> Oh, lend a hammer and a nail,
> Which we want to mend our pail.

FELTON

> The little priest of Felton,
> The little priest of Felton,
> He kill'd a mouse within his house
> And ne'er a one to help him.

SIR RALPH ASHTON

Sweet Jesu, for thy mercy's sake,
  And for thy bitter passion,
Save us from the axe of the Tower,
  And from Sir Ralph of Ashton.

This rhyme is traditionally known in the North of England, and refers, it is said, to Sir Ralph Ashton, who, in the latter part of the fifteenth century, exercised great severity as vice-constable. The ancient custom of *riding the black lad* at Ashton-under-Lyne on Easter Monday, which consists of carrying an effigy on horseback through the town, shooting at it, and finally burning it, is alleged to have taken its origin from this individual, who, according to tradition, was shot as he was riding down the principal street. According to another story, the custom commemorates the valiant actions of Thomas Ashton at the battle of Neville's Cross.

PRESTON

Proud Preston, poor people,
Fine church and no steeple.

LANCASHIRE

Little lad, little lad, where wast thou born?
Far off in Lancashire, under a thorn,
Where they sup sour milk in a ram's horn.

LEYLAND

A village in Lancashire, not far from Chorley. There is, or was sixty years since, a tradition current here, to the effect that the church, on the night following the day in which the building was completed, was removed some distance by supernatural agency, and the astonished inhabitants, on entering the sacred edifice the following morning, found the following metrical command written on a marble tablet on the wall:

184

Here thou shalt be,
    And here thou shalt stand,
And thou shalt be called
    The church of Ley-land.

Leyland church stands on an eminence at the east side of the village. The ancient tower is still standing, but the body of the church is modern.

HUGH OF LINCOLN

He tossed the ball so high, so high,
    He tossed the ball so low;
He tossed the ball in the Jew's garden,
    And the Jews were all below.

Oh, then out came the Jew's daughter,
    She was dressed all in green;
Come hither, come hither, my sweet pretty fellow,
    And fetch your ball again.

These lines refer to the well-known story of the murder of a child at Lincoln by a Jewess. The child was playing at ball, and threw it into the Jew's garden. She enticed him into the house to recover it, killed him, and to conceal her guilt, threw the body into a deep well. According to the ballads on the subject, the spirit of the boy answers his mother's inquiry from the bottom of the well, the bells ring without human aid, and several miracles are accomplished. The above fragment of some old ballad on the subject was given me by Miss Agnes Strickland as current in the country nursery.

CUCKSTONE

If you would go to a church miswent,
You must go to Cuckstone in Kent.

So said because the church is "very unusual in proportion". Lelandi Itin. ed. 1744, ii. 137.

185

SAINT LEVAN

When with panniers astride
A pack-horse can ride
Through St. Levan's stone
The world will be done.

St. Levan's stone is a great rock in the churchyard of St. Levan, co. Cornwall.

ROLLRIGHT

The "Druidical" stones at Rollright, Oxfordshire, are said to have been originally a general and his army who were transformed into stones by a magician. The tradition runs that there was a prophecy or oracle which told the general,

If Long Compton thou canst see,
King of England thou shalt be.

He was within a few yards of the spot whence that town could be observed, when his progress was stopped by the magician's transformation,

Sink down man, and rise up stone!
King of England thou shalt be none.

The general was transformed into a large stone which stands on a spot from which Long Compton is not visible, but on ascending a slight rise close to it, the town is revealed to view. Roger Gale, writing in 1719, says that whoever dared to contradict this story was regarded "as a most audacious freethinker". It is said that no man could ever count these stones, and that a baker once attempted it by placing a penny loaf on each of them, but somehow or other he failed in counting his own bread. A similar tale is related of Stonehenge.

HAMPDEN

The following relation is given in the additions to Camden's Britannia, co. Bucks, p. 318. Tradition says the Black Prince, who held Hartwell, had large possessions at Prince's Risborough, where they show part of a wall of his palace, and a field where his horses were turned called Prince's Field, and repeat these lines on a supposed quarrel between him and one of the family of Hampden:

> Hamden of Hamden did foregoe
> The manors of Tring, Wing, and Ivinghoe,
> For striking the Black Prince a blow.

RIBCHESTER

> It is written upon a wall in Rome
> Ribchester was as rich as any town in Christendom.

Camden says that Ribchester was famous for its remains of ancient art.

HAWLEY

> Blow the wind high, blow the wind low,
> It bloweth good to Hawley's hoe.

These lines are said to relate to one John Hawley, a wealthy merchant of Devon some centuries ago, who was fortunate in his shipping. According to Prince, p. 477, "so was the gentleman's habitation in that town (Dartmouth) call'd the Hoe or Haw".

GOTHAM

> Three wise men of Gotham
> Went to sea in a bowl;
> And if the bowl had been stronger,
> My song would have been longer.

Honour to whom honour is due! Mr. Lower will have it that Sussex is the county of the Gothamites. Gotham is near Pevensey, and many traditionary anecdotes are still current respecting the stupidity of the people of that town. On one occasion, the mayor, having received a letter, was reading it upside down, the messenger very respectfully suggested that he would sooner arrive at the meaning of its contents by reversing its position. "Hold your tongue, sir," replied the chief magistrate; "for while I am mayor of Pemsey, I'll hold the letter which eend uppards I like!"

BUCKLAND

Buckland and Laverton,
Stanway and Staunton,
Childswickham, Wickamford,
Badsey and Aston.

These are places in Gloucestershire, Worcestershire, and Somersetshire. Staunton is pronounced *Stawn*, and Aston is commonly called *Awn*.

COLEBROOK

There were three cooks of Colebrook,
And they fell out with our cook;
And all was for a pudding he took
From the three cooks of Colebrook.

GILLING

Tradition informs us, but leaves us in ignorance as to the nature of the offence offered, that once upon a time, a long time ago, his satanic majesty took dire displeasure at the good folks of Hartforth, for some naughty trick, no doubt played upon him, during one of his visits to that locality; so finding a stone of enormous bulk and weight to the south of Gilling, his majesty, in his rage, raised the ponderous mass in one hand, and uttering this exclamatory couplet,

Have at thee, Black Hartforth,
But have a care o' Bonny Gilling!

cast it from him with all his strength. It would appear that the devil's vision is rather of a telescopic character; for, as luck would have it, he missed his aim, and the stone, which flew whizzing through the air, at last fell harmless far beyond the former place; and now lies, bearing the impression of his unholy fingers, on the rising ground to the north side of Gatherly Moor.*

* Communicated by Mr. M. A. Denham.

SHREWSBURY

The inhabitants of Shropshire, and, it is said, especially Shrewsbury, have an unfortunate habit of misplacing the letter *h*. It is
scarcely necessary to say that the failing is by no means peculiar to
that county. I am unable to vouch for the antiquity of the following
lines on the subject, but they have become proverbial, and are
therefore worth giving:

The petition of the letter *H* to the inhabitants of Shrewsbury,
greeting,

> Whereas I have by you been driven,
> From house, from home, from hope, from heaven,
> And plac'd by your most learn'd society
> In exile, anguish, and anxiety,
> And used, without one just pretence,
> With arrogance and insolence;
> I here demand full restitution,
> And beg you'll mend your elocution.

To this was returned the following answer from the Shrewsburians:

> Whereas we've rescued you, Ingrate,
> From handcuff, horror, and from hate,
> From hell, from horse-pond, and from halter,
> And consecrated you in altar;
> And placed you, where you ne'er should be,
> In honour and in honesty;
> We deem your pray'r a rude intrusion,
> And will not mend our elocution.

JACK ROBINSON

There are few proverbial expressions more common than the saying, "As soon as you can say Jack Robinson", implying excessive
rapidity. I have seen the phrase with the name of *Dick Robinson*,
but failed to take a memorandum of it. It has since occurred to me
that it may have originated in some way or other with the actor of
that name mentioned by Ben Jonson. If, however, the following

189

quotation from an "old play", given by Carr, be genuine, this conjecture must fall to the ground:

> A warke it ys as easie to be doone,
> As 'tys to say, Jack! robys on.

WRANGHAM

> Swing'em, swang'em, bells at Wrangham,
> Three dogs in a string, hang'em, hang'em.

A hit at the Cheshire provincial pronounciation of the *ng*.

LEICESTERSHIRE

> Higham on the hill,
> Stoke in the vale;
> Wykin for buttermilk,
> Hinckley for ale.

BROCKLEY-HILL

> No heart can think, nor tongue can tell,
> What lies between Brockley-hill and Penny-well.

Brockley-hill lies near Elstree, in Hertfordshire, and Penny-well is the name of a parcel of closes in the neighbourhood. See Stukeley's Itin. Cur. 1776, i. 118. This distich alludes to the quantity of old coins found near those places.

STANTON DREW

> Stanton Drew,
> A mile from Peasford,
> Another from Chue.

A Somersetshire proverb, mentioned by Stukeley, in the work above quoted, ii. 169.

SEVERN

Blessed is the eye,
That's between Severn and Wye.

Ray gives this proverb, but appears to misunderstand it, the first line not alluding to the prospect, but to an islet or ait in the river, though I have not met with the word *eye* used in this sense. There can, however, be no doubt as to its meaning; probably from A.-S. eá.

SHERSTON MAGNA

The following very curious observations on this town are extracted from an anonymous MS. in my possession, written forty or fifty years ago. I have never seen the lines in print. Aubrey, in his Natural History of Wiltshire, mentions the plant called *Danes'-blood*, and derives the name from a similar circumstance. Some observations on Sherston may be seen in Camden, ed. Gough, i. 96. It is Sceor-stán, where the celebrated battle between the Anglo-Saxons and the Danes was fought in the year 1016, and prodigies of valour exhibited by the combatants.

"When a schoolboy, I have often traced the intrenchments at Sherston Magna, which are still visible on the north side of the town, and particularly in a field near the brow of a hill which overlooks a branch of the river Avon, which rises a little below Didmarton; and with other boys have gone in quest of a certain plant in the field where the battle was said to have been fought, which the inhabitants pretended dropt blood when gathered, and called Danesblood, corruptly no doubt for *Dane-wort*, which was supposed to have sprung from the blood of the Danes slain in that battle. Among other memorials, the statue of a brave warrior, vulgarly called Rattlebone, but whose real name I could never learn, is still standing upon a pedestal on the east side of the church-porch, as I've been lately informed, where I saw it above fifty years ago: of whose bravery, almost equal to that of Withrington, many fabulous stories are told. One, in particular, like some of the Grecian fables of old, built upon the resemblance his shield bears to the shape of a tile-stone, which he is said to have placed over his stomach after it had been ripped up in battle, and by that means maintained the field; whilst the following rude verses are said to have been repeated by the king by way of encouragement.

> Fight on, Rattlebone,
> And thou shalt have Sherstone;
> If Sherstone will not do,
> Then Easton Grey and Pinkney too."

NORTH ACRE

> The Lord Dacre
> Was slain in North Acre.

North Acre is or was the name of the spot where Lord Dacre perished at the battle of Towton in 1461. He is said to have been shot by a boy out of an elder tree.

BELLASIS*

> Johnny tuth' Bellas daft was thy poll,
> When thou changed Bellas for Henknoll.

This saying, as given by Surtees, is still remembered near Bellasis, and is preferable to Hutchinson's version of it from the east window of the north transept of St. Andrew's Auckland church, where he says, "are remains of an inscription painted on the glass; the date appears 1386; beneath the inscription are the arms of Bellasys, and in a belt round them the following words:

> Bellysys Belysys dafe was thy sowel,
> When exchanged Belysys for Henknowell."

Collins (followed by Hutchinson), who gives the proverb as—

> Belasise, Belassis, daft was thy nowle,
> When thou gave Bellassis for Henknowle,

connects it with a grant dated 1380, from John de Belasye to the convent of Durham, of his lands in Wolveston, in exchange for the Manor of Henknoll. But Bellasyse is not even within the Manor of Wolveston, and, in fact, the Manor of Bellasye was held by the Prior in 1361; and we can only account for the proverb by suppos-

* Communicated by Mr Longstaffe.

ing that, at a former period, Bellasyse had been exchanged for lands, but not the manor of Henknoll. The legend dates the matter in crusading times, and is chivalric in the extreme. John of Bellasis minded to take up the cross, and fight in the Holy Land, found his piety sorely let and hindered by his attachment to the green pastures and deep meadows of his ancestors. With resolution strong, he exchanged them with the Church of Durham, for Henknoll, near Auckland. He went to fight, but lived it seems to return and repent his rash bargain. I descend by one step, from the sublime to the ridiculous, to mention how oddly more recent characters are wound round those of olden time, for a popular notion is that the Red-Cross Knight had enormous teeth, and was passionately addicted to "race-horses"! Children, moreover, have a dark saying when they leap off anything:

> Bellasay, Bellasay, what time of day?
> One o'clock, two o'clock, three and away!

Miss Bellasyse, the heiress of Brancepeth, died for love of Robert Shafto, of Whitworth, whose portrait at Whitworth represents him as very young and handsome, with *yellow* hair. He was the favourite candidate in the election of 1791, when he was popularly called Bonny Bobby Shafto; and the old song of the older Bobby, who, it seems, was also "bright and fair, combing down his *yellow* hair", was revived with the addition of—

> Bobby Shafto's looking out,
> All his ribbons flew about,
> All the ladies gave a shout—
> Hey, for Bobby Shafto!

The most ancient verses of the old song seem to be—

> Bobby Shafto's gone to sea,
> Silver buckles at his knee;
> He'll come back and marry me,
> Bonny Bobby Shafto!
>
> Bobby Shafto's bright and fair,
> Combing down his yellow hair;
> He's my ain for evermair,
> Bonny Bobby Shafto.

193

An apocryphal verse says,

> Bobby Shafto's getten a bairn,
> For to dangle on his arm—
> On his arm and on his knee;
> Bobby Shafto loves me.

KELLOE

> John Lively, Vicar of Kelloe,
> Had seven daughters and never a fellow.

An equivocal rhyme of the bishopric, which may either mean that the parson of the sixteenth century had no son, or that he had no equal in learning, &c. He certainly, however, mentions no son in his will, in which he leaves to his daughter Elizabeth, his best gold ring *with a death's head in it* (Compare Love's Labour Lost, v. 2), and seventeen yards of white cloth for curtains of a bed, and to his daughter Mary his silver seal of arms, his gimald ring, and black gold ring. Another version of the proverb reads "*six* daughters", and indeed *seven* is often merely a conventional number.

ROSEBERRY-TOPPING

"Not far from Gisborough is Ounsberry-hill, or Roseberry-topping, which mounts aloft and makes a great show at a distance, serving unto sailors for a mark of direction, and to the neighbour inhabitants for a prognostication; for as often as the head of it hath its cloudy cap on, there commonly follows rain, whereupon they have a proverbial rhyme,

> When Roseberry-topping wears a cap,
> Let Cleveland then beware a clap.

Near to the top of it, out of a huge rock, there flows a spring of water, medicinable for diseased eyes; and from thence there is a most delightful prospect upon the valleys below to the hills above."
—Brome's Travels, 8vo. Lond. 1700.

LINCOLN

"As for the town, though it flourished mightily for some years together after the Norman Conquest, by reason of a staple for wooll and other commodities, setled here by King Edward the Third; yet it met still with some calamities or other, which hindred its growth and eclipsed its grandeur, for it had its share of sufferings, both by fire and water, in King Stephen's days, about which time, it seems, though the king had at first been conquered and taken prisoner, yet he afterward entred into the city in triumph, with his crown upon his head, to break the citizens of a superstitious opinion they held, that no king could possibly enter into that city after such a manner, but some great disaster or other would befall him; but neither did it then, or by the barons' wars afterwards, sustain half the damages which of late years it hath received from the devouring hands of time, who hath wrought its downfal, and from a rich and populous city hath reduced it almost to the lowest ebb of fortune; and of fifty churches, which were all standing within one or two centuries, hath scarce left fifteen; so that the old proverbial rhymes (which go current amonst them) seem so far to have something of verity in them:

> Lincoln was, and London is,
> And York shall be
> The fairest city of the three."—*Ibid*.

SKIDDAW

"After we had passed these borders we arrived again safe in our own native soil, within the precincts of Cumberland, which, like the rest of the northern counties, hath a sharp piercing air; the soil is fertile for the most part both with corn and cattel, and in some parts hereof with fish and fowl; here are likewise several minerals, which of late have been discovered; not only mines of copper, but some veins of gold and silver, as we were informed, have been found; and of all the shires we have, it is accounted the best furnished with the Roman antiquities. Nor is it less renowned for its exceeding high mountains; for, beside the mountain called Wrynose, on the top of which, near the highway side, are to be seen three shire-stones within a foot of each other, one in this county, another in Westmoreland, and a third in Lancashire, there are three other hills, Skiddaw, Lanvalin, and Casticand, very remarkable. Skiddaw riseth up with two mighty high heads, like Parnassus, and beholds Scruffel Hill, which is in Annandale, in Scotland; and accordingly as mists arise or fall upon these heads, the people thereby prognosticate of the change of weather, singing this rhime:

> If Skiddaw have a cap,
> Scruffel wotts full of that.

And there goes also this usual by-word concerning the height, as well of this hill as of the other two:

> Skiddaw, Lanvellin, and Casticand,
> Are the highest hills in all England."—*Ibid.*

INGLEBOROUGH

"Here are three great hills, not far distant asunder, seeming to be as high as the clouds, which are Ingleborow, Penigent, and Pendle, on the top of which grows a peculiar plant called cloudsberry, as though it came out of the clouds. This hill formerly did the country much harm, by reason of an extraordinary deal of water gushing out of it, and is now famous for an infallible sign of rain whensoever the top of it is covered with a mist; and by reason of the excessive height for which they are all three celebrated, there is this proverbial rhime goes current amongst them:

> Ingleborow, Pendle, and Penigent,
> Are the highest hills betwixt Scotland and Trent."—*Ibid.*

THE KIRBY FEIGHT

> Eighty-eight wor Kirby feight,
> Where nivver a man was slain;
> They yatt ther meaat, an drank ther drink,
> An sae com merrily heaam agayn.

After the abdication of James the Second, in the year 1688, a rumour was spread in the North of England that he was lying off the Yorkshire coast, ready to make a descent with a numerous army from France, in hopes of regaining his lost throne. This report gave the Lord Lieutenant of Westmoreland an opportunity of showing his own and the people's attachment to the new order of things; he accordingly called out the *posse comitatus*, comprising all able-bodied men from sixteen to sixty. The order was obeyed with alacrity; and the inhabitants met armed in a field called Miller's-close, near Kendal, from whence they marched to Kirby Lonsdale. This historical fact explains the above popular rhyme, the meaning of which is, at this day, perhaps not generally understood.—West. and Cumb. Dial. 89.

THORNTON

At the Westgate came Thornton in
With a hap, a halfpenny, and a lambskin.

A Newcastle distich relating to Roger Thornton, a wealthy merchant, and a great benefactor to that town. A *hap* is a coarse coverlet of any kind.

ISLE OF MAN

All the bairns unborn will rue the day
That the Isle of Man was sold away,
And there's ne'er a wife that loves a dram,
But what will lament for the Isle of Man.

EARSDON

Hartley and Hallowell, a' ya' bonnie lassie,
Fair Seaton-Delaval, a' ya';
Earsdon stands on a hill, a' ya',
Near to the Billy-mill, a' ya'.

NINE

Superstition Rhymes

Although the spread of education has doubtlessly weakened in an extraordinary degree the hold which superstition formerly maintained on the mind of the public, yet vestiges of the more innocent portions of superstitious belief are still in considerable repute amongst the lower orders, and may be found in all their force in many of the rural districts. It may be a question how far a complete eradication of these would benefit the cause of religion and morality, treason though it be in these times to doubt the efficacy of argumentative education. But all of us cannot be philosophers; and need we reprove a pretty village maiden for plucking the even-ash or four-leaved clover? The selfish tendencies of the age, in their opposition to every action which partakes of poetry or romantic belief, will effect their mission without the aid of the cynic.

CHARM RHYMES

The subject of rural charms, many of which are lineal descendants from those used by our Anglo-Saxon ancestors, is one of great interest and curiosity; and it were much to be wished that a complete collection of them were formed. The following one is taken from a manuscript of the time of Queen Elizabeth; the others are for the most part still in use.

This charme shall be said at night, or against night, about the place or feild, or about beasts without feild, and whosoever cometh in, he goeth not out for certaine.

On three crosses of a tree,
Three dead bodyes did hang;
Two were theeves,
The third was Christ,
On whom our beleife is;
Dismas and Gesmas;
Christ amidst them was;
Dismas to heaven went,
Gesmas to heaven was sent.
Christ that died on the roode,
For Marie's love that by him stood,
And through the vertue of his blood,
Jesus save us and our good,
Within and without,
And all this place about!
And through the vertue of his might,
Lett noe theefe enter in this night
Noe foote further in this place
That I upon goe,
But at my bidding there be bound
To do all things that I bid them do!
Starke be their sinewes therewith,
And their lives mightles,
And their eyes sightles!
Dread and doubt
Them enclose about,
As a wall wrought of stone;
So be the crampe in the ton (*toes*):
Crampe and crookeing,
And tault in their tooting,
The might of the Trinity
Save these goods and me,
In the name of Jesus, holy benedicité,

All about our goods bee,
Within and without,
And all place about!

Warts.—Whoever will charm away a wart must take a pin and go
to an ash-tree. He then *crosses* the wart with the pin three times,
and, after each crossing, repeats:

Ash-tree, ashen-tree,
Pray buy this wart of me!

After which he sticks the pin in the tree, and the wart soon dis-
appears, and grows on the tree instead. This must be done secretly.
I need scarcely observe that the ash is sacred amongst all the
Teutonic and Scandinavian nations.

Another.—Take a bean-shell, and rub the wart with it; then
bring the bean-shell under an ash-tree, and repeat:

As this bean-shell rots away,
So my wart shall soon decay!

This also must be done secretly.

The Hiccup

Hickup, hickup, go away,
Come again another day:
Hickup, hickup, when I bake,
I'll give to you a butter-cake.

The Ague.—Said on St. Agnes's eve, sometimes up the chimney,
by the oldest female in the family:

Tremble and go!
First day shiver and burn:
Tremble and quake!
Second day shiver and learn:
Tremble and die!
Third day never return.

Cattle.—Reginald Scott relates that an old woman who cured the
diseases of cattle, and who always required a penny and a loaf for
her services, used these lines for the purpose:

My loaf in my lap,
My penny in my purse;
Thou art never the better,
And I am never the worse.

The same writer gives a curious anecdote of a priest who, on one occasion, went out a-nights with his companions, and stole all the eels from a miller's weir. The poor miller made his complaint to the same priest, who desired him to be quiet, for he would so denounce the thief and his confederates by bell, book, and candle, they should have small joy of their fish. Accordingly, on the following Sunday, during the service, he pronounced the following sentences to the congregation:

All you that have stol'n the miller's eels,
Laudate Dominum de cælis;
And all they that have consented thereto,
Benedicamus Domino.

"So," says he, "there is sauce for your eels, my masters!"

An "old woman came into an house at a time whenas the maid was churning of butter, and having laboured long, and could not make her butter come, the old woman told the maid what was wont to be done when she was a maid, and also in her mother's young time, that if it happened their butter would not come readily, they used a charm to be said over it whilst yet it was in beating, and it would come straightways, and that was this:

Come, butter, come,
Come, butter, come;
Peter stands at the gate,
Waiting for a buttered cake;
Come, butter, come!

This, said the old woman, being said three times, will make your butter come, for it was taught my mother by a learned churchman in Queen Marie's days; whenas churchmen had more cunning, and could teach people many a trick that our ministers now-a-days know not."—Ady's "Candle in the Dark", 1656, p. 59.

"There be twenty several ways," says Scot, 1584, "to make your butter come, which for brevity I omit—as to bind your churn with a rope, to thrust therein a red-hot spit, &c.; but your best remedy and surest way is to look well to your dairy-maid or wife, that she neither eat up the cream, nor sell away your butter."

Effusion of Blood.—From Worcestershire.

> Jesus was born in Bethlem,
> Baptized in the river Jordan;
> The water was wild and wood,
> But he was just and good;
> God spake, and the water stood,
> And so shall now thy blood.

Charms were formerly always used when wounds were attempted to be cured. So in the old ballad of Tommy Potts:

> Tom Potts was but a serving-man,
>   But yet he was a doctor good;
> He bound his handkerchief on the wound,
>   And with some words he staunched the blood.

Bed-charm.—The following is one of the most common rural charms that are in vogue. Boys are taught to repeat it instead of a prayer:

> Matthew, Mark, Luke, and John,
> Bless the bed that I lay on;
> Four corners to my bed,
> Four angels round my head,
> One at head and one at feet,
> And two to keep my soul asleep!

There are many variations of it. Ady, in his "Candle in the Dark", 1656, p. 58, gives the first two lines as having been used by an old woman in the time of Queen Mary.

> Matthew, Mark, Luke, and John,
> Bless the bed that I lie on!
> All the four corners round about,
> When I get in, when I get out!

The two following distiches were obtained from Lancashire, but

I cannot profess to explain them, unless indeed they were written by the Puritans to ridicule the above:

> Matthew, Mark, Luke, and John,
> Hold the horse that I leap on!

> Matthew, Mark, Luke, and John,
> Take a stick and lay upon!

Burn.—The following charm, repeated three times, was used by an old woman in Sussex, within the last forty years:

> Two angels from the north,
> One brought fire, the other brought frost:
>> Out fire!
>> In frost!
> In the name of the Father, Son, and Holy Ghost.

Pepys has recorded this, with a slight variation, in his Diary, vol. ii. p. 416.

Thorn.—This rural charm for a thorn was obtained from Yorkshire:

> Unto the Virgin Mary our Saviour was born,
> And on his head He wore a crown of thorn;
> If you believe this true and mind it well,
> This hurt will never fester nor swell!

The following is one given by Lord Northampton in his "Defensative against the Poyson of supposed Prophecies", 1583. as having been used by Mother Joane of Stowe:

> Our Lord was the fyrst man
> That ever thorne prickt upon;
> It never blysted, nor it never belted,
> And I pray God nor this not may.

And Pepys, ii. 415, gives another:

> Christ was of a virgin born,
> And he was pricked with a thorn;
> And it did neither bell nor swell,
> And I trust in Jesus this never will.

Toothache.—A very common one in the North of England but I do not remember to have seen it in print.

> Peter was sitting on a marble-stone,
>   And Jesus passed by;
> Peter said, "My Lord, my God,
>   How my tooth doth ache!"
> Jesus said, "Peter art whole!
> And whoever keeps these words for my sake
> Shall never have the tooth-ache!"*

Aubrey gives another charm for this complaint, copied out of one of Ashmole's manuscripts:

> Mars, hurs, abursa, aburse;
> Jesu Christ, for Mary's sake,
> Take away this tooth-ache!

Against an evil Tongue (from Aubrey, 1696, p. 111).—"Take *unguentum populeum* and vervain, and hypericon, and put a red hot iron into it. You must anoint the backbone, or wear it on your breast. This is printed in Mr. W. Lilly's Astrology. Mr. H. C. hath try'd this receipt with good success.

> "Vervain and dill
> Hinders witches from their will."

Cramp.—From Pepys' Diary, ii. 415:

> Cramp, be thou faintless,
> As our Lady was sinless,
> When she bare Jesus.

Sciatica.—The patient must lie on his back on the bank of a river

---

* It is a fact that within the last few years the following ignorant copy of this charm was used by a native of Craven, recorded by Carr, ii. 264, and I have been informed on credible authority that the trade of selling efficacies of this kind is far from obsolete in the remote rural districts:

"Ass Sant Petter Sat at the Geats of Jerusalem our blesed Lord and Sevour Jesus Crist Pased by and Sead, What Elcth thee hee Sead Lord My Teeth Ecketh he Sead arise and folow Mee and Thy Teeth shall Never Eake Eney Moor, fiat + at + fiat +."

or brook of water, with a straight staff by his side between him and the water, and must have the following words repeated over him—

> Bone-shave right,
> Bone-shave straight;
> As the water runs by the stave,
> Good for bone-shave.

The *bone-shave* is a Devonshire term for the sciatica. See the "Exmoor Scolding", ed. 1839, p. 2.

Night-mare.—The following charm is taken from Scot's "Discoverie of Witchcraft", 1584, p. 87:

> S. George, S. George, our ladies knight,
> He walkt by daie, so did he by night.
> Untill such time as he her found,
> He hir beat and he hir bound,
> Untill her troth she to him plight,
> He would not come to hir that night.

Sore Eyes.—From the same work, p. 246:

> The diuell pull out both thine eies,
> And etish in the holes likewise.

For rest.—From the same work, p. 260:

> In nomine Patris, up and downe,
> Et Filii et Spiritus Sancti upon my crowne,
> Crux Christi upon my brest;
> Sweete ladie, send me eternall rest.

Stopping of Blood.—From the same work, p. 273:

> In the bloud of Adam death was taken +
> In the bloud of Christ it was all to-shaken +
> And by the same bloud I doo thee charge
> That thou doo runne no longer at large.

This charm continued in use long after the publication of Scot's work. A version of it, slightly altered, is given in the "Athenian Oracle", 1728, i. 158, as having been used by a country empiric.

Evil Spirits.—"When I was a boy," says Aubrey, MS. Lansd. 231, "a charme was used for (I thinke) keeping away evill spirits, which was to say thrice in a breath—

> 'Three blew beanes in a blew bladder,
> Rattle, bladder, rattle'."

These lines are quoted by Zantippa in Peele's "Old Wives' Tale", 1595.

BUCKEE BENE

> Buckee, Buckee, biddy Bene,
> Is the way now fair and clean?
> Is the goose ygone to nest,
> And the fox ygone to rest?
> Shall I come away?

These curious lines are said by Devonshire children when they go through any passages in the dark, and are said to be addressed to Puck or Robin Goodfellow as a method of asking permission to trace them. Biddy bene, A.-S. *biddan*, to ask or pray, *bén*, a supplication or entreaty. Buckee, possibly a corruption of Puck.

THE OX

In Herefordshire, on the eve of Twelfth-day, the best ox, white or spotted, has a cake placed on his left horn; the men and girls of the farm-house being present, drink out of a silver tankard to him, repeating this verse—

> We drink to thee and thy white horn,
> Pray God send master a good crop of corn,
> Wheat, rye, and barley, and all sorts of grain:
> If alive at the next time, I'll hail thee again!

The animal is then sprinkled with the libation. This makes him toss his head up and down, and if, in so doing, the cake be thrown forwards, it is a good omen; if backwards, the contrary. Sir S. Meyrick, "Trans. Brit. Arch. Assoc. Glouc. 1848", p. 128, appears to consider this custom a relic of the ancient Pagan religion.

LOVE DIVINATIONS

Butter-dock.—The seeds of butter-dock must be sowed by a young unmarried woman half an hour before sunrise on a Friday morning, in a lonesome place. She must strew the seeds gradually on the grass, saying these words—

> I sow, I sow!
> Then, my own dear,
> Come here, come here,
> And mow and mow!

The seed being scattered, she will see her future husband mowing with a scythe at a short distance from her. She must not be frightened, for, if she says "Have mercy on me", he will immediately vanish. This method is said to be infallible, but it is looked upon as a bold, desperate, and presumptuous undertaking.

True-love.—Two young unmarried girls must sit together in a room by themselves, from twelve o'clock at night till one o'clock the next morning, without speaking a word. During this time each of them must take as many hairs from her head as she is years old, and, having put them into a linen cloth with some of the herb true-love, as soon as the clock strikes one, she must burn every hair separately, saying—

> I offer this my sacrifice
> To him most precious in my eyes;
> I charge thee now come forth to me,
> That I this minute may thee see.

Upon which her first husband will appear, and walk round the room, and then vanish. The same event happens to both the girls, but neither sees the other's lover.

Gerard says of the herb true-love or moonwort, p. 328, that "witches do wonders withall, who say that it will loose locks, and make them to fall from the feete of horses that grase where it doth growe".

A charm-divination on the 6th of October, St. Faith's day, is still in use in the North of England. A cake of flour, spring water, salt and sugar, is made by three girls, each having an equal hand in the composition. It is then baked in a Dutch oven, silence being strictly preserved, and turned thrice by each person. When it is well baked, it must be divided into three equal parts, and each girl must cut her share into nine pieces, drawing every piece through a wedding-ring which had been borrowed from a woman who has been married seven years. Each girl must eat her piece of cake while she is undressing, and repeat the following verses:

> O good St. Faith, be kind to-night,
> And bring to me my heart's delight;
> Let me my future husband view,
> And be my visions chaste and true!

All three must then get into one bed, with the ring suspended by a string to the head of the couch. They will then dream of their future husbands, or if perchance one of them is destined to lead apes, she will dream of wandering by herself over crags and mountains.

On the 28th of the same month, another divination is practised by the paring of an apple, which is taken by a girl in the right hand, who recites the following lines, standing in the middle of a room:

> St. Simon and Jude, on you I intrude,
> By this paring I hold to discover,
> Without any delay, to tell me this day
> The first letter of my own true lover.

She must then turn round three times, casting the paring over her left shoulder, and it will form the first letter of her husband's name; but if the paring breaks into many pieces so that no letter is discernible, she will never marry. The pips of the apple must then be placed in cold spring water and eaten by the girl; but for what further object my deponent sayeth not.

A very singular divination practised at the period of the harvest-moon is thus described in an old chap-book. When you go to bed, place under your pillow a prayer-book open at the part of the matrimonial service "With this ring I thee wed"; place on it a key, a ring, a flower, and a sprig of willow, a small heart-cake, a crust of bread, and the following cards: the ten of clubs, nine of hearts, ace of spades, and ace of diamonds. Wrap all these in a thin handkerchief of gauze or muslin, and on getting into bed, cross your hands, and say—

> Luna, every woman's friend,
> To me thy goodness condescend
> Let me this night in visions see
> Emblems of my destiny.

If you dream of storms, trouble will betide you; if the storm ends in a fine calm, so will your fate; if of a ring or the ace of diamonds, marriage; bread, an industrious life; cake, a prosperous life; flowers, joy; willow, treachery in love; spades, death; diamonds, money; clubs, a foreign land; hearts, illegitimate children; keys, that you will rise to great trust and power, and never know want; birds, that you will have many children; and geese, that you will marry more than once.

In Dorsetshire, the girls have a method of divination with their shoes for obtaining dreams of their future husbands. At night, on going to bed, a girl places her shoes at right angles to one another, in the form of a T, saying—

> Hoping this night my true love to see,
> I place my shoes in the form of a T.

On St. Luke's day, says Mother Bunch, take marigold flowers, a sprig of marjoram, thyme, and a little wormwood; dry them before a fire, rub them to powder; then sift it through a fine piece of lawn, and simmer it over a slow fire, adding a small quantity of virgin honey, and vinegar. Anoint yourself with this when you go to bed, saying the following lines three times, and you will dream of your partner "that is to be":

> St. Luke, St. Luke, be kind to me,
> In dreams let me my true love see.

If a girl desires to obtain this information, let her seek for a green peascod in which there are full nine peas, and write on a piece of paper—

> Come in, my dear,
> And do not fear;

which paper she must inclose in the peascod, and lay it under the door. The first person who comes into the room will be her husband. Does Shakespeare allude to some notion of this kind by the wooing of a peascod in "As You Like it", ii. 4?

ST. AGNES' NIGHT

"The women have several magical secrets handed down to them by tradition, as on St. Agnes' night, 21st January. Take a row of pins, and pull out every one, one after another, saying a pater-noster, sticking a pin in your sleeve, and you will dream of him or her you shall marry. You must lie in another county, and knit the left garter about the right-legg'd stockin (let the other garter and stockin alone), and as you rehearse these following verses, at every comma knit a knot:

> This knot I knit
> To know the thing I know not yet:
> That I may see
> The man that shall my husband be,
> How he goes and what he wears,
> And what he does all the days.

Accordingly in your dream you will see him, if a musitian with a lute or other instrument; if a scholar, with a book, &c. A gentlewoman that I knew confessed in my hearing, that she used this method, and dreamt of her husband whom she had never seen. About two or three years after, as she was on Sunday at church, up pops a young Oxonian in the pulpit. She cries out presently to her sister, 'This is the very face of the man that I saw in my dream'."
—Aubrey's Miscellanies, ed. 1696, p. 105.

On St. Agnes' day, take a sprig of rosemary, and another of thyme, and sprinkle them thrice with water. In the evening put one in each shoe, placing a shoe on each side of the bed, and when you retire to rest, say the following lines, and your future husband will appear "visible to sight":

> St. Agnes, that's to lovers kind,
> Come ease the trouble of my mind.

KALE

The young women of some districts in the North of England have a method of divination by *kale* or broth, which is used for the purpose of learning who are to be their future husbands. The plan followed is this. The maiden at bedtime stands *on something on which she never stood before*, holding a pot of cold kale in her hand, and repeating the following lines. She then drinks nine times, goes to bed backwards, and of course dreams of her partner:

> Hot kale or cold kale, I drink thee;
> If ever I marry a man, or a man marry me,
> I wish this night I may him see,
> To-morrow may him ken
> In church, fair, or market,
> Above all other men.

On Valentine's day take two bay-leaves, sprinkle them with rose-water, and lay them across your pillow in the evening. When you go to bed, put on a clean nightgown turned wrong side outwards, and, lying down, say these words softly to yourself—

> Good Valentine, be kind to me,
> In dreams let me my true love see.

After this go to sleep as soon as you can, and you will see in a dream your future husband.

Schoolboys have several kinds of divination-verses on going to bed, now repeated "more in mock than mark", but no doubt originating in serious belief—

> Go to bed first,
> A golden purse;
> Go to bed second,
> A golden pheasant;
> Go to bed third,
> A golden bird.

The positions they occupy in the bed are suggestive of the following fortunes:

> He that lies at the stock,
> Shall have the gold rock:
> He that lies at the wall,
> Shall have the gold ball;
> He that lies in the middle,
> Shall have the gold fiddle.

BALL-DIVINATION

Cook a ball, cherry-tree;
Good ball, tell me
How many years I shall be
Before my true love I do see?
One and two, and that makes three;
Thank'ee, good ball, for telling of me.

Cook is to toss or throw, a provincialism common in the midland counties. The ball is thrown against a wall, and the divination is taken from the number of rebounds it makes. Another version is—

Cuckoo, cherry-tree*
Good ball, tell me
How many years I shall be
Before I get married?

And this is probably correct, for we appear to have formed this method of divination in some indirect manner from a custom still prevalent in Germany of addressing the cuckoo, when he is first heard, with a view of ascertaining the duration of life, by counting the number of times it repeats its note. The lines used on this occasion are given by Grimm:

Kukuk, Beckenknecht!
   Sag mir recht,
Wie viel jahr Ich leben soll?

An old story is told of a man who was on his road towards a monastery, which he was desirous of entering as a monk for the salvation of his soul, and hearing the cuckoo, stopped to count the number of notes. They were twenty-two. "Oh!" said he, "since I shall be sure to live twenty-two years, what is the use of mortifying myself in a monastery all that time? I'll e'en go and live merrily for twenty years, and it will be all in good time to betake me to a

---

* The following lines reached me without an explanation. They seem to be analogous to the above:
> Cuckoo, cherry-tree,
> Lay an egg, give it me;
> Lay another.
> Give it my brother!

213

monastery for the other two." See Wright's Essays, i. 257; and "Latin Stories", p. 42, de cuculo; p. 74, de muliere in extremis quæ dixit *kuckuc*. Both these tales curiously illustrate the extent to which faith in the divination extended.

If a maid desires to attach the affections of her lover unalterably to her, she must wait till she finds him asleep with his clothes on. She must then take away one of his garters without his perceiving it, and tie it to her own in a true-love knot, saying—

> Three times this knot
> I tie secure;
> Firm is the knot
> Firm his love endure.

In many parts of the country, it is considered extremely unlucky to give a person anything that is sharp, as a knife, razor, &c., but the bad fortune may be averted if the receiver gives something, however trifling, in return, and exclaims—

> If you love me as I love you,
> No knife shall cut our love in two!

In counting the buttons of the waistcoat upwards, the last found corresponding to one of the following names indicates the destiny of the wearer:

> My belief,—
> A captain, a colonel, a cow-boy, a thief.

THE EVEN-ASH

A girl must pluck a leaf from the even-ash, and, holding it in her hand, say—

> This even-ash I hold in my hand,
> The first I meet is my true man.

She carries it in her hand a short distance, and if she meets a young man, he will be her future husband. If not, she must put the leaf in her glove, and say—

> This even-ash I hold in my glove,
> The first I meet is my true love.

She carries it in her glove a short time, with the same intention as before, but if she meets no one, she places the leaf in her bosom, saying—

> This even-ash I hold in my bosom,
> The first I meet in my husband.

And the first young man she meets after this will infallibly be her future partner. There are a great variety of rhymes relating to the even-ash. Another is—

> If you find even-ash or four-leaved clover,
> You will see your love afore the day's over.

DOCK

> Nettle in, dock out,
> Dock rub nettle out!

If a person is stung with a nettle, a certain cure will be effected by rubbing dock leaves over the part, repeating the above charm very slowly. Mr. Akerman gives us another version of it as current in Wiltshire:

> Out 'ettle, in dock,
> Dock zhall h' a new smock;
> 'Ettle zhant ha' narrun!

THE YARROW

This plant, in the eastern counties, is termed *yarroway*, and there is a curious mode of divination with its serrated leaf, with which you must tickle the inside of your nose, repeating the following lines. If the operation causes the nose to bleed, it is a certain omen of success:

> Yarroway, yarroway, bear a white blow,
> If my love love me, my nose will bleed now.

Another mode of divination with this plant caused a dream of a future husband. An ounce of yarrow, sewed up in flannel, must be placed under your pillow when you go to bed, and having repeated the following words, the required dream will be realized:

215

Thou pretty herb of Venus' tree,
Thy true name it is yarrow;
Now who my bosom friend must be,
Pray tell thou me to-morrow.

Boys have a variety of divinations with the kernels of pips of fruit. They will shoot one with their thumb and forefinger, exclaiming—

Kernel come kernel, hop over my thumb,
And tell me which way my true love will come;
East, West, North, or South,
Kernel, jump into my true love's mouth.

This is taken from Mr. Barnes's "Dorset Gl.", p. 320, but the author does not inform us in what way the divination was effected. I remember throwing apple-pips into the fire, saying—

If you love me, pop and fly,
If you hate me, lay and die!

addressing an imaginary love, or naming some individual whose affection was desired to be tested.

Girls used to have a method of divination with a "St. Thomas's onion",* for the purpose of ascertaining their future partners. They peeled the onion, wrapped it up in a clean handkerchief, and then placing it under their heads, said the following lines:

Good St. Thomas, do me right,
And let my true love come to-night,
That I may see him in the face,
And him in my kind arms embrace;

which were considered infallible for procuring a dream of the beloved one.

To know if your present sweetheart will marry you, let an unmarried woman take the bladebone of a shoulder of lamb, and borrowing a penknife, without on any account mentioning the purpose for which it is required, stick it through the bone when she

---

* One of the old cries of London was, "Buy my rope of onions—white St. Thomas's onions". They are also mentioned in "The Hog hath lost his Pearl", i. 1.

goes to bed for nine nights in different places, repeating the following lines each time:

> 'Tis not this bone I mean to stick,
> But my love's heart I mean to prick,
> Wishing him neither rest nor sleep,
> Until he comes to me to speak.

Accordingly at the end of nine days, or shortly afterwards, he will ask for something to put to a wound he will have met with during the time he was thus charmed.—Another method is also employed for the same object. On a Friday morning, fasting, write on four pieces of paper the names of three persons you like best, and also the name of Death, fold them up, wear them in your bosom all day, and at night shake them up in your left shoe, going to bed backwards; take out one with your left hand and the other with your right, throw three of them out of the shoe, and in the morning whichever name remains in the shoe is that of your future husband. If Death is left, you will not marry any of them.

VERVAIN

The herb vervain was formerly held of great efficacy against witchcraft, and in various diseases. Sir W. Scott mentions a popular rhyme, supposed to be addressed to a young woman by the devil, who attempted to seduce her in the shape of a handsome young man:

> Gin you wish to be leman mine,
> Leave off the St. John's wort and the vervine.

By this repugnance to these sacred plants, his mistress discovered the cloven foot. Many ceremonies were used in gathering it. "You must observe," says Gerard, "Mother Bumbies rules to take just so many knots or sprigs, and no more, least it fall out so that it do you no good, if you catch no harme by it; many odde olde wives' fables are written of vervaine, tending to witchcraft and sorcerie, which you may reade elsewhere, for I am not willing to trouble your eares with reporting such trifles as honest earcs abhorre to heare." An old English poem on the virtue of herbs, of the fourteenth century, says:

As we redyn, gaderyd most hym be
With iij. pater-noster and iij. ave,
Fastand, thow the wedir be grylle,
Be-twen mydde March and mydde Aprille,
And get awysyd moste the be,
That the sonne be in ariete.

A magical MS. in the Chetham Library at Manchester, of the time of Queen Elizabeth, furnishes us with a poetical prayer used in gathering this herb:

All hele, thou holy herb vervin,
Growing on the ground;
In the mount of Calvery
There was thou found;
Thou helpest many a greife,
And stenchest many a wound,
In the name of sweet Jesus,
I take thee from the ground.
O Lord, effect the same
That I doe now go about.

The following lines, according to this authority, were to be said when pulling it:

In the name of God, on Mount Olivet
First I thee found;
In the name of Jesus
I pull thee from the ground.

Two hogsheads full of money were concealed in a subterraneous vault at Penyard Castle, in Herefordshire. A farmer undertook to drag them from their hiding-place, a matter of no small difficulty, for they were protected by preternatural power. To accomplish his object, he took twenty steers to draw down the iron doors of the vault in which the hogsheads were deposited. The door was partially opened, and a jackdaw was seen perched on one of the casks. The farmer was overjoyed at the prospect of success, and as soon as he saw the casks, he exclaimed, "I believe I shall have it." The door immediately closed with a loud clang, and a voice in the air exclaimed—

Had it not been
  For your quicken-tree goad
And your yew-tree pin,
  You and your cattle
Had all been drawn in!

The belief that the quicken-tree is of great efficacy against the power of witches is still in force in the North of England. The yew-tree was formerly employed in witchcraft, a practice alluded to in Macbeth:

Liver of blaspheming Jew,
Gall of goats, and slips of yew,
Sliver'd in the moon's eclipse.

FINGER-NAILS

There is a superstition, says Forby, ii. 411, respecting cutting the nails, and some days are considered more lucky for this operation than others. To cut them on Tuesday is thought particularly auspicious. Indeed if we are to believe an old rhyming-saw on this subject, every day of the week is endowed with its several and peculiar virtue, if the nails are invariably cut on that day and no other. The lines are as follow:

Cut them on Monday, you cut them for health:
Cut them on Tuesday, you cut them for wealth;
Cut them on Wednesday, you cut them for news;
Cut them on Thursday, a new pair of shoes;
Cut them on Friday, you cut them for sorrow;
Cut them on Saturday, see your true love to-morrow;
Cut them on Sunday, the devil will be with you all the week.

The following divination rhymes refer to the *gifts*, or white spots on the nails, beginning with the thumb, and going on regularly to the little finger. The last gift will show the destiny of the operator *pro tempore*,

A gift—a friend—a foe—
A journey—to go.

219

DAYS OF BIRTH

Monday's child is fair in face,
Tuesday's child is full of grace,
Wednesday's child is full of woe,
Thursday's child has far to go,
Friday's child is loving and giving,
Saturday's child works hard for its living;
And a child that's born on a Sunday
Is fair and wise, good and gay.

COLOURS

Blue is true,
Yellow's jealous,
Green's forsaken,
Red's brazen,
White is love,
And black is death!

THE MAN IN THE MOON

The Man in the Moon
Sups his sowins with a cutty-spoon.

A Northumberland dish called *sowins* is composed of the coarse
parts of oatmeal, which are put into a tub and covered with water,
and then allowed to stand till it turns sour. A portion of it is then
taken out, and sapped with milk. It may easily be imagined that
this is a substance not very accessible to the movements of a cutty
or very small spoon.

Grimm, "Deutsche Mythologie", p. 412, informs us that there
are three legends connected with the Man in the Moon; the first,
that his personage was Isaac carrying a bundle of sticks for his
own sacrifice: the second, that he was Cain; and the other, which
is taken from the history of the Sabbath-breaker, as related in the
Book of Numbers. The last is still generally current in this country,
and is alluded to by Chaucer, and many early writers. The second

is mentioned by Dante, "Inferno", xx., Cain sacrificing to the Lord *thorns*, the most wretched production of the ground,

> ——chè già tiene 'l confine
> D'amenduo gli emisperi, e tocca l'onda
> Sotto Sibilia, Caino e le spine.

It appears that sowins were not the only food of the lunary inhabitant, for it is related by children he once favoured middle-earth with his presence, and took a fancy to some pease-porridge, which he was in such a hurry to devour that he scalded his mouth:

> The Man in the Moon
> Came tumbling down,
> And asked his way to Norwich;
> He went by the south,
> And burnt his mouth
> With supping hot pease-porridge.

His chief beverage, as everybody knows, was claret:

> The Man in the Moon drinks claret,
> But he is a dull Jack-a-Dandy;
> Would he know a sheep's head from a carrot,
> He should learn to drink cyder and brandy.

Another old ballad commences,

> The Man in the Moon drinks claret,
> With powder-beef, turnip, and carrot.

TEN

Custom Rhymes

It is greatly to be feared that, notwithstanding the efforts made within the last few years by individuals who have desired to see the resuscitation of the merry sports and customs of old England, the spirit which formerly characterized them is not to be recovered. The mechanical spirit of the age has thrown a degree of ridicule over observances which have not been without use in their day; and might even now be rendered beneficial to the public, were it possible to exclude the influence which tells the humbler subject such matters are below his regard. Yet it must be confessed that most of our ancient customs are only suited to the thinly-populated rural districts, where charity, good-will, and friendship may be delicately cultivated under the plea of their observance.

CHRISTMAS

Ha wish ye a merry Chresamas,
    An a happy new year,
A pantry full a' good rost beef,
    And a barril full a' beer.

To these lines we may add the following north-country nursery song:

Now Christmas is come, and now Pappy's come home,
    Wi' a pegtop for Tammie, a hussif for Sue;
A new bag o' marbles for Dick; and for Joan
    A workbox; for Phœbe a bow for her shoe:
For Cecily singing a humming-top comes,
    For dull drowsie Marie a sleeping-top meet;
For Ben, Ned, and Harry, a fife and two drums,
    For Jennie a box of nice sugar-plums sweet.

CHRISTMAS MUMMER'S PLAY

A rude drama is performed at Christmas by the guisers or mummers
in most parts of England and Scotland, but the versions are
extremely numerous, and no less than six copies have reached me
differing materially from each other. In the following copy, which
is the most perfect one I have been able to procure, the *dramatis
personæ* consist of a Fool, St. George, Slasher, a Doctor, Prince of
Paradine, King of Egypt, Hector, Beelzebub, and little Devil Doubt.
I am informed that this drama is occasionally acted at Easter as
well as at Christmas.

Enter Actors

    Fool. Room, room, brave gallants, give us room to sport,
For in this room we wish for to resort,
Resort, and to repeat to you our merry rhyme;
For remember, good sirs, this is Christmas time!
The time to cut up goose-pies now doth appear,
So we are come to act our merry Christmas here;
At the sound of the trumpet and beat of the drum,
Make room, brave gentlemen, and let our actors come!
We are the merry actors that traverse the street,
We are the merry actors that fight for our meat;
We are the merry actors that show pleasant play.
Step in, St. George, thou champion, and clear the way.

Enter St. George

I am St. George, who from old England sprung,
My famous name throughout the world hath rung;
Many bloody deeds and wonders have I made known,

And made the tyrants tremble on their throne.
I followed a fair lady to a giant's gate,
Confined in dungeon deep to meet her fate;
Then I resolved, with true knight-errantry,
To burst the door, and set the prisoner free;
When a giant almost struck me dead,
But by my valour I cut off his head.
I've searched the world all round and round,
But a man to equal me I never found.

Enter Slasher

Slasher. I am a valiant soldier, and Slasher is my name,
With sword and buckler by my side I hope to win the game;
And for to fight with me I see thou art not able,
So with my trusty broad-sword I soon will thee disable!
St. George. Disable! disable! it lies not in thy power,
For with my glittering sword and spear I soon will thee devour.
Stand off, Slasher! let no more be said,
For if I draw my sword, I'm sure to break thy head!
Slasher. How canst thou break my head?
Since it is made of iron,
   And my body's made of steel;
My hands and feet of knuckle-bone;
   I challenge thee to field.

[*They fight, and* Slasher *is wounded. Exit* St. George.

Enter Fool

Fool. Alas! alas! my chiefest son is slain!
What must I do to raise him up again?
Here he lies in the presence of you all,
I'll lovingly for a doctor call!
(*Aloud.*) A doctor! a doctor! ten pounds for a doctor!
I'll go and fetch a doctor.   [*Going.*

Enter Doctor

Doctor. Here am I.
Fool. Are you the doctor?
Doctor. Yes, that you may plainly see,
By my art and activity.
Fool. Well, what's your fee to cure this man?

Doctor. Ten pounds is my fee; but Jack, if thou be an honest man, I'll only take five of thee.

Fool. You'll be wondrous cunning if you get any. (*Aside.*)
Well, how far have you travelled in doctrineship?

Doctor. From Italy, Titaly, High Germany, France, and Spain,
And now am returned to cure the diseases in old England again.

Fool. So far, and no farther?

Doctor. O yes! a great deal farther.

Fool. How far?

Doctor. From the fireside cupboard, upstairs and into bed.

Fool. What diseases can you cure?

Doctor. All sorts.

Fool. What's all sorts?

Doctor. The itch, the pitch, the palsy, and the gout.
         If a man gets nineteen devils in his skull
         I'll cast twenty of them out.

I have in my pockets crutches for lame ducks, spectacles for blind humble-bees, pack-saddles and panniers for grasshoppers, and plaisters for broken-backed mice. I cured Sir Harry of a nang-nail almost fifty-five yards long; surely I can cure this poor man.

Here, Jack, take a little out of my bottle,
And let it run down thy throttle;
If thou be not quite slain,
Rise, Jack, and fight again.   [Slasher *rises.*

Slasher. Oh, my back!

Fool. What's amiss with thy back?

Slasher. My back it is wounded,
And my heart is confounded.
To be struck out of seven senses into four score;
The like was never seen in Old England before.

Enter St. George

Oh, hark! St. George, I hear the silver trumpet sound,
That summons us from off this bloody ground;
Down yonder is the way (*pointing*).
Farewell, St. George, we can no longer stay.

                    [*Exeunt* Slasher, Doctor, *and* Fool.

St. George. I am St. George, that noble champion bold,
And with my trusty sword I won ten thousand pounds in gold;

226

'Twas I that fought the fiery dragon, and brought him to the
    slaughter,
And by those means I won the King of Egypt's daughter.

Enter Prince of Paradine

Prince. I am Black Prince of Paradine, born in high renown;
Soon I will fetch St. George's lofty courage down.
Before St. George shall be received by me,
St. George shall die to all eternity!
    St. George. Stand off, thou black Morocco dog,
Or by my sword, thou'lt die;
I'll pierce thy body full of holes,
And make thy buttons fly.
    Prince. Draw out thy sword and slay,
Pull out thy purse and pay;
For I will have a recompense
Before I go away.
    St. George. Now, Prince of Paradine, where have you been?
And what fine sights, pray, have you seen?
Dost think that no man of thy age
Dares such a black as thee engage?
Lay down thy sword; take up to me a spear,
And then I'll fight thee without dread or fear.

[*They fight,* and Prince of Paradine *is slain.*

St. George. Now Prince of Paradine is dead,
And all his joys entirely fled;
Take him, and give him to the flies,
And never more come near mine eyes.

Enter King of Egypt

King. I am the King of Egypt, as plainly doth appear;
I'm come to seek my son, my son and only heir.
    St. George. He is slain.
    King. Who did him slay, who did him kill,
And on the ground his precious blood did spill?
    St. George. I did him slay, I did him kill,
And on the ground his precious blood did spill!
Please you, my liege, my honour to maintain,
Had you been there, you might have fared the same.

227

King. Cursed Christian! what is this thou'st done?
Thou hast ruined me, and slain my only son.
   St. George. He gave me a challenge, why should I it deny?
How high he was, but see how low he lies!
   King. O Hector! Hector! help me with speed,
For in my life I never stood more need!

Enter Hector

And stand not there with sword in hand,
But rise and fight at my command!
   Hector. Yes, yes, my liege, I will obey,
And by my sword I hope to win the day;
If that be he who doth stand there,
That slew my master's son and heir,
If he be sprung from royal blood,
I'll make it run like Noah's flood!
   St. George. Hold, Hector! do not be so hot,
For here thou knowest not who thou'st got,
For I can tame thee of thy pride,
And lay thine anger, too, aside;
Inch thee, and cut thee as small as flies,
And send thee over the sea to make mince-pies;
Mince-pies hot, and mince-pies cold;
I'll send thee to Black Sam before thou'rt three days old.
   Hector. How canst thou tame me of my pride,
And lay mine anger, too, aside?
Inch me, and cut me as small as flies,
Send me over the sea to make mince-pies?
Mince-pies hot, mince-pies cold;
How canst thou send me to Black Sam before I'm three days old?
Since my head is made of iron,
   My body's made of steel,
My hands and feet of knuckle-bone,
   I challenge thee to field.

[*They fight, and* Hector *is wounded.*

I am a valiant knight, and Hector is my name,
Many bloody battles have I fought, and always won the same;
But from St. George I received this bloody wound.

(*A trumpet sounds.*)

228

Hark, hark! I hear the silver trumpet sound,
Down yonder is the way (*pointing*).
Farewell, St. George, I can no longer stay.　　　　　[*Exit.*

Enter Fool

St. George. He comes from post, old Bold Ben.
Fool. Why, master, did ever I take you to be my friend?
St. George. Why, Jack, did ever I do thee any harm?
Fool. Thou proud saucy coxcomb, begone!
St. George. A coxcomb! I defy that name!
With a sword thou ought to be stabbed for the same.
　Fool. To be stabbed is the least I fear!
Appoint your time and place, I'll meet you there.
　St. George. I'll cross the water at the hour of five,
And meet you there, sir, if I be alive.　　　　　[*Exit.*

Enter Beelzebub

Here come I, Beelzebub,
And over my shoulders I carry my club;
And in my hand a dripping-pan,
And I think myself a jolly old man;
And if you don't believe what I say,
Enter in, Devil Doubt, and clear the way.

Enter Devil Doubt

Here come I, little Devil Doubt,
If you do not give me money, I'll sweep you all out:
Money I want, and money I crave;
If you do not give me money, I'll sweep you all to the grave.

NEW YEAR'S DAY

God bless the master of this house,
　　The mistress also,
And all the little children
　　That round the table go;
And all your kin and kinsmen,
　　That dwell both far and near;
I wish you a merry Christmas,
　　And a happy new year.

Wassel or *Wassal*.—A remnant of this part of our Saxon manners still exists at Yarmouth, and strange to say, in no other part of the Isle of Wight. On the first day of the new year the children collect together and sing wassel or wassal through the streets; the following is their song (see p. 241):

> Wassal, wassal, to our town!
> The cup is white and the ale is brown;
> The cup is made of the ashen tree,
> And so is the ale of the good barley;
>
> Little maid, little maid, turn the pin,
> Open the door and let us come in;
> God be here, God be there!
> I wish you all a happy new year!

TWELFTH-NIGHT

The following verses are said to be in some way or other connected with the amusements of this festival. They refer probably to the choosing the king and the queen on Twelfth-night:

> Lavender's blue, dilly dilly, lavender's green,
> When I am king, dilly dilly, you shall be queen.
> Who told you so, dilly dilly, who told you so?
> 'Twas mine own heart, dilly dilly, that told me so.
>
> Call up your men, dilly dilly, set them to work,
> Some with a rake, dilly dilly, some with a fork;
> Some to make hay, dilly dilly, some to thresh corn,
> Whilst you and I, dilly dilly, keep ourselves warm.
>
> If you should die, dilly dilly, as it may hap,
> You shall be buried, dilly dilly, under the tap.
> Who told you so, dilly dilly, pray tell me why?
> That you might drink, dilly dilly, when you are dry.

Another version may be given for the sake of adding the traditional tune to which it was sung:

Lav - en - der blue, fid - dle, fad - dle Lav - en - der green.

When I am king, fid - dle fad - dle, You shall be queen.

Call up your men, fid - dle fad - dle; Set them to work—

Some with a rake, fid - dle fad - dle— Some with a fork—

Some to make hay, fid - dle fad - dle— Some to the farm

Whilst you and I, fid - dle fad - dle Keep our - selves warm.

CATHERNING

Catherine and Clement, be here, be here,
Some of your apples, and some of your beer:
Some for Peter, and some for Paul,
And some for Him that made us all:
Clement was a good man,
For his sake give us some,
Not of the worst, but some of the best,
And God will send your soul to rest.

These lines are sung by the children of Worcestershire on St.
Catherine's day, when they go round to the farmhouses collecting
apples and beer for a festival. This is no doubt the relic of a Popish
custom; and the Dean of Worcester informs me that the Chapter

have a practice of preparing a rich bowl of wine and spices, called the "Cathern bowl", for the inhabitants of the College Precincts upon that day.

VALENTINE'S DAY

In the western counties, the children, decked with the wreaths and true-lovers' knots presented to them, gaily adorn one of their number as their chief, and march from house to house, singing—

> Good morrow to you, Valentine!
> Curl your locks as I do mine;
> Two before and three behind;
> Good morrow to you, Valentine!

They commence in many places as early as six o'clock in the morning, and intermingle the cry, "To-morrow is come!" Afterwards they make merry with their collections. At Islip, co. Oxon, I have heard the children sing the following when collecting pence on this day:

> Good morrow, Valentine!
> I be thine and thou be'st mine,
> So please give me a Valentine!

And likewise the following:

> Good morrow, Valentine!
> God bless you ever!
> If you'll be true to me,
> I'll be the like to thee.
> Old England for ever!

Schoolboys have a very uncomplimentary way of presenting each other with these poetical memorials:

> Peep, fool, peep,
> What do you think to see?
> Every one has a valentine
> And here's one for thee!

Far different from this is a stanza which is a great favourite with young girls on this day, offered indiscriminately, and of course quite innocently, to most of their acquaintances:

> The rose is red,
>   The violet's blue;
> Pinks are sweet,
>   And so are you!

The mission of valentines is one of the very few old customs not on the wane; and the streets of our metropolis practically bear evidence of this fact in the distribution of love-messages on our stalls and shop-windows, varying in price from a sovereign to one halfpenny. Our readers, no doubt, will ask for its origin, and there we are at fault to begin with. The events of St. Valentine's life furnish no clue whatever to the mystery, although Wheatley, in his "Illustration of the Common Prayer", absurdly disposes of the question in this way: "St. Valentine was a man of most admirable parts, and so famous for his love and charity, that the custom of choosing valentines upon his festival, which is still practised, took its rise from thence." We see no explanation here in any way satisfactory, and must be contented with the hope that some of our antiquaries may hit on something more to the purpose.

Valentine's day has long been popularly believed to be the day on which birds pair. Shakespeare alludes to this belief:

> Good morrow, friends: St. Valentine is past;
> Begin these wood-birds but to couple now?

It was anciently the custom to draw lots on this day. The names of an equal number of each sex were put into a box, in separate partitions, out of which every one present drew a name, called the Valentine, which was regarded as a good omen of their future marriage. It would appear, from a curious passage quoted in my "Dictionary of Archaisms", that any lover was hence termed a valentine; not necessarily an affianced lover, as suggested in Hampson's "Calendarium", vol i. p. 163. Lydgate, the poet of Bury, in the fifteenth century, thus mentions this practice:

> Saint Valentine, of custom year by year
> Men have an usance in this region
> To look and search Cupid's calendere,

And choose their choice by great affection:
Such as be prick'd with Cupid's motion
Taking their choice as their lot doth fall:
But I love one which excelleth all.

Gay alludes to another popular notion referring to the same day:

Last Valentine, the day when birds of kind
Their paramours with mutual chirpings find,
I early rose, just at the break of day,
Before the sun had chas'd the stars away;
Afield I went, amid the burning dew,
To milk my kine, for so should housewives do.
Thee first I spied; and the first swain we see,
In spite of fortune shall our true love be.

The divinations practised on St. Valentine's day is a curious subject. Herrick mentions one by rose-buds:

She must no more a-maying;
Or by rose-buds divine
Who'll be her valentine.

Perhaps the poet may here allude to a practice similar to the following, quoted by Brand: "Last Friday was Valentine day; and the night before I got five bay-leaves, and pinned four of them to the four corners of my pillow, and the fifth to the middle; and then, if I dreamt of my sweetheart, Betty said we should be married before the year was out. *But to make it more sure* I boiled an egg hard, and took out the yolk, and filled it with salt; and when I went to bed, ate it shell and all, without speaking or drinking after it. We also wrote our lovers' names upon bits of paper, rolled them up in clay, and put them into water; and the first that rose up was to be our valentine. Would you think it? Mr. Blossom was my man. I lay abed, and shut my eyes all the morning, till he came to our house, for I would not have seen another man before him for all the world." According to Mother Bunch, the following lines should be said by the girl on retiring to rest the previous night:

Sweet guardian angels, let me have
What I most earnestly do crave,
A valentine endow'd with love,
That will both kind and constant prove.

We believe the old custom of drawing lots on this eventful day is obsolete, and has given place to the favourite practice of sending pictures, with poetical legends, to objects of love or ridicule. The lower classes, however, seldom treat the matter with levity, and many are the offers of marriage thus made. The clerks at the post-offices are to be pitied, the immense increase of letters beyond the usual average adding very inconveniently to their labours.

"This iz Volantine day, mind, an be wot ah can see theal be a good deal a hanksiaty a mind sturrin amang't owd maids an't batchillors; luv sickness al be war than ivver wor nawn, espeshly amang them ats gettin raither owdish like; but all al end weel, so doant be daan abaght it. Ah recaleckt, when ah wor a yung man, ah went tut poast-office an bowt hauf a peck a volantines for tuppance, an when ah look't em ovver, thear wor wun dereckted for mesen, an this wor wot thear wor it inside:

> Paper's scarce, and luv iz dear,
> So av sent ye a bit a my pig-ear;
> And if t'same bit case we yo, my dear,
> Pray send me a bit a yor pig-ear.

Ha, ah wor mad, yo mind, ah nivver look't at a yung womman for two days at after for't; but it wor becos ah hedant a chonce."— Yorkshire Dial.

YOULING

In Rogation week there is or was an old custom in the country about Keston and Wickham, in Kent. A number of young men meet together for the purpose, and, with a most hideous noise, run into the orchards, and, encircling each tree, pronounce these words:

> Stand fast, root; bear well, top;
> God send us a youling sop!
> E'ry twig, apple big;
> E'ry bough, apple enow.
> Hats full, caps full,
> Full quarter sacks full.

For this incantation the confused rabble expect a gratuity in money, or drink, which is no less welcome; but if they are disappointed in both, they, with great solemnity, anathematize the owners and trees with altogether as insignificant a curse.

"It seems highly probable," says Hasted, in his "History of Kent", "that this custom has arisen from the ancient one of per-ambulation among the heathens, when they made their prayers to the gods, for the use and blessing of the fruits coming up, with thanksgiving for those of the preceding year; and as the heathens supplicated Eolus, the god of the winds, for his favourable blasts, so in this custom they still retain his name, with a very small variation, the ceremony being called *yeuling*; and the word is often used in their invocations."

BOY'S BAILIFF

An old custom, formerly in vogue at Wenlock, in Shropshire, thus described by Mr. Collins: "I am old enough to remember an old custom, and the last time it took place was about sixty years ago; it was called the 'boy's bailiff', and was held in the Easter week, Holy Thursday, or in Whitsun week, and I have no doubt was for the purpose of going a bannering the extensive boundaries of this franchise, which consists of eighteen parishes. It consisted of a man, who wore a hair-cloth gown and was called the bailiff, a recorder, justices, town-clerk, sheriff, treasurer, crier, and other municipal officers. They were a large retinue of men and boys mounted on horseback, begirt with wooden swords, which they carried on their right sides, so that they must draw the swords out of the scabbards with their left hands. They, when I knew them, did not go the boundary, but used to call at the gentlemen's houses in the franchise, where they were regaled with meat, drink, and money; and before the conclusion they assembled at the pillory at the guildhall, where the town-clerk read some sort of a rigmarole which they called their charter, and I remember one part was—

We go from Bickbury and Badger to Stoke on the Clee,
To Monkhopton, Round Acton, and so return we.

Bickbury, Badger, and Stoke on the Clee, were and are the two extreme points of the franchise, north and south; Monkhopton and Round Acton are two other parishes on the return from Stoke

St. Millborough, otherwise Stoke on the Clee (or perhaps Milburga, the tutelar saint of the Abbey of Wenlock), to Much Wenlock. This custom I conceive to have originated in going a bannering, unless it should have been got up as a mockery to the magistracy of the franchise; but I rather think the former."

PACE-EGGING

It is a custom in some parts of England for boys to go round the village on Easter eve begging for eggs or money, and a sort of dramatic song is sometimes used on the occasion. The following copy was taken down from recitation some years ago in the neighbourhood of York; but in another version we find Lords Nelson and Collingwood introduced, by a practice of adaptation to passing events which is fortunately not extensively followed in such matters. A boy, representing a captain, enters and sings—

> Here's two or three jolly boys all o' one mind,
> We've come a pace-egging, and hope you'll be kind;
> I hope you'll be kind with your eggs and your beer,
> And we'll come no more pace-egging until the next year.

Then old Toss-pot enters, and the captain, pointing him out, says—

> The first that comes in is old Toss-pot, you see,
> A valiant old blade for his age and degree;
> He is a brave fellow on hill or in dale,
> And all he delights in is a–drinking of ale.

Toss-pot then pretends to take a long draught from a huge quart-pot, and, reeling about, tries to create laughter by tumbling over as many boys as he can. A miser next enters, who is generally a boy dressed up as an old woman in tattered rags, with his face blackened. He is thus introduced by the captain:

> An old miser's the next that comes in with her bags,
> And to save up her money wears nothing but rags.

Chorus. Whatever you give us we claim for our right,
> Then bow with our heads, and wish you good night.

237

This is repeated twice, and the performance concludes by the whole company shouting at the top of their voice—

> Now, ye ladies and gentlemen, who sit by the fire,
> Put your hands in your pockets, 'tis all we desire;
> Put your hands in your pockets, and lug out your purse,
> We shall be the better, you'll be none the worse!

"Pase-day, Easter-day, Pase-eggs, Easter-eggs. Corrupt. from Pasch. They have a proverbial rhyme in those parts for the Sundaies in Lent:

> Tid, Mid, Misera,
> Carl, Paum, good Pase-day."
>
> Kennett, MS. Lansd. 1033.

COLLOP MONDAY

> Collop Monday,
> Pancake Tuesday,
> Ash Wednesday,
> Bludee Thursday,
> Friday's lang, but will be dune,
> And hey for Saturday afternune!

Verses for Shrove-tide, Collop-Monday being a north-country name for Shrove-Monday, because eggs and collops compose a standard dish for that day. At Islip, in Oxfordshire, the children, on Shrove-Tuesday, go round to the various houses, to collect pence, saying:

> Pit-a-pat, the pan is hot,
> We are come a-shroving;
> A little bit of bread and cheese
> Is better than nothing.
> The pan is hot, the pan is cold;
> Is the fat in the pan nine days old?

"*Collap Munday.*—This time reminds me on a bit ov a consarn at happand abaght two year sin, to a chap at thay call Jeremiah Fudgemutton. This Jerry, yo mun naw, went ta see a yung womman, a sweetheart a hiz, an when he put hiz arms raand her neck ta gie her a cus, it happand shood been hevin sum fried bacon to her dinner, an fagettan ta wipe t' grease off on her magth at after. Thear hiz faice slip't off on her chin-end, an slap went hiz head reight throot winda, an cut tip ov hiz noaze off."—Yorshire Dial.

ISLE OF WIGHT SHROVERS

Until within about the last fifty years, it had been the custom in the Isle of Wight from time immemorial at all the farms and some other charitable houses to distribute cakes on Shrove-Tuesday, called Shrove-cakes, to the poor children of the parish or neighbourhood, who assembled early in the morning at the different villages, hamlets, and cottages, in parties of from two to thirty or more, for the purpose of what was denominated "Going Shroving", and the children bore the name of *Shrovers*. At every house they visited they had a nice Shrove-cake each given them. In those days the winters were much more inclement and of longer duration than at the present time, and it often happened that, in addition to a severe frost, the ground was covered several inches high with snow, yet however cold or intense the weather, it did not prevent these little ones from what they called in the provincial dialect *Gwine a Shrovun*, and they jogged merrily along hand in hand from one house to another to obtain their cakes; but, before receiving them, it was expected and deemed necessary that they should all sing together a song suitable to the occasion; those who *sang the loudest* were considered the *best Shrovers*, and sometimes had an extra cake bestowed on them; consequently, there was no want of noise (whatever there might have been of harmony) to endeavour to get another Shroving gift. There were many different versions of the song, according to the parishes they lived in. The one generally sang by the children of the East Medina was as follows:

A Shrovun, a Shrovun,
I be cum a Shrovun,
A piece a bread, a piece a cheese,
A bit a your fat beyacun,
Or a dish of doughnuts,
Aal of your own meyacun!

A Shrovun, a Shrovun,
I be cum a Shrovun,
Nice meeat in a pie,
My mouth is verrey dry!
I wish a wuz zoo well a-wet,
I'd zing the louder for a nut!*

Chorus. A Shrovun, a Shrovun,
We be cum a Shrovun!

The song of the children of the West Medina was different:

A Shrovun, a Shrovun,
I be cum a Shrovun,
Linen stuff es good enuff,
Vor we that cums a Shrovun.
Vine veathers in a pie,
My mouth is verrey dry.
I wish a wuz zoo well a-wet,
Then I'd zing louder vor a nut!

Dame,† dame, a igg, a igg,‡
Or a piece a beyacun.
Dro awaay§ the porridge pot,
Or crock to bwile the peeazun.
Vine veathers in a pie,
My mouth is verrey dry.
I wish a wuz zoo well a-wet,
Then I'd zing louder vor a nut!

Chorus. A Shrovun, a Shrovun,
We be cum a Shrovun!

If the song was not given sufficiently loud, they were desired to sing

---

* Composed of flour and lard, with plums in the middle, and made into round substances about the size of a cricket-ball. They were called *nuts* or *dough-nuts*, and quite peculiar to the Isle of Wight.
† Dame. The mistress of the house, if past the middle age, was called Dame, *i.e.*, Madame.
‡ An egg, an egg.
§ Throw away.

it again. In that case it very rarely required a second repetition. When the Shrovers were more numerous than was anticipated, it not infrequently happened that, before the time of the arrival of the latter parties, the Shrove-cakes had been expended; then dough-nuts, pancakes, bread and cheese, or bread and bacon, were given, or halfpence were substituted; but in *no instance* whatever were they sent from the door empty-handed. It is much to be regretted that this charitable custom should have become almost extinct; there being very few houses at the present time where they dis-tribute shrove-cakes.

"There was another very ancient custom somewhat similar to the Shroving, which has also nearly, if not quite, disappeared; probably it began to decay within the last half-century: this was a gift of cakes and ale to children on *New Year's Day*, who, like the Shrovers, went from house to house singing for them; but, if we may judge from the song, those children were for the most part from the towns and larger villages, as the song begins, '*A sale, a sale in our town*'; there is no doubt but it was written for the occasion some centuries since, when 'a sale' was not a thing of such common occurrence as now, and when there was one, it was often held in an open field in or near the town." So writes my kind and valued correspondent, Captain Henry Smith; but *town* is, I think, merely a provincialism for *village*. It is so, at least, in the North of England. As for the phrase *a seyal*, it seems to be a corruption of *wassail*, the original sense having been lost. The following was the song:

> A seyal, a seyal in our town,
> The cup es white and the eal es brown;
> The cup es meyad from the ashen tree,
> And the eal es brew'd vrom the good barlie.

> *Chorus.* Cake and eal, cake and eal,
> A piece of cake and a cup of eal;
> We zing merrily one and aal
> For a piece of cake and a cup of eal.

> Little maid, little maid, troll the pin,*

* That is, turn the pin inside the door in order to raise the latch. In the old method of latching doors, there was a pin inside which was turned round to raise the latch. An old Isle of Wight song says,

Lift up the latch and we'll aal vall in;†
Ghee us a cake and zum eal that es brown,
And we dont keer a vig vor the seyal in the town.

Chorus. W'ill zing merrily one and aal
Vor a cake and a cup of eal;
God be there and God be here,
We wish you aal a happy New Year!

The above was the original song, but as the custom began to fall off, the chorus or some other part was often omitted.

EASTER GLOVES

Love, to thee I send these gloves,
If you love me,
Leave out the G,
And make a pair of loves!

It appears from Hall's Satires, 1598, that it was customary to make presents of gloves at Easter. In "Much Ado about Nothing", the Count sends Hero a pair of perfumed gloves, and they seem to have been a common present between lovers. In Devonshire, the young women thus address the first young man they happen to meet on St. Valentine's day—

Good morrow, Valentine, I go to-day,
To wear for you what you must pay—
A pair of gloves next Easter-day.

In Oxfordshire I have heard the following lines, intended, I believe, for the same festival:

The rose is red, the violet's blue,
The gilly-flower sweet, and so are you;
These are the words you bade me say
For a pair of new gloves on Easter-day.

Then John he arose,
And to the door goes,
And he trolled, and he trolled at the pin.
The lass she took the hint,
And to the door she went,
And she let her true love in.

† "Aal vall in", stand in rank to receive in turn the cake and ale.

LENT CROCKING

Parties of young people, during Lent, go to the most noted farm-houses, and sing, in order to obtain a *crock* or cake, an old song beginning—

> I see by the latch
> There is something to catch;
> I see by the string
> The good dame's within;
> Give a cake, for I've none;
> At the door goes a stone.
> Come give, and I'm gone.

"If invited in," says Mrs. Bray, "a cake, a cup of cider, and a health followed. If not invited in, the sport consisted in battering the house door with stones, because not open to hospitality. Then the assailant would run away, be followed and caught, and brought back again as a prisoner, and had to undergo the punishment of roasting the shoe. This consisted in an old shoe being hung up before the fire, which the culprit was obliged to keep in a constant whirl, roasting himself as well as the shoe, till some damsel took compassion on him, and let him go; in this case he was to treat her with a little present at the next fair."

CARE SUNDAY

> Care Sunday, care away,
> Palm Sunday and Easter-day.

Care Sunday is the Sabbath next before Palm Sunday, and the second before Easter. Etymologists differ respecting the origin of the term. It is also called Carling Sunday, and hence the Nottinghamshire couplet:

> Tid, Mid, Misera,
> Carling, Palm, Paste-egg day.

APRIL-FOOL DAY

The custom of making fools on the 1st of April is one of the few old English merriments still in general vogue. We used to say on the occasion of having entrapped anyone—

> Fool, fool, April fool,
> You learn nought by going to school!

The legitimate period only extends to noon, and if anyone makes an
April-fool after that hour, the boy on whom the attempt is made
retorts with the distich—

> April-fool time's past and gone:
> You're the fool, and I'm none!

MAY DAY

> Rise up, fair maidens, fie, for shame,
> For I've been four lang miles from hame;
> I've been gathering my garlands gay.
> Rise up, fair maids, and take in your May!

This old Newcastle May-day song is given by Brockett, ii. 32. At
Islip, near Oxford, the children go round the village on this day
with garlands of flowers, singing—

> Good morning, missus and measter,
>   I wish you a happy day;
> Please to smell my garland,
>   'Cause it is the first of May.

HARVEST HOME

> Here's a health unto our maister,
> The founder of the feast,
> And I hope to God wi' all my heart
>   His soul in heaven mid rest.
>
> That everything mid prosper
>   That ever he tiak in hand,
> Vor we be all his sarvants,
>   And all at his command.

These verses were sometimes said in proposing the health of the
farmer at a harvest-home supper. Another version of them is given

in Hone's "Table Book", ii. 334. When they have had a fortunate harvest, and the produce has been carried home without an accident, the following lines are sung at the harvest-home:

Harvest home, harvest home,
Ne'er a load's been overthrown.

THE BARLEY MOW

Here's a health to the barley mow,
  Here's a health to the man,
  Who very well can
Both harrow, and plough, and sow.

When it is well sown,
  See it is well mown,
Both raked and gravell'd clean,
And a barn to lay it in:

Here's a health to the man,
  Who very well can
Both thresh and fan it clean.

ALL-SOULS' DAY

"November 2nd is All Souls, a day instituted by the Church of Rome in commemoration of all the faithful departed this life, that by the prayers and suffrages of the living they may be discharged of their purging pain, and at last obtain life everlasting. To this purpose the day is kept holy till noon. Hence proceeds the custom of Soul-mass cakes, which are a kind of oat-cakes that some of the richer sort of persons in Lancashire and Herefordshire (among the Papists there) use still to give the poor on this day; and they, in retribution of their charity, hold themselves obliged to say this old couplet:

'God have your saul,
Beens and all'."

—"Festa Anglo-Romana", 1678, p. 109.

FIFTH OF NOVEMBER

The fifth of November,
Since I can remember,
   Gunpowder treason and plot:
This was the day the plot was contriv'd,
To blow up the King and Parliament alive;
But God's mercy did prevent
To save our King and his Parliament.
   A stick and a stake
   For King James's sake!
If you won't give me one,
   I'll take two,
The better for me,
   And the worse for you!

This is the Oxfordshire song chanted by the boys when collecting sticks for the bonfire, and it is considered quite lawful to appropriate any old wood they can lay their hands on after the recitation of these lines. If it happen that a crusty chuff prevents them, the threatening finale is too often fulfilled. The operation is called *going a progging*, but whether this is a mere corruption of *prigging*, or whether *progging* means collecting sticks (*brog*, Scot. Bor.), I am unable to decide. In some places they shout, previously to the burning of the effigy of Guy Fawkes—

A penn'orth of bread to feed the Pope,
   A penn'orth of cheese to choke him;
A pint of beer to wash it down,
   And a good old faggot to burn him.

The metropolis and its neighbourhood are still annually visited by subdued vestiges of the old customs of the bonfire-day. Numerous parties of boys parade the streets with effigies of Guy Fawkes, but pence, not anti-popery, is the object of the exhibition, and the evening fires have generally been exchanged for the mischievous practice of annoying passengers with squibs and crackers. The spirit and necessity of the display have expired, and the lover of old customs had better now be contented to hear of it in history.

BARBERS' FORFEITS

————————laws for all faults,
But faults so countenanced, that the strong statutes
Stand like *the forfeits in a barber's shop*,
As much in mock as mark.

Steevens and Henley, in their notes on Shakespeare, bear testimony to the fact that barbers were accustomed to expose in their shops a list of forfeits for misbehaviour, which were "as much in mock as mark", because the barber had no authority of himself to enforce them, and they were in some respects of a ludicrous nature. "Barbers' forfeits," says Forby, in his "Vocabulary of East Anglia", p. 119, "exist to this day in some, perhaps in many, village shops. They are penalties for handling the razors, &c., offences very likely to be committed by lounging clowns waiting for their turn to be scraped on a Saturday night or Sunday morning. They are still, as of old, 'more in mock than mark'. Certainly more mischief might be done two hundred years ago, when the barber was also a surgeon."

Dr. Kenrick* was the first to publish a copy of *barbers' forfeits*, and, as I do not observe it in any recent edition of Shakespeare, I here present the reader with the following homely verses obtained by the Doctor in Yorkshire:

Rules for seemly Behaviour

First come, first serve—then come not late;
And when arrived, keep your state;
For he who from these rules shall swerve,
Must pay the *forfeits*—so observe.

Who enters here with boots and spurs,
Must keep his nook, for if he stirs,
And give with armed heel a kick,
A pint he pays for ev'ry prick.

Who rudely takes another's turn,
A forfeit mug may manners learn.

* Review of Johnson's Shakespeare, 1765, p. 42.

Who reverentless shall swear or curse,
Must lug seven farthings from his purse.

Who checks the barber in his tale,
Must pay for each a pot of ale.

Who will or can not miss his hat
While trimming, pays a pint for that;
And he who can or will not pay,
Shall hence be sent half-trimm'd away.
For will he nill he, if in fault
He forfeit must in meal or malt.
But mark, who is alreads in drink,
The cannikin must never clink!

It is not improbable that these lines had been partly modernized from an older original before they reached Dr. Kenrick, but Steevens was certainly too precipitate in pronouncing them to be forgeries. Their authenticity is placed beyond a doubt by the testimony of my late friend, Major Moor, who, in his "Suffolk Words", p. 133, informs us that he had seen a version of these rules at the tonsor's, of Alderton, near the sea.

COCKLE-BREAD

My granny is sick, and now is dead,*
And we'll go mould some cockle-bread;
Up with my heels and down with my head,
And this is the way to mould cockle-bread.

A very old practice of young women, moving as if they were knead-ing dough, and repeating the above lines, which are sometimes varied thus:

Cockeldy bread, mistley cake,
When you do that for our sake.

---

* Another version says, "and I wish she was dead, that I may go mould", &c., which, if correct, may be supposed to mean, "My granny is ill, and I wish she was dead, that I may use a charm for obtaining a husband".

The entire explanation of this, which is not worth giving here, may be seen in Thoms's "Anecdotes and Traditions", p. 95. An allusion to cockle-bread occurs as early as 1595, in Peele's singular play of the "Old Wives' Tale".

A DRINKING CUSTOM

A pie sat on a pear-tree,
A pie sat on a pear-tree,
A pie sat on a pear-tree,
Heigh ho! heigh ho! heigh ho!

These lines are sung by a person at the table after dinner. His next neighbour then sings "Once so merrily hopped she", during which the first singer is obliged to drink a bumper; and should he be unable to empty his glass before the last line is sung, he must begin again till he succeeds. The next line is "Twice so merrily hopped she", sung by the next person under a similar arrangement, and so on; beginning again after "Thrice so merrily hopped she, heigh ho! heigh ho! heigh ho!" till the ceremony has been repeated around the table. It is to be hoped so absurd a practice is not now in fashion.

When a boy finds anything, and another sees him stoop for it, if the latter cries *halves* before he has picked it up, he is, by school-boy law, entitled to half of it. This right may, however, be negatived, if the finder cries out first—

Ricket, racket, find it, tack it,
And never give it to the aunder.

Or, sometimes the following:

No halfers,
Findee, keepee;
Lossee, seekee.

Boys leaving the schoolroom are accustomed to shout—

Those that go my way, butter and eggs,
Those that go your way, chop off their legs.

A sort of persuasive inducement, I suppose, for them to follow the speaker for the sake of forming a party for a game.

ELEVEN

Nursery Songs

The earliest and simplest form in which the nursery song appears is the lullaby, which may be defined a gentle song used for the purpose of inducing sleep. The term was generally, though not exclusively, confined to nurses:

> Philomel, with melody
> Sing in our sweet lullaby;
> Lulla, lulla, lullaby;
> Lulla, lulla, lullaby.

The etymology is to be sought for in the word *lull*, to sing gently, which Douce thinks is connected with λαλεω or λαλλη. One of the earliest nursery lullabies that have descended to our day occurs in the play of "Philotimus", 1583:

> Trylle the ball againe, my Jacke,
>   And be contente to make some play,
> And I will lull thee on my lappe,
> With hey be bird now say not nay.

Another is introduced in the comedy of "Patient Grissel", printed in the year 1603:

Hush, hush, hush, hush!
And I dance mine own child,
And I dance mine own child,
Hush, hush, hush, hush!

BILLY, MY SON

The following lines are very common in the English nursery, and resemble the popular German ditty of Grandmother Addercook, inserted in the "Knaben Wunderhorn", and translated by Dr. Jamieson in the "Illustrations of Northern Antiquities". The ballad of the "Crowden Doo", Chambers, p. 205, bears, however, a far greater similarity to the German song. Compare, also, the ballad of "Willie Doo", in Buchan's "Ancient Songs", ii. 179.

Where have you been to-day, Billy, my son?
Where have you been to-day, my only man?
I've been a wooing, mother, make my bed soon,
For I'm sick at heart, and fain would lay down.

What have you ate to-day, Billy, my son?
What have you ate to-day, my only man?
I've ate eel-pie, mother, make my bed soon,
For I'm sick at heart, and shall die before noon.

It is said that there is some kind of fairy legend connected with these lines, Billy having probably been visited by his mermaid mother. Nothing at all satisfactory has, however, yet been produced. It appears to bear a slight analogy to the old ballad, "Where have you been all the day, my boy Willie?" printed from a version obtained from Suffolk, in the "Nursery Rhymes of England", p. 177;* and on this account we may here insert a copy of the pretty

* Another version was obtained from Yorkshire:

Where have you been all the day,
My boy Billy?
Where have you been all the day,
My boy Billy?
I have been all the day
Courting of a lady gay;
Although she is a young thing,
And just come from her mammy!

Scottish ballad, intitled "Tammy's Courtship":

> Oh, where ha' ye been a' day,
> > My boy Tammy?
> Where ha' ye been a' day,
> > My boy Tammy?
> I've been by burn and flow'ry brae,
> Meadow green and mountain grey,
> Courting o' this young thing,
> > Just come frae her mammy.
>
> And where gat ye that young thing,
> > My boy Tammy?
> And where gat ye that young thing,
> > My boy Tammy?
> I gat her down in yonder how,
> Smiling on a broomy knowe,
> Herding ae wee lamb and ewe
> > For her poor mammy.
>
> What said ye to the bonny bairn,
> > My boy Tammy?
> What said ye to the bonny bairn,
> > My boy Tammy?
> I praised her een sae lovely blue,
> Her dimpled cheek and cherry mou';
> I preed it aft, as ye may trow—
> > She said she'd tell her mammy.

> Is she fit to be thy love,
> > My boy Billy?
> She is as fit to be my love
> As my hand is for my glove,
> Although she is, &c.
>
> Is she fit to be thy wife,
> > My boy Billy?
> She is as fit to be my wife,
> As my blade is for my knife;
> Although she is, &c.
>
> How old may she be,
> > My boy Billy?
> Twice six, twice seven,
> Twice twenty and eleven;
> Although she is, &c.

I held her to my beating breast,
   My young, my smiling lammy;
I held her to my beating breast,
   My young, my smiling lammy:
I hae a house, it cost me dear,
I've wealth o' plenishing and gear,
Ye'se get it a', war't ten times mair,
   Gin ye will leave your mammy:

The smile gaed aff her bonny face,
   I maunna leave my mammy;
The smile gaed aff her bonny face,
   I maunna leave my mammy:
She's gi'en me meat, she's gi'en me claise,
She's been my comfort a' my days;
My father's death brought mony waes—
   I canna leave my mammy.

We'll tak' her hame, and mak' her fain,
   My ain kind-hearted lammy;
We'll tak' her hame, and mak' her fain,
   My ain kind-hearted lammy:
We'll gie her meat, we'll gie her claise,
We'll be her comfort a' her days;
The wee thing gi'es her han', and says—
   There! gang and ask my mammy.

Has she been to the kirk wi' thee,
   My boy Tammy?
Has she been to the kirk wi' thee,
   My boy Tammy?
She's been to kirk wi' me,
And the tear was in her e'e;
But, oh! she's but a young thing,
   Just come frae her mammy!

The ballad of Lord Randal, printed by Sir Walter Scott, may after all furnish the true solution to the meaning of our nursery rhyme, and I am therefore induced to insert a version of it still popular in Scotland, in which the hero of the song is styled Laird Rowland:

254

Ah! where have you been, Lairde Rowlande, my son?
Ah! where have you been, &c.
> I've been in the wild-woods;
>> Mither, mak my bed soon,
> For I'm weary wi' hunting,
>> And faine would lie down.

Oh! you've been at your true love's, Lairde Rowlande, my son!
Oh! you've been at your true love's, &c.
> I've been at my true love's;
>> Mither, mak my bed soon,
> For I'm weary wi' hunting,
>> And faine would lie down.

What got you to dinner, Lairde Rowlande, my son?
What got you to dinner, &c.
> I got eels boil'd in brue;
>> Mither, mak my bed soon,
> For I'm weary wi' hunting,
>> And faine would lie down.

What's become of your Warden, Lairde Rowlande, my son?
What's become of your Warden, &c.
> He died in the muirlands;
>> Mither, mak my bed soon,
> For I'm weary wi' hunting,
>> And faine would lie down.

What's become of your stag-hounds, Lairde Rowlande, my son?
What's become of your stag-hounds, &c.
> They swelled and they died!
>> Mither, mak my bed soon,
> For I'm weary wi' hunting,
>> And faine would lie down.

The fable or plot of this seems to be, that Lord Rowlande, upon a visit at the castle of his mistress, has been poisoned by the drugged viands at the table of her father, who was averse to her marriage with the lord. Finding himself weary, and conscious that he is poisoned, he returns to his home, and wishes to retire to his chamber without raising in his mother any suspicions of the state of his body and mind. This may be gathered from his short and evasive answers, and the importunate entreaties with which he requests his mother to prepare his chamber.

In Swedish there are two distinct versions: one, the Child's Last Wishes, in "Geijer and Afzelius", iii. 13, beginning—

> Hvar har du varit så länge,
>   Dotter, liten kind?
> Jag har varit hos min Amma.
>   Kär styf-moder min!
> För aj aj! ondt hafver jag—jag!
>
> (Where hast thou been so long now,
>   My sweet wee little child?
> Sure with my nurse I've tarried,
>   My own step-mother mild!
> For oh! oh! sore pains have I—I!)

The second is in "Afzelius", ii. 90, under the same title, and beginning—

> Hvar har du va't så länge,
>   Lilla dotter kind?
> Jag har va't i Bänne,
> Hos broderen min!
>   Aj, aj, ondt hafver jag, jag!
>
> (Where hast thou been so long now,
>   Wee little daughter fine?
> In Bänne have I tarried,
>   With brother mine!
> Oh! oh! sore pains have I—I!)

Both are sung to exquisitely melancholy melodies.

Dr. Jamieson makes some very just observations on this ballad, and the importance of tracing this class of tales. "That any of the Scotch, English, and German copies of the same tale have been borrowed or translated from another seems very improbable: and it would now be in vain to attempt to ascertain what it originally was, or in what age it was produced. It has had the good fortune in every country to get possession of the nursery, a circumstance which, from the enthusiasm and curiosity of young imaginations, and the communicative volubility of little tongues, has insured its preservation. Indeed, many curious relics of past times are preserved in the games and rhymes found amongst children, which are on that account by no means beneath the notice of the curious traveller, who will be surprised to find after the lapse of so many ages, and so many changes of place, language, and manners, how little these differ among different nations of the same original stock, who have been so long divided and estranged from each other."

MY COCK LILY-COCK

An inferior version of the following, which was obtained from Essex, is printed in Mr. Chambers's "Popular Rhymes of Scotland", ed. 1847, p. 190. A Swedish version, or rather a variation, in "Lilja", p. 17, commences as follows: "I served a farmer for four years, and he paid me with a hen. 'Skrock, skrock!' said my hen. I served a farmer for four years, and he paid me with a cock. 'Kucklilo!' said my cock. 'Skrock, skrock!' said my hen, &c."

> I had a cock, and a cock loved me,
> And I fed my cock under a hollow tree;
>   My cock cried—cock-cock-coo—
> Everybody loves their cock, and I love my cock too!
>
> I had a hen, and a hen loved me,
> And I fed my hen under a hollow tree;
>   My hen went—chickle-chackle, chickle-chackle—
>   My cock cried—cock-cock-coo—
> Everybody loves their cock, and I love my cock too!
>
> I had a goose, and a goose loved me,
> And I fed my goose under a hollow tree;
>   My goose went—qua'k, qua'k—
>   My hen went—chickle-chackle, chickle-chackle—
>   My cock cried—cock-cock-coo—
> Everybody loves their cock, and I love my cock too!
>
> I had a duck, and a duck loved me,
> And I fed my duck under a hollow tree;

My duck went—quack, quack, quack—
My goose went—qua'k, qua'k—
My hen went—chickle-chackle, chickle-chackle—
    My cock cried—cock-cock-coo—
Everybody loves their cock, and I love my cock too!

I had a drake, and a drake loved me,
And I fed my drake under a hollow tree;
    My drake went—ca-qua, ca-qua, ca-qua—
    My duck went—quack, quack, quack—
    My goose went—qua'k, qua'k, qua'k—
    My hen went—chickle-chackle, chickle-chackle—
        My cock cried cock-cock-coo—
Everybody loves their cock, and I love my cock too!

I had a cat, and a cat loved me,
And I fed my cat under a hollow tree;
    My cat went—miow, miow, miow—
    My drake went—ca-qua, ca-qua, ca-qua—
    My duck went—quack, quack, quack—
    My goose went—qua'k, qua'k, qua'k—
    My hen went—chickle-chackle, chickle-chackle—
        My cock cried—cock-cock-coo—
Everybody loves their cock, and I love my cock too!

I had a dog, &c. My dog went—bow, wow, wow—
I had a cow, &c. My cow went—moo, moo, moo—
I had a sheep, &c. My sheep went—baa, baa, baa—
I had a donkey, &c. My donkey went—hi-haugh, hi-haugh—
I had a horse, &c. My horse went—whin-neigh-h-h-h-h—

    I had a pig, and a pig loved me,
    And I fed my pig under a hollow tree;
        And my pig went—hoogh, hoogh, hoogh—
        My horse went—whin-neigh-h-h-h-h—
        My donkey went—hi-haugh, hi-haugh—
        My sheep went—baa, baa, baa—
        My cow went—moo, moo, moo—
        My dog went—bow, bow, wow—
        My cat went—miow, miow, miow—

My drake went—ca-qua, ca-qua, ca-qua—
My duck went—quack, quack, quack—
My goose went—qua'k, qua'k, qua'k—
My hen went—chickle-chackle, chickle-chackle—
   My cock cried—cock-cock-coo—
Everybody loves their cock, and I love my cock too!

    And so the pig—grunted,
    The horse—neigh'd
    The donkey—bray'd
    The sheep—bleated,
    The cow—low'd,
    The dog—bark'd,
    The cat—mew'd.
    The drake—quackled,
    The duck—cackled,
    The goose—gobbled,
    The hen—chuckled,
    The cock—crow'd—
  And my cock cried—cock-cock-coo!
Everybody loves their cock, and I love my cock too!

JACK SPRAT

Fragments of this tale are common in the nursery, but I have only met with one copy of the following poem, which appears to be of some antiquity, although it is here printed from a modern chap-book:

    Jack Sprat could eat no fat,
      His wife could eat no lean,
    And so between them both,
      They licked the platter clean.
    Jack ate all the lean,
      Joan ate all the fat,
    The bone they picked clean,
      Then gave it to the cat.
    When Jack Sprat was young
      He dressed very smart,

He courted Joan Cole,
    And he gained her heart.
In his fine leather doublet
    And old greasy hat,
Oh, what a smart fellow
    Was little Jack Sprat!
Joan Cole had a hole
    In her petticoat,
Jack Sprat, to get a patch,
    Gave her a groat;
The groat bought a patch,
    Which stopped the hole,
"I thank you, Jack Sprat,"
    Says little Joan Cole.
Jack Sprat was the bridegroom,
    Joan Cole was the bride,
Jack said, from the church
    His Joan home should ride.
But no coach could take her
    The lane was so narrow,
Said Jack, then I'll take her
    Home in a wheelbarrow.
Jack Sprat was wheeling
    His wife by the ditch,
The barrow turned over,
    And in she did pitch.
Says Jack, she'll be drown'd,
    But Joan did reply,
I don't think I shall,
    For the ditch is quite dry.
Jack brought home his Joan,
    And she sat in a chair,
When in came his cat,
    That had got but one ear.
Says Joan, I'm come home, Puss,
    Pray, how do you do?
The cat wagg'd her tail,
    And said nothing but "mew".

Jack Sprat took his gun,
　And went to the brook,
He shot at the drake,
　But he killed the duck.
He brought it to Joan,
　Who a fire did make
To roast the fat duck,
　While Jack went for the drake.
The drake was swimming
　With his curly tail,
Jack Sprat came to shoot him,
　But happened to fail;
He let off his gun,
　But missing his mark,
The drake flew away
　Crying, "Quack, quack, quack."
Jack Sprat to live pretty,
　Now bought him a pig,
It was not very little,
　It was not very big;
It was not very lean,
　It was not very fat,
It will serve for a grunter
　For little Jack Sprat.
Then Joan went to market
　To buy her some fowls,
She bought a jackdaw
　And a couple of owls.
The owls they were white,
　The jackdaw was black,
They'll make a rare breed,
　Says little Joan Sprat.
Jack Sprat bought a cow,
　His Joan for to please,
For Joan she could make
　Both butter and cheese,
Or pancakes or puddings,
　Without any fat;

A notable housewife
  Was little Joan Sprat.
Joan Sprat went to brewing
  A barrel of ale,
She put in some hops
  That it might not turn stale;
But as for the malt,
  She forgot to put that;
This is brave sober liquor,
  Said little Jack Sprat.
Jack Sprat went to market,
  And bought him a mare,
She was lame of three legs,
  And as blind as she could stare;
Her ribs they were bare,
  For the mare had no fat,
She looks like a racer,
  Says little Jack Sprat.
Jack and Joan went abroad,
  Puss took care of the house,
She caught a large rat
  And a very small mouse:
She caught a small mouse,
  And a very large rat;
You're an excellent hunter,
  Says little Jack Sprat.
Now I have told you the story
  Of little Jack Sprat,
And little Joan Cole,
  And the poor one-ear'd cat.
Now Jack loved Joan,
  And good things he taught her,
Then she gave him a son,
  Then after a daughter.
Now Jack has got rich
  And has plenty of pelf;
If you know any more,
  You may tell it yourself.

DABBLING IN THE DEW

The following pretty ballad appears to be a humorous imitation of an Elizabethan eclogue-song. Its style guarantees its antiquity:

Oh, where are you going,
  My pretty maiden fair,
With your red rosy cheeks,
  And your coal-black hair?

I'm going a-milking,
  Kind sir, says she;
And it's dabbling in the dew,
  Where you'll find me.

May I go with you,
  My pretty maiden fair, &c.
Oh, you may go with me,
  Kind sir, says she, &c.

If I should chance to kiss you,
  My pretty maiden fair, &c.
The wind may take it off again,
  Kind sir, says she, &c.

If I should chance to lay you down,
  My pretty maiden fair, &c.
Then you must pick me up again,
  Kind sir, says she, &c.

If I should chance to run away,
  My pretty maiden fair, &c.
The De'el may then run away wi' you,
  Kind sir, says she, &c.

And what is your father,
  My pretty maiden fair, &c.
My father is a farmer,
  Kind sir, says she, &c.

263

And what is your mother,
   My pretty maiden fair, &c.
My mother is a dairy-maid,
   Kind sir, says she, &c.

And what is your sweetheart,
   My pretty maiden fair, &c.
William the carpenter,
   Kind sir, says she, &c.

———

There was an old couple, and they were poor,
      Fa la, fa la la lee!
They lived in a house that had but one door;
  Oh! what a poor couple were they.

The old man once he went far from his home,
      Fa la, fa la la lee!
The old woman afraid was to stay alone:
  Oh! what a weak woman was she.

The old man he came home at last,
      Fa la, fa la la lee!
And found the windows and door all fast.
  Oh! what is the matter? quoth he.

Oh! I have been sick since you have been gone.
      Fa la, fa la la lee!
If you'd been in the garden you'd heard me groan.
  Oh! I'm sorry for that, quoth he.

I have a request to make unto thee;
      Fa la, fa la la lee!
To pluck me an apple from yonder tree.
  Ay, that will I, marry, quoth he.

The old man tried to get up in the tree,
      Fa la, fa la la lee!
But the ladder it fell, and down tumbled he.
  That's cleverly done! said she.

HEY DIDDLE DIDDLE*

Hey diddle diddle,
The cat scraped the fiddle,
The cow jump'd over the moon;
The little dog bayed
To see such sports played,
And the dish ran away with the spoon.

Ἄδ' ἄδηλα, δῆλα δ ᾆδε,
Πῶς γαλῆ λύραν ἔτριβε,
Βοῖς δὲ μήνην ὑπερεπήδτ.
Κυνίδιον δ' ἔκλαγξεν, αὖ, αὖ,
Παιδιάν γ̓ δρῶν τοιάνδε,
Καὶ τορύνην
Ἔφυγε κάρδοπος λαβών.

The unmeaning "Hey diddle diddle" is a corruption of the very intelligible Ἄδ' ἄδηλα, δῆλα δ' ᾆδε, which is literally "Sing words not clear, and Sing words clear"; with which may be compared a Sibylline verse in Greek, Δῆλος ἄρ' οὐκ ἔτι δῆλος· ἄδηλα δὲ πάντα τὰ Δήλου.

TOMMY LINN

Tommy Linn is a Scotchman born,
His head is bald and his beard is shorn;
He has a cap made of a hare skin,
An alderman is Tommy Linn.

Tommy Linn has no boots to put on,
But two calves' skins, and the hair it was on.
They are open at the side and the water goes in:
Unwholesome boots, says Tommy Linn.

Tommy Linn no bridle had to put on,
But two mouses' tails that he put on;
Tommy Linn had no saddle to put on,
But two urchin skins, and them he put on.

* The above ingenious translation and remarks were communicated by Mr. George Burges.

Tommy Linn's daughter sat on the stair,
Oh, dear father, gin I be not fair?
The stairs they broke, and she fell in:
You're fair enough now, says Tommy Linn.

Tommy Linn had no watch to put on,
So he scooped out a turnip to make himself one;
He caught a cricket, and put it within;
It's my own ticker, says Tommy Linn.

Tommy Linn, his wife, and wife's mother,
They all fell into the fire together;
Oh, said the topmost, I've got a hot skin:
It's hotter below, says Tommy Linn.

An immense variety of songs and catches relating to Tommy Linn are known throughout the country. The air of "Thom of Lyn" is one of those mentioned in the "Complaynt of Scotland", 1549. See Chambers, p. 192, who gives a Scotch version of the above song. The song itself is quoted in Wager's play, "The longer thou livest the more foole thou art", written about the year 1560. Dr. Leyden conjectures that the hero is the same with Tamlene, who is introduced into a well-known fairy ballad published by Sir W. Scott.

THE BEGGARS OF RATCLIFFE FAIR

As I went to Ratcliffe Fair, there I met with a jolly beggáre,
Jolly beggáre, and his name was John, and his wife's name was
    Jumping Joan;
        So there was John and Jumping Joan,
        Merry companions every one.

As I went to Ratcliffe Fair, there I met with a jolly beggáre,
Jolly beggáre, and his name was Richard, and his wife's name was
    Mrs. Ap Richard;
        So there was Richard, and Mrs. Ap Richard,
        And there was John and Jumping Joan,
        Merry companions every one.

As I went to Ratcliffe Fair, there I met with a jolly beggáre,
Jolly beggáre, and his name was Robert, and his wife's name was
    Mrs. Ap Robert;
        So there was Robert and Mrs. Ap Robert,
        And there was Richard and Mrs. Ap Richard,
        And there was John and Jumping Joan,
        Merry companions every one.

As I went to Ratcliffe Fair, there I met with a jolly beggáre,
Jolly beggáre, and his name was Rice, and his wife's name was
    Mrs. Ap Rice;
        So there was Rice and Mrs. Ap Rice.
        And there was Richard and Mrs. Ap Richard,
        And there was Robert and Mrs. Ap Robert,
        And there was John and Jumping Joan,
        Merry companions every one.

As I went to Ratcliffe Fair, there I met with a jolly beggáre,
Jolly beggáre, and his name was Jones, and his wife's name was
    Mrs. Ap Jones;
        So there was Jones and Mrs. Ap Jones,
        And there was Rice and Mrs. Ap Rice,
        And there was Robert and Mrs. Ap Robert,
        And there was Richard and Mrs. Ap Richard,
        And there was John and Jumping Joan,
        Merry companions every one.

As I went to Ratcliffe Fair, there I met with a jolly beggáre,
Jolly beggáre, and his name was Lloyd, and his wife's name was
    Mrs. Ap Lloyd;
        So there was Lloyd and Mrs. Ap Lloyd,
        And there was Jones and Mrs. Ap Jones,
        And there was Rice and Mrs. Ap Rice,
        And there was Robert and Mrs. Ap Robert,
        And there was Richard and Mrs. Ap Richard,
        And there was John and Jumping Joan,
        Merry companions every one.

As I went to Ratcliffe Fair, there I met with a jolly beggáre,
Jolly beggáre, and his name was Owen, and his wife's name was
    Mrs. Ap Owen;

       So there was Owen and Mrs. Ap Owen,
       And there was Lloyd and Mrs. Ap Lloyd,
       And there was Jones and Mrs. Ap Jones,
       And there was Rice and Mrs. Ap Rice,
       And there was Robert and Mrs. Ap Robert,
       And there was Richard and Mrs. Ap Richard,
       And there was John and Jumping Joan,
       Merry companions every one.

As I went to Ratcliffe Fair, there I met with a jolly beggáre,
Jolly beggáre, and his name was Lewin, and his wife's name was
    Mrs. Ap Lewin;

       So there was Lewin and Mrs. Ap Lewin,
       And there was Owen and Mrs. Ap Owen,
       And there was Lloyd and Mrs. Ap Lloyd,
       And there was Jones and Mrs. Ap Jones,
       And there was Rice and Mrs. Ap Rice,
       And there was Robert and Mrs. Ap Robert,
       And there was Richard and Mrs. Ap Richard,
       And there was John and Jumping Joan,
       Merry companions every one.

As I went to Ratcliffe Fair, there I met with a jolly beggáre,
Jolly beggáre, and his name was Shenkyn, and his wife's name was
    Mrs. Ap Shenkyn;

       So there was Shenkyn, and Mrs. Ap Shenkyn,
       And there was Lewin and Mrs. Ap Lewin,
       And there was Owen and Mrs. Ap Owen,
       And there was Lloyd and Mrs. Ap Lloyd,
       And there was Jones and Mrs. Ap Jones,
       And there was Rice and Mrs. Ap Rice,
       And there was Robert and Mrs. Ap Robert,
       And there was Richard and Mrs. Ap Richard,
       And there was John and Jumping Joan,
       Merry companions every one.

As I went to Ratcliffe Fair, there I met with a jolly beggáre,
Jolly beggáre, and his name was Howell, and his wife's name was
    Mrs. Ap Howell;
        So there was Howell and Mrs. Ap Howell,
        And there was Shenkyn and Mrs. Ap Shenkyn,
        And there was Lewin and Mrs. Ap Lewin,
        And there was Owen and Mrs. Ap Owen,
        And there was Lloyd and Mrs. Ap Lloyd,
        And there was Jones and Mrs. Ap Jones,
        And there was Rice and Mrs. Ap Rice,
        And there was Robert and Mrs. Ap Robert,
        And there was Richard and Mrs. Ap Richard,
        And there was John and Jumping Joan,
        Merry companions every one.

This singular accumulative tale produces great amusement amongst children when rapidly repeated. Mr. Chambers, p. 197, has given a Scotch version, very different from the above, commencing—

        The first time that I gaed to Coudingham fair,
        I fell in with a jolly beggar;
        The beggar's name O it was Harry,
        And he had a wife, and they ca'd her Mary:
            O Mary and Harry, and Harry and Mary,
            And Janet and John,
            That's the beggars one by one;
            But now I will gie you them pair by pair,
            All the brave beggars of Coudingham fair.

Our collection of vernacular scraps, which, like the "brave beggars of Coudingham fair", have been gathered from the lanes and byeways, is now brought to a conclusion. They are, it must be confessed, but literary vagrants at the best; but they breathe of country freshness, and may impart some of their spirit to our languishing home-life. The cottage with its traditional literature is but a poor feature in the landscape that is loved by the poet. The legend or antique rhyme emanating from its door expresses a characteristic he would not willingly see perish. It may be that little of this now remains in

England, but the minutest indications should be carefully chronicled ere they disappear.

Many of the fragments in the preceding pages are, in fact, rather indications of what formerly existed than complete specimens of their class. It is beyond a doubt that, two centuries ago, our rural districts were rich in all kinds of popular and traditional literature, in legends and ancient rhymes. Unfortunately, the antiquaries of the old school considered such matters beneath their notice; and instead of conferring a very important benefit on literature by preserving them, occupied a great portion of their time in essays of very questionable utility. It thus happened that allusions in our old poets, intelligible enough in those days, became enigmas when the memory of these trifles disappeared. We should fall into a similar error did we neglect those which still remain, merely because their value is not always immediately apparent, or be alarmed at a suggestion that we are "suckling fools, and chronicling small beer".

Let us hope the reader may view these trifles with more indulgence, and enlist these sympathies with our own; for if literary value is insisted upon as the sole use of their publication, the critic may require an abler apologist. He may refuse to admit the importance of preserving a large collection for the sake of the few which may illustrate the works of our ancient authors. But we trust this opinion will not be general; that their natural simplicity will compensate in some respects for deficiency of literary elegance; and that the universal and absorbing prevalence of one pursuit has not put to flight all kindly memory of the recreations of a happier age:

The sports of childhood's roseate dawn
Have passed from our hearts like the dew-gems from morn:
We have parted with marbles—we own not a ball,
And are deaf to the hail of a "whoop and a call".
But there's an old game that we all keep up,
When we've drunk much deeper from life's mixed cup;
Youth may have vanished, and manhood come round,
Yet how busy we are on "Tom Tidler's ground
      Looking for gold and silver!"

Index of First Lines

Index of Subjects and Titles

MY VISIT TO THE DENTIST

Diana Bentley

Reading Consultant
University of Reading

Photographs by
Paul Seheult

Wayland

My Visit

My Visit to the Airport
My Visit to the Birthday Party
My Visit to the Dentist
My Visit to the Doctor
My Visit to the Hospital
My Visit to the Seaside
My Visit to the Supermarket
My Visit to the Swimming Baths
My Visit to the Zoo

First Published in 1989 by
Wayland (Publishers) Limited
61 Western Road, Hove
East Sussex, BN3 1JD, England

Editor: Sophie Davies

British Library Cataloguing in Publication Data
Bentley, Diana
     My visit to the dentist.
     1. English language, – Readers, – For
     children
     I. Title II. Seheult, Paul
     428.6

ISBN 1 85210 716 2

Typeset by: Lizzie George, Wayland
Printed and bound by Casterman S.A., Belgium

Contents

All words that appear in **bold** are explained in the glossary on page 22.

Hello, my name is Sebastian.

Here I am with my brother Ben.

This is a letter from the dentist. It says it is time for me to go for a **check-up**. Mum phones the dentist's surgery to make an **appointment**.

Today I am going to the dentist.

Mum takes me to visit the dentist. Ben comes too. Here we are at the door. My dentist's name is written on a shiny plate outside the door. I ring the bell.

This is the **receptionist**. She comes to let us in. Her badge says her name is Tracey. Tracey says hello. She remembers me from last time I came to the dentist. Mum tells her the time of my appointment.

We play with the toys in the waiting room.

Tracey checks my appointment. She tells us to wait in the waiting room. There are lots of toys in the waiting room. I draw on the blackboard, and Ben reads a book all about teeth.

This is the **dental nurse**. She says it is time
to see the dentist.

This is my dentist.

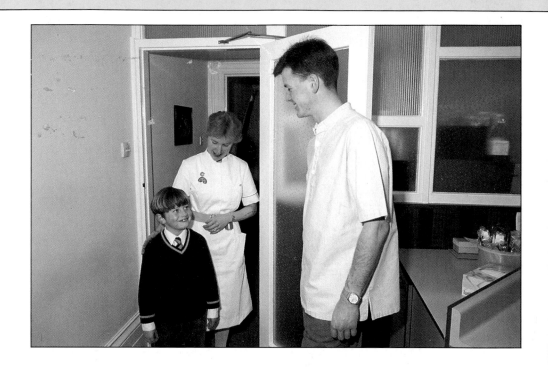

The nurse takes me in to see the dentist. My dentist is called Patrick Nayler. He lets me sit in this special chair. The dentist can make it go up and down, or tip backwards.
I like this chair. There is a lamp over the chair. The dentist switches it on.

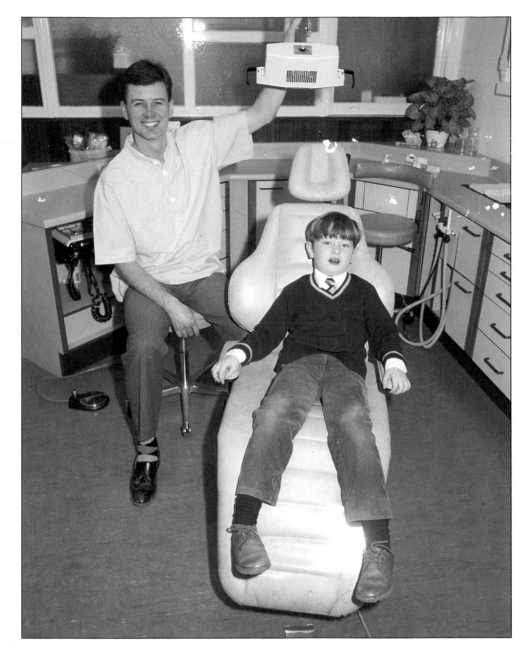

The dentist looks at my teeth with a special mirror.

The nurse gives me some plastic glasses. They stop anything from getting in my eyes. The dentist wears plastic gloves to keep his hands clean. He looks at my teeth with a mirror.

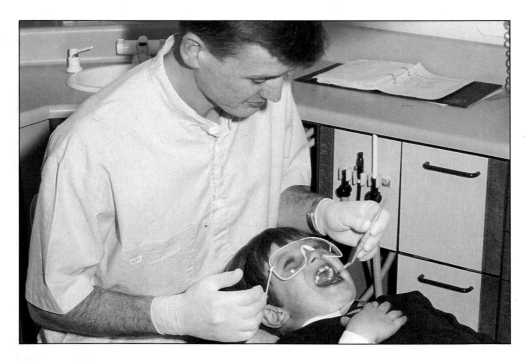

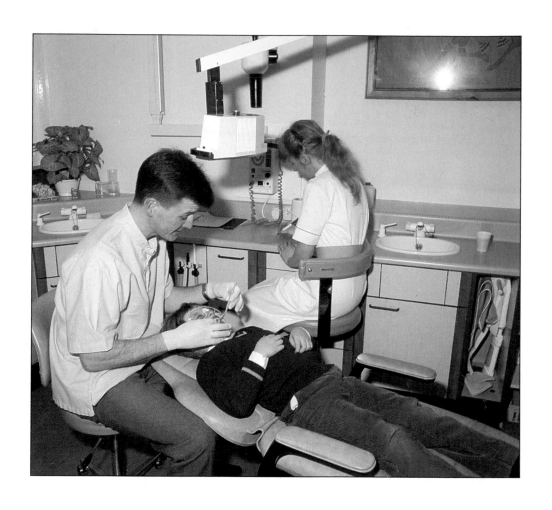

Each tooth has a number or a letter. The
dentist calls out the numbers to the nurse. The
nurse writes them down on a special chart.
She would also mark any that needed
attention, but this time they are all fine.

The dentist shows me how to clean my teeth.

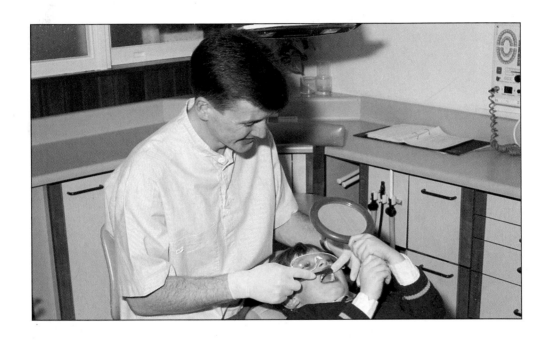

The dentist gives me a mirror, and shows me how to clean my teeth. He says that teeth have **plaque** on them. This is made from germs left over from food. Plaque is very bad for your teeth.

Plaque grows most of all near your gums, so you must brush really well here. Don't forget to brush the backs of your teeth too! Now the dentist cleans my teeth for me with a special tool.

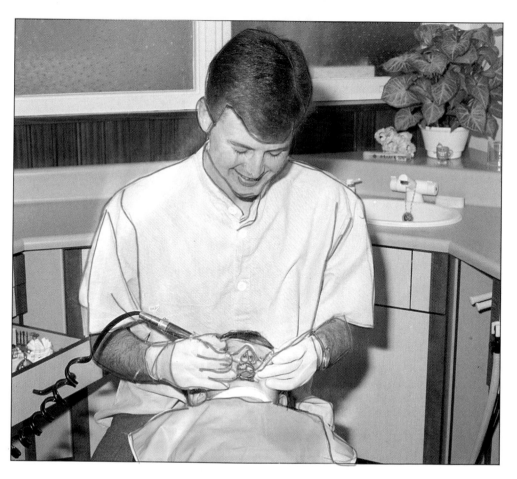

The nurse cleans the tools.

The nurse cleans all the tools the dentist has used. She scrubs them with water and a brush.

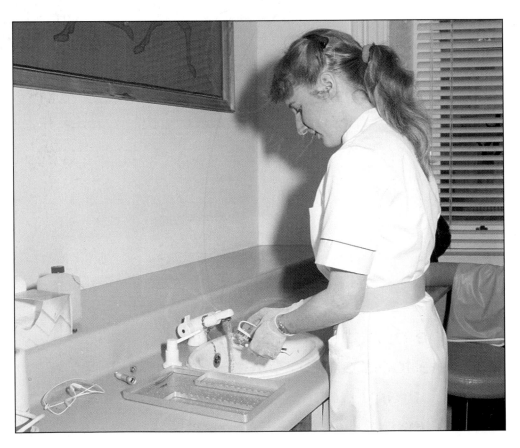

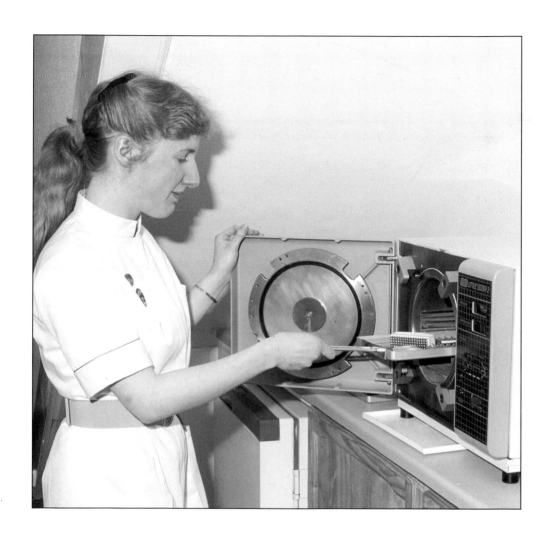

Then she puts them in a special machine.
Here the tools are sprayed with steam. This
cleans off any germs. Now the tools are ready
for the next patient.

The dentist gives me a toothbrush.

I wash my mouth out with pink mouthwash.

18

The dentist tells Mum how I must look after my teeth. I must not eat too many sugary things like sweets, cakes and fizzy drinks. Then I won't need any fillings. He gives me a toothbrush and a mirror to help me clean my teeth.

I clean my teeth with my new toothbrush.

At home I look in the mirror, and clean my teeth the way the dentist showed me.

You need good, strong teeth to eat an
apple like this!

Glossary

Appointment The time that you arrange to see someone, like your doctor or dentist.

Check-up The time when you visit your dentist to make sure that your teeth are healthy. You should have a check-up every four months.

Dental nurse The person who cares for the patient and helps the dentist. The dental nurse fills in charts, passes tools to the dentist, cleans the tools, and mixes up pastes.

Plaque Plaque is made by germs that stick to your teeth, near the gums. It comes from the sugar in your food. It is very bad for teeth and gums.

Receptionist The person at the dentist's surgery who tells you when to come, and when the dentist is ready to see you.

Books to read

Going to the Dentist Anne Civardi (Usborne, 1986)
Teeth John Gaskin (Franklin Watts, 1984)
Teeth Sandra Halford (Ladybird, 1978)
Your Teeth Joan Iveson-Iveson (Wayland, 1985)

Acknowledgements

The author and publishers would like to thank Patrick Nayler and everyone at his surgery, and Sue, Sebastian and Ben Trower for their help with this book.

Index

24